MIDNIGHT RANGER

BROTHERHOOD PROTECTORS WORLD

KRIS NORRIS

Twisted Page Press LLC

Midnight Ranger

To the men and women who risk their lives so civilians don't have to. You're a special breed. Thank you for your sacrifice. It won't be forgotten.

And special thanks to Elle James for allowing me to play in her world. It's been a blast, and I can't wait to revisit her Brotherhood Protectors series. Look for Russel "Ice" Foster's story coming soon.

PROLOGUE

Afghanistan, Nangarhar Province.

"Hey, jackass, you ready?"

First Lieutenant Samuel "Midnight" Montgomery grunted as his buddy punched him in the shoulder, nearly knocking his compass out of his hand. He fumbled with it, shoving the guy back once he'd clipped the unit onto his vest. "You are such a mother fucking pain in my ass, you know that, Gray?"

Gray laughed. "Fuck off. We both know you love me."

"Yeah, like a freaking STD."

Sam turned but grinned. First Lieutenant Rick Lawson—or "Gray" as everyone called him—was a thorn in Sam's side. And the closest thing to a brother he'd ever had. They'd been together since their initial ranger training, and he couldn't imagine a mission without the other jerk having his back.

"They're called STIs now, you ass. Speaking of

which…" He kicked at Sam's ruck sack. "Did you pack your spare pair of boxers? We both know you're gonna shit your pants on this one."

"Got'em right beside your special cream." He motioned to his buddy's crotch. "Doesn't look like it's making anything bigger, though, bro."

"Good." Gray grabbed his junk. "Because if this gets any bigger, I'll be splitting the ladies in half."

Sam chuckled, checking his straps then closing his sack and tossing it over one shoulder. "I swear this shit gets heavier with every jump."

"Just wait until you get the rest clipped on." Gray's smile faded as he pressed his lips together. "So…thirty big ones tonight."

"Is there even air up that high?"

"Even with the oxygen tanks, it's kind of crazy. Can't the plane avoid detection enough at twenty-five? Do you know how fucking cold it is at thirty-thousand feet?"

"Minus forty."

Gray rolled his eyes. "I *know* how cold it is. It was a rhetorical question."

"I just hope the intel's worth it. The last couple of missions have been a bust."

"Who cares? After this, we've got two weeks off before we train with Regimental." Gray inhaled. "Dude. We *need* to hit Vegas."

A flutter of anticipation clenched Sam's gut. They'd been waiting for months to get a shot at the Regimental Reconnaissance Company. A chance to take their training to the extreme—if they made the cut.

He snorted. No way they'd fail. Gray wouldn't let them, and his buddy was solid grit.

Sam arched a brow. "Vegas? Really? Aren't you banned from like, half the casinos?"

"That still leaves the other half. And I bet we can find a couple of college babes lookin' for a man in uniform."

"Do you ever stop thinking with either your stomach or your dick?"

"I have a fast metabolism, and not all of us are stuck pinning away for some high school sweetheart. Which reminds me. It's way past time you fucked that girl right out of your mind, bro. It's been what? Ten years?"

"Twelve."

Gray snorted. "And the fact you corrected me without hesitating... You need help, Midnight."

Sam flipped Gray the bird. But it wasn't the ribbing that pissed Sam off. It was the fact Gray was right. Not that Sam hadn't done his best to move on. To let his heart whither and die in the desert sun. But somehow, she'd invaded his head. Hidden pieces of herself like a scattering of landmines just waiting to explode when he thought he was safe. Free.

Not that it mattered. He'd burned that bridge—obliterated it. And the sooner he let those memories fade—let *her* fade—the better.

Sam gave the guy another shove. "Let's just get through this mission, then we can chat about Vegas."

"You know, haters are just gonna hate..."

"Jerk."

Gray just kept on talking, teasing the other guys once they'd taken their seats. The easy banter helped pass the time until they were standing in front of the open door—wind eddying through the space, nothing but inky darkness beyond the doorway. Gray looked back at him, giving him a guarded nod, before moving ahead. Just another couple of minutes, and they'd be out the door.

Sam steadied his breathing in the mask, frowning when Gray stumbled on his next step forward. He nudged his buddy, motioning to him as he activated his mike. "You okay?"

Gray arched his brow. "Is there something other than oxygen in your mask? Of course, I'm okay. Why wouldn't I be?"

"It's not like you to stumble."

"These packs don't exactly make walking easy."

"Still…" He grabbed Gray this time. "Is your hand shaking?"

Gray tugged his arm free, shoving his hand in his pocket. "I'm fine, Sam. Done this a hundred times before."

"Doesn't matter. You know it's different every time. Any one of us could have adverse effects to the altitude on any given mission." He held up his hand. "How many fingers."

"Would you stop it? I'm fine. Better than fine, actually. I feel invincible. Now, let's do this."

Sam looked over to the PT tech going down the line, nodding at Gray. The man focused on his friend, checking his gear then rattling off some questions. He gave Gray a nod, then shifted over to Sam.

"First Lieutenant Lawson seems fine."

Sam narrowed his gaze, watching Gray take another unsteady step. "Are you sure?"

"As sure as I can be. If you think…"

His words died beneath a series of shouts as the light flashed above the door, and their commander motioned for them to go. Gray shuffled forward when the men in front stepped out, disappearing into the clouds as Sam moved to the door. He clenched his jaw, hoping he'd only been imaging things, then jumped, inhaling at the rush of adrenaline through his body. He fell, weightless, surrounded by darkness before getting jerked upwards by the chute. The damn things packed a punch. It didn't matter how many times he jumped, he'd still be sore for days after.

Sam gathered his bearings. His team appeared in his night vision googles, or NVGs—ghostly green images amidst the black. He adjusted his trajectory, heading toward them as they sounded off, nothing but silence when Gray's turn came. Sam scanned the area, catching a glimpse of movement below him. A chute billowed upwards, the tangled strings keeping it from properly deploying.

He hit the button on his headset. "Gray! You're tangled. Release the main chute and deploy your reserve. We'll adjust our descent rate to meet up with you." He waited, but Gray didn't answer him. "Gray!"

A beep sounded in his ear. "I don't see any movement, Midnight. I think he's out."

Shit. "I'll intercept. Stay on target. We'll reevaluate once I've got him."

"Roger."

Sam cursed then released his chute, dropping into free fall. He fanned out his body, then drew his arms together, increasing his speed as he angled toward his friend. The cold burned through his layers of clothing, numbing any exposed skin and slowing his reactions. If he waited much longer, he wouldn't have enough dexterity to manipulate Gray's chute.

Gray's limp form rushed toward Sam as he closed the distance. He needed to slow his approach, or the impact could kill them both. Sam waited until he was close then spread his limbs, using the friction as a brake.

He aimed for Gray's waist, propelling them both forward as he locked his arms around his friend. The impact tumbled them over until Sam was able to get them stabilized. His vision blurred for a bit before he managed to shake it off. He released his friend's chute, clipping them together before pulling his reserve. The material fluttered out behind him, once again jerking him up. Gray moaned, squirming against Sam's hold.

"Easy. You're suffering from hypoxia. Just...hold still."

Gray mumbled something Sam couldn't make out, his body going limp, again. Sam talked to the others, doing his best to follow behind them. But the added weight coupled with the extreme loss in altitude altered their path enough he knew they wouldn't make it to the landing zone. Hell, he was happy the chute was working at all, aware they were pushing the upward limits of the damn thing's useful load.

The land raced past, every minute drawing them closer to the ground. Sam cursed under his breath, constantly recalculating their new arrival zone, when lights flashed from the ground.

His radio buzzed a second before one of his

teammates sounded in his headset. "Ground fire. Defensive maneuvers."

Sam angled them to the right, hoping to get clear, when bullets ripped through the canopy above him, dropping them toward the ground. He pulled on the ropes, slowing them as best he could. Jagged rocks rushed up toward him, the unforgiving landscape stretching out beneath him. He made one last attempt to veer clear before parts of the chute caught on a sharp out jut, halting their descent and slamming them against the cliff.

A rush of pain stole his next breath, dulling the voices shouting in his headset before he managed to blink away the fuzzy feeling in his head. Gray had slipped farther down Sam's chest, the dead weight making it hard to breathe. That, or he'd crushed a few ribs.

"Gray! Shit, buddy, talk to me."

He reached to check for a pulse, clenching his jaw at the stab of pain in his shoulder when his right arm wouldn't move. He used his left, cursing the slick glide of fluid against his fingertips. He didn't need to see the red color to know it was blood.

Fuck.

He looked up, hoping there was a way to untangle the cords, when a gust of wind slammed them against the rock, again. His knee connected with the stone, the dull crack echoing inside his head.

Sam clawed at the rocks, searching for an anchor point. "Hold on, brother. We'll find a way out of this, just…"

His words trailed into a shout as the straps gave way

above him, dropping them into the darkness below. There was a frenzied moment of free fall…then nothing.

"Sir?"

Sam jolted back, blinking against the wash of scenery until it cleared. A young woman stood beside the booth, coffee pot in one hand, a slice of pie in the other. Lines creased her forehead as she stared at him, her fingers white-knuckled around the plate.

He scanned the diner, the few people still in there looking over at him before turning away. Sam swallowed hard, nodding at the woman. "Sorry. I guess I dozed off. It's been a long day."

Fuck the day. It had been a long six months.

She gave him a timid smile. "You were talking. Calling for someone named Gray. I wasn't sure—"

"It's fine. I could use some more coffee, though. And a slice of that pie."

"Sure. You can have this one." She placed the plate in front of him as she refilled his mug. "Are you sure you're okay?"

"Fine, just…tired."

She nodded, but it was obvious she didn't quite believe him, as she wandered off, moving to another table.

Sam stared down at his hands, hating the way they shook as he took a swig of his drink. His hands had always been rock steady. Had to be to make it through training. Yet, there was no denying the tremor. The slight slosh of the coffee inside the mug.

The damn dream.

Six months and it still haunted him—used every opportunity to chip away at what little sanity he had left. And god knew, he didn't have any to spare.

He scrubbed a hand down his face, catching a hint of movement in the window beside him. He looked out, inhaling at the figure wavering by the lamppost next to his truck. A familiar set of eyes stared back at him, the ghosted echo of his name curling around him.

Sam closed his eyes. It wasn't real. Just a figment of his imagination. A by-product of guilt, fatigue, and pain that manifested as the image of his dead teammate. His dead brother. He'd been told it would go away—fade like Gray's voice inside Sam's head. He just needed to be patient.

Sam stood, tossing some money on table before heading out into the snowy night. Another six hours and he'd be in Montana. The one place he swore he'd never return, and the only place that might save what was left of his soul.

A new job. A new beginning. He only hoped there was enough of him left to save.

"Midnight?"

Sam looked up, nodding at the two men standing off to his left. He'd made it to the small town of Eagle Rock, Montana in good time considering the poor road conditions and had stopped at the local diner, sitting in a booth similar to the one he had the previous night— the one where he'd questioned his sanity to the point he'd considered turning around. Or maybe just continue driving until he ran out of land.

He stood, extending his hand. "Sam Montgomery."

The larger of the two men smiled, shaking Sam's hand firmly. "Hank Patterson. Some of the guys call me Montana. It's great to finally meet you in person." He thumbed at the other guy. "Taz, here, has been driving me nuts since he heard via the grapevine you were going civilian. Told me I'd be crazy not to hire you."

Sam nodded at the other man, shaking his hand next. "Thanks, though, I don't recall us ever meeting."

Taz chuckled. "We haven't. Not officially. The name's Alex Davila, but as Hank said, most folks call me Taz. As for knowing you… The 75th Ranger Regiment is a small community, and I've heard you mentioned a lot from some mutual buddies overseas. Seems you made quite the name for yourself over the past twelve years. It's great to have you joining the team."

Sam nodded, again, not quite sure how to respond. He hadn't actually accepted the job—hadn't really been offered it, if he were honest—though, it seemed as if this was far more than just an interview. "Um—"

Hank cursed, giving Taz a shove. "Nice, Davila. You're gonna scare off our new recruit before he even signs up. Let's have some coffee. Chat."

Sam took his seat, eyeing both men from across the table. While Taz seemed like more of an open book where Sam was concerned, Hank definitely kept a tight fist on his emotions. Nothing registered beyond the firm press of the man's lips or his steady gaze as he relaxed against the seat cushion.

Hank waited until the waitress had brought them all

coffee before leaning forward, his hands folded together on top of the table. "So, I gotta ask. Why do they call you Midnight?"

Some of the tension eased from Sam's muscles as he took a gulp of coffee, cradling the mug between his hands. "While I consider Montana home, I was born and raised in Barrow, Alaska. My father was a bush pilot, and he set up shop there for about fifteen years. Unfortunately, he died when I was ten. My mom tried to make a go of it on her own but decided to move back to her hometown of Livingston when I was twelve. But once the guys learned where I was originally from…"

Hank laughed. "Land of the midnight sun."

"Shortened to Midnight."

"I'm sure all those night maneuvers you did only made it stick more." He glanced at Taz. "If I may…why the move to civilian life? From what Taz had heard, you'd planned on making the rangers your life's work. And my contacts at Walter Reed said you'd returned to your regiment—something about RRC training. It sounded as if things were okay."

Sam steeled himself against the rush of images that flashed in his mind—against the ghosted feel of rock beneath his palms, and the lingering sound of him and Gray hitting the ground, Gray's body crushed beneath his.

The air thickened, aggravating the side of his ribs that hadn't quite healed. He forced in a few quick breaths, breaking eye contact when the other men frowned, looking as if they were going to reach for him.

Hank sighed. "Look, Midnight. I didn't mean to pry."

Sam made a conscious effort of raising his gaze to theirs. "I got hurt on my last mission. The jump went sideways, and I ended up with four broken ribs, and a punctured lung, amongst other issues. Despite making a full recovery, the doctors felt the residual damage from the pneumothorax made future HAHO and HALO jumps too risky. To be honest, they thought any jump was probably too risky. I argued—spent the past four months trying to get some kind of waiver, prove to them it hadn't slowed me down—anything to change their minds, but…"

He didn't mention that he'd screwed his knee and shoulder, or the part where he was seeing his dead friend. He already thought he was crazy. He didn't need strangers to confirm it.

Taz muttered something under his breath. "But what you got was a one-way ticket stateside."

Sam snorted. "Hard to be a ranger when you can't jump out of a damn plane. And changing specialties now… It didn't appeal to me—not when I was exactly where I'd wanted to be. That's if they even would have allowed it. You'd heard right. I was supposed to head off to RRC after the mission, but…" He shook his head. "Of course, I hadn't really considered how hard it would be to integrate back into civilian life. The Army Rangers was supposed to see me through to my golden years, if I lived that long. Who knew there weren't many job prospects for guys like us?"

Hank nodded. "Which is exactly why I created Brotherhood Protectors. There are far too many veterans who have the same issues. They want to continue to fight the good fight, but they don't know how to go about it."

"So what, exactly, do you and the other men do?"

"In a nutshell? We provide protective services for clients who have problems beyond the scope of the police. Everything from stalkers to covert assignments where we've been hired by someone close to the client to see they aren't put in harm's way. Taz, here, started off posing as a patient for the Brighter Days rehab ranch." Hank cleared his throat. "Not only did he stop the perpetrator, he and Hannah have been together ever since."

Taz laughed. "I was luckier than most. But the point is, the work we do has a way of making us feel worthy. It definitely helped me with the transition."

Sam crossed his arms over his chest, focusing on Hank. "And you think I'll be a good fit?"

Hank shrugged. "Wouldn't have asked you to come here if I didn't. But the real question is...do you?"

Sam stared at his coffee for a few moments, ignoring the memories that hovered at the edge of his consciousness, before giving Hank a nod. "I'd like to accept your offer."

"Perfect." Hank reached into his pocket and removed a folded up manila envelope. "Then let's get you started. I have a client right up your alley." He smiled. "Welcome to the Brotherhood Protectors, Midnight."

CHAPTER ONE

Seattle. Ten months later…

"Don't you ever keep regular hours?"

Bridgette Hayward looked up from her desk, smiling at the man standing in her doorway. Tall, dark, handsome, dressed in Armani with his hair perfectly styled—Jeremy Brenner was the classic image of an assistant U.S. attorney. In the two years she'd been working for the United States Attorney's Office, she'd never once seen the guy sweat or lose the calm demeanor he wore like a shield, regardless of the circumstances. And the man had gone up against some intimidating clients.

Bridgette leaned back, twirling her pen around her fingers. "Says the man standing in my doorway at…oh, nine o'clock on a Friday night."

"I just came back because I forgot a brief I needed. You, on the other hand, haven't left, yet."

"Big case means extra time, and I can't afford to screw this one up."

Jeremy's eyes narrowed, and he glanced around as if looking for others despite the fact the office had been closed for hours, before stepping through the doorway. "You know I think you're one of the best lawyers we've had come through here, right?"

She frowned. "Why do I sense a 'but' at the end of that statement?"

"Not a 'but'. I'm just...worried about you."

"That's sweet."

"Seriously, Bridgette. Alexander Stevens has been heading his family's drug business for longer than you've been alive. It's taken that many years to make a case against him, and it was essentially a fluke. Which means he's got more connections than anyone knows. The kind that's kept him out of jail and gotten other people killed." He nodded at her. "You still getting threats? Calls? Letters?"

A chill beaded her skin, the ghostly echo of a gravelly voice on her cell sounding inside her head before she shoved it aside. "Nothing I haven't gotten before. And, as usual, I'm being cautious."

"If you were being cautious, you'd either have a bodyguard or you'd be working remotely until the trial starts, and we can petition for police protection."

"I'm fine, Jeremy. Promise."

He shook his head. "I realize this is a huge leap forward in your career, and you deserve every bit of it. Your record here is more than impressive. I'd just hate to see you get hurt over it."

"I promise I'll be more vigilant. And if things escalate—"

"If things escalate, it'll be too damn late." He huffed, running his fingers through his hair. "You *are* stubborn. Anyway, I'm heading out. You ready to go? I'll walk you to your car like a perfect gentleman." He winked. "Or not, if you'd prefer."

She smiled—the guy had been trying to get into her pants for months. "Thanks, but I have a few things left. I'll be out of here soon, though."

"All right. Be careful."

"Always."

He shook his head then left, his footsteps fading down the hallway. Bridgette focused on the written testimonies, again, noting any concerns or questions she wanted to discuss, until the words started blurring together. She sat back and glanced at the clock—nine forty-five. She closed her eyes for a moment, rubbing the bridge of her nose in the hopes of lessening the ache building between her eyes. Jeremy was right about one thing. She needed a break. She could look at the files, again, in the morning, but reading the same paragraph over and over wasn't helping.

She stood and stretched, hoping to ease the tight press between her shoulder blades. A few more weeks like this and her colleagues would start calling her Quasimodo. Maybe she'd take a hot bath. Spend the night curled up on the couch watching a movie. Anything not related to Alexander Stevens or this case.

The thought made her smile as she packed some folders into her briefcase then placed it on her desk. She filed any remaining papers then grabbed her case and her purse. A quick trip to the ladies' room, and she could head out.

The building was eerily quiet as she walked down the hallway then into the bathroom. Usually, she enjoyed the silence after everyone else had left, but tonight felt different. Whether it was the storm raging outside or Jeremy's words, she wasn't sure. But she'd be happy to get home—lock herself inside.

Her boots clicked across the floor as she made her way back to grab her jacket. If she'd been thinking clearly, she would have taken it with her and locked up, already, saving her the return trip. But the long days were definitely taking a toll, and it seemed as if she forgot simple things more often, lately.

She sighed, stepping inside, before coming to a halt. A large yellow envelope sat kitty-corner on her desk, her name scribbled across the front. She glanced around, staring at the shadows lining the hallway. She'd been gone less than ten minutes.

Her heart rate kicked up as she walked over to her desk, staring down at the offering. No return address. No mail stamp. She thumbed the corner, debating on whether to open it or call the cops. Though, if it turned out to be nothing, she'd never live it down. And she hadn't been there long enough to bring that kind of attention to herself.

Bridgette took a breath then gently lifted the tab. It hadn't even been sealed, which hopefully meant it didn't contain any kind of deadly virus. Her pulse thundered in her head as she slipped her hand inside and removed a collection of photographs. A small note was stuck to the front, the same handwriting scrawled across it.

I'm coming for you.

The words glared up at her, the simple statement making her stomach roil. She bit her bottom lip then flipped through the images. Whoever had taken them had followed her from her apartment to her office. There were even a few of her at the boxing club—her hands in gloves as she moved around the ring. They'd obviously been taken over a few days, which meant someone was stalking her. *Had* been stalking her for some time, and she hadn't even noticed.

Memories surfaced in the background. Distant like a clock ticking in another room. But there, just the same. She pursed her lips then stuffed the photos back into the envelope. If Alex Stevens thought some creepy phone calls and a few pictures would be enough to intimidate her, the man had a hard lesson ahead of him.

First, she'd go home. Lock up. Double check her alarm system. Then, she'd make copies of everything. She knew firsthand that evidence had a way of "disappearing" with the right amount of motivation. And Stevens had more than enough motivation at his disposal.

In the morning, she'd head to the police station. She'd give them the envelope and half of the photos. Have them add the images to her growing file of harassment since she'd first been handed the case months ago. But she'd send the note and the other pictures to her friend, Special Agent Jack Taylor. See if the Bureau could match the handwriting or get some kind of DNA off the paper. It wasn't that she didn't trust the local precinct, she just trusted Jack more.

Her briefcase felt heavy as she slipped the envelope inside then headed for the bank of elevators at the opposite end of the hallway. Different scenarios bounced around in her head, trying to take shape, when a distant noise stopped her. She paused, trying to pinpoint it when the dull echo sounded, again.

Footsteps. Behind her.

Bridgette swallowed against the punch of fear cooling her skin and began walking. Faster this time. The footsteps followed her—two for every one of hers. She reached the elevator and hit the button. The arrow lit up, accompanied by the hum of machinery as the unit began moving.

She glanced down the hallway. Had she only imagined the footsteps? Wouldn't the person have rounded the corner by now? Was it another coworker returning to their office?

No. There hadn't been any other lights on. All the doors had been closed. She looked at the number pad click off the floors then made for the stairwell. At least she'd have some control by taking the stairs. No surprises when the silver doors opened, and she could easily detour to another floor if she heard someone approaching from below.

The heavy metal fire door clicked shut behind her as she bustled through, descending as fast as she could without making too much noise. She'd gotten two floors down when another click resonated through the air above her, followed by hurried steps.

Bridgette raced down the stairs, sticking to the outer

wall in case anyone tried to see her over the railing. She didn't stop, winding her way down to the bottom level. Why had she decided to park in the damn garage today? It was like asking to become a victim. But the rain had been falling in steady sheets, and she'd been too rushed to try and find a spot on the road or in a neighboring lot. So, she'd opted for the staff parking. A key-activated sensor and garage door were supposed to make the area secure. But no such thing existed. There were always ways in, and if someone wanted her bad enough, they would have found one.

The exit door squeaked as she shoved on it, darting to her right once she'd cleared the small glass enclosure. Only a scattering of cars dotted the large space, a patchwork of shadows masking the glare of the overhead lights. She headed for the wall, keeping herself between it and the front of a few vehicles in case she needed to disappear. She'd made it halfway to her Jeep when the inner door bounced open.

Bridgette hit the concrete, crouching behind the grill of a large Suburban. The plate caught on her pants, ripping a line across her hip. She cursed under her breath, yanking the fabric free then slowing peering around the left side of the SUV. A dark figure moved down the outer edge of the parking stalls, head swiveling from side to side.

A man. No question. Wide, thick shoulders with a broad chest and narrow waist, the guy looked athletic beneath the snug black clothing and matching ski mask. As if he could chase her for hours and never get tired. Judging by the size of his biceps, she had no doubts that he packed one hell of a punch. The kind that would knock her out with only a single blow. Something glinted off one of the lights, the silver gleam winking at her.

He had a gun, though the barrel looked strangely thick—shit. A suppressor. This guy meant business. He wasn't there to threaten her. To beat a warning into her. He was there to kill her. Period.

Bridgette weighed her options. She could call for help, but with the garage so empty, her voice was sure to echo. And the police wouldn't be able to reach her before her stalker would.

She could make a run for her Jeep. She was quick.

Not faster than a bullet, girl. Think!

It wouldn't take the man long to figure out she'd hidden behind one of the available cars. All he'd have to do was systematically check. Her best bet was to double back. Wait until she had enough distance to dash inside the building. She could head upstairs and find another way out. Or hide in a bathroom while she called for help. Anything but sit there and wait for the asshole to shoot her.

Footsteps.

He was moving. Each step carefully orchestrated as if he'd done this a hundred times before. He stopped at every vehicle, checked underneath then moved on.

Shit. He'd see her feet unless she could somehow balance on the bumper with her boots pressed to the wall. Sweat slicked her palms as she tried to judge how to bridge her weight, when a noise sounded from across the lot.

The guy turned, staring into the deep shadows, his body rigid. Alert. She didn't know how long he'd stay focused on other side of the garage. A second. Five. All night. She chanced it and quickly scrambled over to the bank of cars he'd already checked, doing her best to hide her feet behind the wheel on the left side.

Silence stretched out, the utter nothingness making her heart pound. Could he hear it? She could. Frantically beating inside her chest—making it hard to breathe.

A step.

Continuing in the same direction. She matched his movements, shuffling toward the doorway every time he took a step—hoping to mask her sounds in his. He kept going, kept allowing her to get closer to the door, until she'd reached the last car. Bridgette crept to the tail end, stealing a look beneath the vehicle. Black boots faced away from her, the guy's shadow stretching out like a snake behind him.

She glanced at the doorway. Nothing but an oversized pillar stood between her and the glass. If he caught her movement, she'd be wide open. Bile crested her throat, burning at her resolve. One chance.

She moved as soon as he took another step, surging to her feet then dashing behind the column. Her boots scuffed the cement, the dull sound echoing off the walls.

He stopped.

Damn. He'd heard her. She knew he had. Were those his footsteps toward her, now? Getting closer? Louder. She couldn't check. Couldn't risk he'd see her. She was pretty sure her body fit behind the pillar, but it wouldn't keep her safe. And soon, he'd be there. Beside her. Nothing but a couple feet of concrete between her and a bullet.

The steady click of his boots stopped on the other side of the column, his harsh breath whispering close by. She held hers, inching around the column as he slowly picked his way toward the wall, keeping the pillar between them. What happened once he'd checked behind the cars? If he headed toward the door, she'd never be able to stay hidden. It nothing else, he'd see her shadow.

A cold sweat broke out across her skin, dripping down her forehead despite the near freezing temperature. He was on the other side, about to move past the edge of the column. Bridgette clenched her jaw, waiting for him to suddenly jump out at her, when the garage door started rolling. She startled, barely stopping the scream clawing at her throat from joining the grating sound of metal chains moving along a pulley as the door rose, exposing a flash of light from the street beyond.

The man stopped, quickly walking back the way he'd come. Bridgette moved with him, once again, darting behind the car. Headlights cut through the shadows as the approaching vehicle rounded the corner, pulling into an empty stall just down from where she was crouched against the wall. Music blared through the closed windows then cut off, easy laughter filling the void.

A couple stepped out, still engrossed in conversation as they talked over the top of the car. Bridgette glanced at where she'd last seen the man, but he was gone. Most likely out through the employee door beside the exit ramp.

Her hands shook as she straightened then leaned against the wall, bracing her palms on her knees. A dull roar sounded inside her head, blocking out everything until a hand landed on her shoulder. She jumped, tripping sideways as she swung toward the person, her fist glancing off a torso.

"Whoa, Bridgette. Easy. Christ, it's just me."

Air wheezed through her lungs, the steady supply finally clearing her vision. Jeremy stood off to her right, brow furrowed, his lips turned into a frown.

He glanced around then looked back at her. "Are you okay?"

"I thought you'd left?"

The words rushed out, all melding together to form one long incoherent word.

"I got halfway home before I realized I'd left my damn cell on the counter in the men's room." He leaned a bit closer. "Did something happen? You look like a damn ghost."

She opened her mouth, but nothing made it past the lump in her throat. She scanned the garage, again, but it looked like it always had. Deserted. Safe. One of the overhead lights buzzed then winked out, blanketing them in dull gray.

Jeremy reached into his pocket, retrieving his phone. "I'm calling an ambulance."

"No." She managed to grasp his wrist—draw his attention. "I'm fine, I'm..."

Just terrified. Nearly died at the hands of a gunman. But I'm fine.

"You don't look fine."

She snorted, the aftermath of adrenaline making her shake. "I..."

She paused. While she didn't think there was any

chance Jeremy had been bought—that he *could* be bought—she'd been fooled before. Betrayed. And she'd promised herself she'd never fall victim to that, again. Better to play it safe until she could talk to Jack. Jack couldn't be bought, and he wouldn't ever betray her. It was a given. A knowledge that ran soul deep.

She cleared her throat. "I thought I heard something. Saw someone. But...I must have been imagining it."

"Do yourself a favor and take a couple of days off. Or a week. But get some rest. You keep going like this and you'll burn yourself out." He motioned toward her Jeep. "Can I walk you to your car, now?"

"That would be great. Thanks."

She moved in beside him as he headed toward her vehicle, still searching the area. But they were definitely alone. Though for how long...

She stopped when his hand shot out and grabbed her arm, dragging her back a step. She snapped out of her thoughts, following his gaze until it landed on her Jeep. Two perfectly round holes were punched through the windshield, both front tires flat against the concrete.

"Shit." Jeremy turned toward her. "You still think this is nothing you haven't dealt with before?"

She opened her mouth to answer, but he was already on his phone, talking to the cops. Bridgette looked toward the exit door, wondering if the guy was on the other side. Waiting. Planning.

It didn't matter. She'd been given a second chance to get her head out of her ass and make better decisions. Jeremy was right. She needed to distance herself for a while. Stop giving Stevens' men an easy target. And she knew just where to go.

Montana.

The house her grandmother had left her.

The one still registered in her father's name. The last place anyone would ever look for her, and the only place she might be safe.

CHAPTER TWO

Livingston, Montana. A few weeks later.

"Don't worry, Mr. Hayward." Sam shook the older man's hand, giving him a reassuring smile. "I'll keep Bridg—"

"What the hell is *he* doing here?"

Sam paused mid-sentence, twisting to gaze at the woman standing partway down the broad staircase. He didn't miss the tight press of her lips, or the hint of color high on her cheeks. She glared at him as she continued down the stairs, her boots clicking across the old hardwood floors as she walked halfway into the parlor. After all this time, he wasn't sure she'd even remember him—not that he'd forgotten her. He'd tried. He just hadn't been able to get her out of his head. Though, based on her expression, she remembered him a bit too well.

Her father gave her a wide smile, extending his hand

toward Sam. "Ah, Bridgette, just the person I needed to see. This is—"

"Sam Montgomery. Yeah, I know who the jerk is. What I don't know is why he's standing in *my* house."

Her father frowned. "You two know each other?"

She glared at Sam, crossing her arms over her chest. "I realize it's been what…twelve years? But it's hard to forget your ex-boyfriend, who took you to prom, then slept with Jenny Stinson instead of driving you home. So, yeah…we've met before."

"Oh, I see." George Hayward shifted on his feet, his cheeks turning slightly pink, before he cleared his throat. "It's been a few years, and I didn't make the connection with the name. So, I suppose there's no need for introductions."

"No. You need to answer my question. What is he doing here?"

The man sighed. "He's here because it's been two weeks since you promised me you'd hire a suitable security detail, and you're still walking around on your own as if nothing's wrong."

Her jaw hinged open, her gaze sliding to Sam's. It swept the length of his body, openly assessing him before settling on his face. Stunning blue eyes stared back at him, the corners creased in irritation. It didn't take a genius to tell she'd found him lacking, though he wasn't quite sure in which department. All of them, he supposed, especially if she still believed he'd been a jerk to her all those years ago.

He sighed inwardly. He'd *definitely* been a jerk in high school. Had more than a few regrets inked across his do-over list—her name right there at the top. But those mistakes were a large part of why he'd become an Army Ranger, and he had to believe he'd changed for the better over the past decade—had become the kind of man she'd proud to know, now. Though, it didn't mean Bridg would see it that way, or that she'd let him explain.

He drew a calming breath, studying the way she stared at him. She wasn't anything like the shy, small town girl he remembered. Confidence radiated from the firm line of her jaw to the way she held her shoulders back, owning her space. She'd definitely come into her own over the past twelve years. But despite the change, she couldn't hide the slight twitch of her mouth, or the way she shifted on her feet, as if she couldn't quite stand still. The girl was nervous, and he'd bet his ass it wasn't because he was standing in her house, uninvited.

Bridgette watched him for another few moments before breaking eye contact and glancing at her father "Dad. While I appreciate you're only trying to help, I'm not a kid anymore. I'm thirty. I can take care of myself. Have been for some time, now."

Her father furrowed his brows. "Age doesn't make you any less my child. Which means, I'm not too old to worry, or to want to see you have proper protection." He turned to address Sam. "See what I'm up against? Death threats. Vandalism. Photographs. And she still thinks it's all some kind of joke."

Her expression softened, genuine compassion shaping her eyes. "I never said it was a joke, but it sounds worse than it is. This is just posturing. One of Stevens' underlings flexing their muscles. Attempting to unnerve me. Knock me off my game, or get me to step down from the case. It's a common tactic with the kind of people I deal with on a daily basis. It's just their way of trying to intimidate me. But I don't scare easily."

She relaxed a bit, leaning her hip against the arm of a chair, but Sam noticed the way her skin paled. She wasn't being completely honest. He just wasn't sure if it was regarding the threats she'd received or the way she'd tried to brush them off.

"Besides, all of that happened at work. That's why I came back to stay here until the court date." She snorted. "Trust me, no one's following me to this blip in the map. Livingston, Montana isn't exactly a tourist mecca, especially this time of year."

George frowned, turning to Sam as he pointed to his daughter. "Samuel. Please talk to her. Tell her I'm not being some overprotective, helicopter parent. That she should take these threats seriously."

Sam focused at Bridgette, again. God, she was stunning. More so by the minute, it seemed. Not in a New York model sort of way, but more of a homegrown, girl-next-door kind of beauty. Long, golden hair, smooth, creamy skin with a hint of natural blush, and curves that put any back road in the county to shame, she didn't strike him as a hot-shot, big city lawyer who worked for the U.S.'s office. But then, he'd learned not to judge people by how they looked—it usually came back to bite him in the ass. And he'd definitely misjudged her all those years ago.

He braced his feet apart, crossing his arms over his chest this time. "Your father's right. You need to stop being so stubborn."

Her left eye twitched as she stared at him. "Stubborn? You think this is me throwing a tantrum?"

He shrugged. "Your words, not mine, Bridg. But since you brought it up—I've seen the photographs. Read the letters. They aren't idle threats. And denying help because you don't want to choke on your pride isn't a wise choice."

Her eyes rounded, then narrowed, as she took a calculated step forward. "Choke on my pride? Who the hell are you to judge me?"

"The guy who deals with this kind of situation on a regular basis. Who might just be able to keep your ass in one piece. That's if you stop whining long enough to actually listen to what I have to say."

"Okay. Wow. Can we just pretend, for one second, that you're not a complete douchebag?" She spun, glancing at him over her shoulder. "Oh, wait. We both know that's impossible."

Bridgette took a few quick steps away, stopping when he lunged forward and hooked her elbow. She hissed out her next breath, jerking her arm free then palming his chest and giving him a shove. "Don't touch me."

"Then stop acting like a child and running away. We're not done discussing this."

"There's nothing to discuss. This is my house, and you're not welcome in it."

"I'm not leaving until you realize how serious this is."

"First of all, other than the fact this is none of your business, I never said I wasn't taking it seriously. That's why I'm here—working out of a drafty home office, with less than stellar internet speed. I'm distancing myself from the case—from my life—to let things cool down a bit. Second... If I still thought my life was in danger, I'd hire a professional bodyguard. One I actually trusted. And third..." She shook a finger at him. "If I freaked out and hired someone every time a defendant threatened me, I'd never live alone. A certain amount of risk comes with the job. That's just a fact of life."

A loud ringing sounded in Sam's head before he inched closer, noting how she tensed from the small step. "If you *still* thought your life was in danger? Are you implying it's been in danger, already? Are there incidents you haven't mentioned? Escalated attacks? And did you just say this isn't the first time you've been overtly threatened on the job?"

She crossed her arms over her chest, though he wasn't sure if it was in response to his question or the fact he was only a couple feet away from her. "Sam—"

"Answer the question."

She exhaled, fluttering some strands of hair against her cheek. "I'm an assistant U.S. Attorney. I prosecute people involved in organized crime, including murderers, mafia henchmen, and drug dealers. People who aren't worried about breaking the law to send me a message. So yes, I've been threatened before—pretty much every case I've had for the past couple years. Sometimes it's photos. Sometimes vandalism. Or a creepy ass message on my cell. And every time, I increase my vigilance a little more. Make sure I lock my doors, don't wander down dark alleys at night." She quirked her lips. "Don't pick up strange men at bars and take them home, or go for a run in the park after sunset." She poked his chest with one delicate finger. "Not a damsel. Don't need some alpha male to ride to the rescue."

Sam placed his palm over her finger, pressing her entire hand against him. "Oh, darling. If only I had a dollar for every time a client has assured me they didn't need my services, I'd be one rich son of a bitch." He eased away just enough to reach into his pocket and remove an envelope. "Your dad didn't want to upset you, but these were waiting on your doorstep when he arrived this morning. It's the reason he called my employer. Because what's in here—it's so much more than some pissed off lackey throwing smoke bombs your way. This—it's serious."

She frowned as she took the envelope, staring at it as if it might suddenly burst into flames. "This was on my front step? Here? In Montana?"

"Looks like your little hideout isn't quite as secret as you thought it was."

She broke eye contact, thumbing the envelope before turning then walking into the hallway. She paused at the bottom of the stairs then ripped open the end of the envelope. Sam didn't miss the way her hands shook ever so slightly as she removed the photos stashed inside, slowly shuffling through them.

Bridgette closed her eyes for a moment, then glanced over at him. "While it's...disconcerting that these were sent here, they're still just more photos of me at work, or coming out of my apartment."

Sam shook his head. "I think the fact your *admirer* hand delivered them to your house is proof enough that you're not fooling anyone by holing up in this place."

"If they really wanted to send a message, they would have sent pictures of me at the general store. Or out running."

"Damn it, Bridg. This is so much more than what you've faced before, and you know it. You just don't want to admit that maybe, this time, it's out of your league."

Bridgette swallowed with effort, worrying her bottom lip before tilting her head and staring at him. "Why are you even here? I thought you joined the military? Became some special ops soldier or ranger or something."

Heat burned beneath his skin as scattered memories flashed through his mind, the telltale echo of gunfire and Gray's voice sounding in his head before he managed to shove the sensations aside. Avoid the gut-wrenching episode that generally followed. Now wasn't the time to show any weakness, not when he needed Bridgette to understand this wasn't a prank.

He nodded as he walked over to her. "I did. I'm not anymore. I work for Hank Patterson's company, Brotherhood Protectors. He hires veterans with…unique skills to provide security services for people who are in difficult situations. And yours is pretty damn difficult."

She eyed him, again, looking even more unhappy with whatever she found this time. "While that's all very interesting, I'm positive you have to be hired by the person with the 'difficult situation' before you get to provide your services. And I'm not hiring you."

"You don't have to. Your father already paid Hank in full." He smiled. "Looks like you're stuck with me."

A deep flush slashed across her cheeks, as her

breathing roughened. "Fine. You want to be my bodyguard? You can watch my every move—from the road. Anything else will be considered trespassing. And I happen to know a kick-ass attorney."

Sam clenched his jaw, mentally counting to ten before blowing out a steady breath. Obviously, reasoning with her wasn't going to work—not when she was upset and making decisions based on her emotions. Ones he knew were largely because of him. Ancient history that turned out, wasn't quite ancient enough. But it seemed intimidating her wasn't an option, either. Not that he'd intentionally tried to. It was merely a go-to tactic leftover from his military days. But she wasn't a new recruit. In fact, he'd be lying to himself if he said her tenacious spirit didn't impress the hell out of him. This was obviously the lawyer side of her. The part that never backed down, and damn, he could only imagine how ruthless she was in the courtroom.

"I think we got off on the wrong foot, here. Maybe we could start, again." He held out his hand. "Hey, Bridgette, it's great to see you, even if it is under unfortunate circumstances. You and I need to talk."

She frowned, glancing at his hand then back to his face. "I appreciate your concern, but like I said—I don't need protection."

Her father cleared his throat, gaining her attention. "While it's apparent you two have history, it's not worth getting yourself killed over."

"Your father's right. Dying isn't an option. Besides, he already told me this house is in his name. Which means, he decides whether I stay or not."

George sighed. "I don't want to upset you, Bridgette, but like it or not, Samuel stays."

Bridgette's eyes widened as her breathing hitched, her lips pressing into a thin line. She glanced at Sam. "If you'd like Sam to stay, that's perfectly fine. I was about to head home, anyway."

Sam glanced at her father then closed the distance between him and Bridgette, again, grabbing the photos from her hand then holding one of them up. "This was taken outside your apartment. The same place you're planning to go. Does that sound like the decision of someone who's looking out for themselves?"

He motioned to the door. "I'm leaving for exactly five minutes to get my equipment out of my truck. I suggest you jump onboard in the time I'm gone because whether you like it or not, I'm going to be shadowing your ass until you head back for the trial. And before you lose your shit—I've already cleared it with your office. They agree. This is way past *their* comfort zone, too. So, whether it's here in Montana or in your apartment in Seattle is up to you. But I think you'd be more comfortable here, where there's an extra room for me to sleep in instead of the floor of your bedroom."

He shoved the pictures back into her hand then turned, stopping at the doorway. "And for the record, I never called you a damsel. But I'm fairly certain those kick-boxing classes you've been taking don't compare to my level of training."

Sam marched out, smiling when something hit the door just after he closed it. While running into Bridgette hadn't been something he'd ever expected would happen—especially with how he had broken things off—

he was having a hard time being as upset as he'd originally thought he'd be. Maybe it was her feisty personality or her obvious intelligence. Either way, he needed to find a way to work with her, because if the people who sent those threats turned up, things were going to get bloody.

CHAPTER THREE

This couldn't be happening. Of all the people Bridgette's father could have hired to be her over-qualified bodyguard, surely Fate hadn't somehow aligned the stars and allowed Samuel Montgomery to be the guy. Yet, here she was, staring at the door where the man in question had just left, the shoe she'd tossed at him lying on the floor, and his last few words still ringing in her head.

She leaned against the wall, using it to brace her weight as she glanced at the photos in her hand. She still couldn't believe someone had followed her all the way to Montana. To this two-bit town that lasted all of a few minutes as you drove down Main Street. Surely, there had to be another explanation. Maybe one of her colleagues had forwarded them on?

A quick glance at the corner of the envelope dashed those hopes. The damn thing had been dropped off, not sent through the post office. Which meant *someone* knew where she was. She just wasn't sure who that someone was.

Images of the man clad in black, the gun glinting in his hand as he searched for her in the garage, pushed at her resolve. When the threats had stopped once she'd returned home, she'd assumed she didn't need to worry about better protection. Staring at the photographs made her question that. If there was a chance that guy had tracked her here…

Her father stopped beside her, pursing his lips together before drawing himself up. "I know you're upset, but—"

"I didn't ask for you to hire someone."

"You didn't have to. I'm your father. It's my job as a parent to keep you safe. And while I'll concede I didn't always execute that job very well in the past, I'm not going to stand by while you risk your life for nothing." He held up his hand. "There's nothing I can do to stop you from choosing to work for the U.S. Attorney's office. For taking those kinds of risks. But I'll be damned if I allow you to blatantly ignore these threats when I have the means to do otherwise."

"I wasn't ignoring them. I was taking additional precautions as the situation warranted. You didn't give me a chance to see the new evidence before you called Brotherhood…whatever, and hired the one guy I'd love to stab through the heart."

"It's Brotherhood Protectors, and I find it hard to believe there's only one man that has earned that distinction in your books."

She resisted the smile that twitched her lips. "The

point is, had I known that someone had delivered an envelope to *this* house—"

"You would have given me yet another excuse as to why extra security wasn't required." His expression softened as he gave her a smile. "Just because I'm old, Bridgette, doesn't mean I've forgotten who you are. Or what you're like. I'm proud of the woman you've become, but you're as stubborn as your mother ever was."

Bridgette cursed under her breath. Her father knew she had a soft spot whenever he mentioned her mom, and that she'd have a hard time staying mad at him.

She sighed. "You're not old. And I'll take the stubborn comment as a compliment. Mom was a real ass kicker, and I'm happy that I'm anything like her."

"Too much, if you ask me." Her father looked toward the door when it opened, nodding as Sam appeared, a collection of bags at his feet. "Now, I'm going to head out. The roads aren't getting any better, and I want to stop by the store before it closes. I've got Billy manning the helm, and I'm never quite sure he'll remember to turn everything off." He snorted. "Kids today."

Bridgette grinned, despite the anger still burning beneath her skin. She knew her dad meant well, it was just... She blew out a calming breath, watching Sam talk quietly to her father before the man continued onto the porch, then down the few short steps to the walkway. Cold air gusted through the open space, curling around her feet before Sam shut the door. She shivered, rubbing her hands along her arms—praying it was the chill and not the man standing in front of her that had her on edge.

Sam stared at her, and she swore he looked right through the walls she'd built around her like armor, before bending to grab her shoe. His perfectly full lips quirked into a smile as he walked over to her, holding out her shoe. "Yours, darling?"

She snatched it out of his hand, half considering using it to smack his smug smile off his face. "Just because my father's suddenly your biggest fan doesn't mean I am. Or that I'm onboard with…" She waved her hand between them. "This."

She scrunched up her nose, staring at the bags still resting by the door. "What is all of that, anyway?"

"Alarm system." He shook his head. "I can't believe you don't have one."

Her breath caught. "You brought an alarm system? But—"

"It's wireless." He nudged her. "Relax, Bridg. I'm not going to drill holes or ruin your paint scheme. But I need to know if there's anyone other than us in here. I'll set up detectors in each room and secure the entry points. If one goes off, it'll ring my cell. If I don't answer, it'll call a few of my colleagues. Depending on the code, I'll also program it to notify the local police or fire station. But it shouldn't come to that."

She snagged her lip, groaning inwardly. "Is that really necessary?"

Sam edged closer. "It's my job to keep you safe. This is just the beginning. Don't worry, I'll show you how it all works."

"I know how to work an alarm system. Christ, give me some credit. I have one at my apartment."

His brows drew together. "Then, why the face? And

trust me. You're making a face. The same one you used to make when I wanted you to go skinny dipping with me in the river."

"There were leaches in that water."

He chuckled. "I swear it was only a leaf. So, why the fuss, then?"

She exhaled, leaning against the wall, again. God, she was tired. While she'd put up a good front, the truth was—she hadn't really slept since the threats had started. Then after the incident in the garage, she'd orchestrated a full fledged retreat—running all the way to Montana. Even with less security, she'd felt better. Had managed to fool herself into thinking that the distance, alone, was enough to guarantee her safety. That she didn't need fancy alarm systems or muscle-bound bodyguards—until someone had apparently followed her there.

Strong fingers brushed along her jaw, jerking her back from her thoughts. She jumped, worrying her lip, again, when Sam narrowed his eyes, studying every fine line on her face.

"Hey. You okay?"

She swallowed, coughing as it rasped against the sudden dryness. "Fine. And I'm just disappointed I have to deal with all this, again. I came here to get away from the constant codes and checks. My grandparents lived in this house for sixty-five years. And my grandmother's parents for the same before them. They never locked their doors let alone had motion sensors and window alarms. I'd just hoped it would be the same. That when she left me this place, I'd be able to keep it pure."

She sighed. "I guess what I really mean is that I'd

assumed no one would find me. But you're right." She held up the envelope. "I should have installed an alarm system as soon as I got here."

His thumb skimmed across the corner of her mouth as his furrow eased. "I know it's upsetting, and frustrating, and I really am sorry. But your grandparents didn't get death threats, or spend their days convincing a jury to convict a person of multiple murders. As long as you put yourself into those kinds of situations, you need to take the appropriate precautions. Especially living alone."

Sam backed up a step then crossed his arms over his chest. "Which is actually the real mystery here. Your dad told me you're still single. Why isn't there some guy tagging along?"

She huffed. "Seriously, Sam? You're one of those people that think every woman needs a man to complete her?"

"Shit. Are you going to take everything I say as some kind of sexist remark?"

"Only the ones that sound that way."

"I didn't..." He blew out a long, slow breath. "What I meant was...you're beautiful, smart, successful. Surely the men in Seattle are lining up to ask you out."

"Says the guy who looks like he should be on the cover of some male fitness magazine. I noticed you're not wearing a ring. Do you have someone waiting at home?"

"No."

"Why not?"

He laughed. "And there's the lawyer in you. Can't answer a simple question without asking a few in return. Fine, my answer is that I really haven't had much time. While I was in the Ranger Regiment, I trained for months on end, only to move on to more training. Then it was one mission after another... I guess I thought there'd be time later. Or that I should wait until the chance of getting killed wasn't as big a factor as it seemed to be."

His words extinguished any residual anger. Christ, she hadn't been expecting him to actually answer. Not honestly. A well-rehearsed line, sure. But this...

She straightened. "What about now? I'm sure the ladies are lining up for you, too."

"If only. Truth is...not much has changed. Or maybe it's changed too much. I'm not really sure." He leaned toward her. "Your turn."

Dread washed over her, and she knew he'd done that on purpose. She steadied herself, plastering on the fake smile she'd perfected over the past few years. "My answer's the same."

"You were worried about getting killed?"

She stilled. Surely he hadn't picked up on that. "No, you jerk. I haven't really had any time, either. Do you know how hard it is to get into law school? How many hours I had to work as a public defender to get to the place where I was able to get my job at the U.S. Attorney's office? Maybe some people can juggle all that *and* a relationship, but... I couldn't."

He tilted his head to the side, still watching her closely. "You're lying."

Panic teased her senses, but she managed to push it aside. "Excuse me?"

"I said, you're lying." He took a step closer. "Yes,

you've been busy, and I believe that it would have been hard to make it all work. But there's another reason. Your eye twitches a bit when you're trying to fake your way out of a corner, just like it did earlier. And your hands are trembling. Not much, but I noticed. So... what's the real reason?"

She had a tell? How the hell had he recognized that from a minute-long conversation? One she'd uttered so many times she didn't even have to think about it, anymore. It played like a recording inside her head. And no one had ever questioned her before.

Sam arched a brow. "Well, Bridg? You started this. And I was completely honest with you. I've had my share of furlough flings. One night stands I'm not exactly proud of, but the women always knew where I stood. It was always mutual. So...is that what you've been doing? Is it just sex? A physical release without getting emotionally attached? Is there a reason you don't *want* to get emotionally attached?"

"I..."

She wet her lips, shuffling sideways until she'd put some much-needed space between them. God, it was as if he'd read her mind. Knew that her only sexual encounters over the past several years had been with cops or feds who were attending the same, boring symposium she was. The 'safest' guys she could find to scratch the itch.

She squared her shoulders. "I have some work to do. And you apparently have to turn this place into Fort Knox."

He gently snagged her arm. "Bridgette. You don't have to answer me, but...are you sure you're okay?"

She glanced down at where his fingers curled around her arm. How long had it been since she'd allowed a man to touch her without it being part of a one-off? Since her ex had literally changed her life—sent her down a path she hadn't considered before. Not that she regretted becoming a lawyer, but it hadn't been her first love. What she'd planned on doing with her life. Memories clawed at her bravado, a few fleeting moments breaking through before she managed to draw herself up—seal away her past.

She tugged softly against Sam's hold, thankful when he released her. "Fine."

"Well, when you say it like that…"

"I'm fine, Sam, all things considered." She slipped on her shoe then took a few steps back only to stop when he called out to her. She glanced at him over her shoulder, waiting to see what he wanted, now.

"I get that you're still pissed, and not just about this situation. Maybe later, we could talk? Clear the air?"

The two of them? Alone? Talking? Her stomach fluttered, making her acutely aware of how handsome he was. How he'd lost any trace of boyhood—the hard planes and angles accentuating how much of a man he'd become. He wore his hair longer, the brown color more chestnut than the almost dirty blond she remembered. But it wasn't just his looks that had changed. His personality seemed different. He'd lost the playboy charm he'd carried with him, replacing it with inner confidence and something she couldn't quite place. Honor, maybe. Though, he might have just gotten better at playing people.

She shrugged. "Nothing to talk about. Water under the bridge and all that."

"If it was water under the bridge, you wouldn't have introduced me to your father as the ex who'd cheated on you back in high school."

"Facts are facts, Sam."

"Which is why I'd like to talk. You don't have all of them."

"And I don't need them." She cut him off with a wave of her hand. "Seriously. I'm past it. In fact, you did me a favor that night."

Shadows lined his face as he frowned. "And what favor was that?"

"You taught me that men couldn't be trusted. That they'll say and do anything if it means they'll get their prize. That in the end, the only person I can ever truly count on is myself. A lesson I've...unfortunately had to learn more than once. But it definitely made me open my eyes. See the world differently than I had before. Made me realize I'd been sheltered, and that the only person I was hurting by staying in my safe little bubble was me."

She pushed back her shoulders, digging deep for the strength she'd developed over the years. "So...forget it. You're here to do a job. And I've only got two more weeks, so...this will all be over quickly." She took another few steps. "Let me know when you're done and what code I have to use. I'll be in my office for a bit, then working out. Can't let those kick-boxing classes go to waste."

CHAPTER FOUR

"Bridgette, wait... Fuck."

Sam shook his head as Bridgette kept walking, disappearing into another room. While he'd expected a certain level of animosity from her when he'd learned he'd been hired as her bodyguard—and that she wasn't exactly fond of the idea. He hadn't thought their relationship in high school had scarred her. Not like this.

He reran their interaction in his mind, doing his best to isolate anything that might point toward an answer. She'd been every inch the determined, confident woman he'd expected after learning she'd become a very successful prosecutor in one of Seattle's toughest districts—right up until he'd hooked her arm when she'd tried to leave.

He'd noticed the way she'd shied away from him when he'd gotten close. How she'd glanced at wherever he'd touched her as if the contact, itself, scared her. Judging on the brief snippets of information she'd let slip, he'd bet his right nut that someone had hurt her since he'd last seen her. And not just her heart—he recognized the lingering effects of being physically abused. The only question was whether it had been an isolated incident, or if she'd somehow gotten trapped in that kind of relationship.

He glanced at the hallway. She didn't seem like the type to fall for token promises—ones she had to know weren't worth the breath used to make them. So he doubted she'd actually stay with a guy after any show of aggression. Still...

He slipped his cell from his pocket, stepping out onto the porch as he dialed the office, asking for Hank when his wife, Sadie, answered. The silence scratched at Sam's control until a familiar voice sounded in his ear.

"Please don't tell me she's kicked your sorry ass out already, Midnight, because I think that'll be a company record."

"Great to talk to you, too. And no, Bridgette hasn't tossed me out." He chuckled. "I mean, she tried, of course...hadn't expected any less from her. But that's not why I'm calling. I need your connections to gather some information for me."

"I thought you had everything we could get about her current case?"

"I do. That's not what I'm referring to. I need information on Bridgette. I'd like to know if she was involved in any...personal lawsuits or criminal cases since she left Livingston."

Hank cleared his throat. "Did you say personal? As in her being the victim?"

Sam sighed. "Just...humor me. I have this gut

feeling, and I've learned to always trust my instincts. But I also don't think she'll tell me. At least, not right away. And I'd like to know if there are any other threats out there, besides the people she's put away, that might want to hurt her."

"All right. I'll see what my guys can dig up. It'll take a few days, though."

"Understood. I'll do what I can on this end."

"You do realize that it's most likely connected directly to the case, right? The fact the threats started as soon as the court date was set can't be a coincidence."

"Agreed, it's just… I'm missing a piece of the puzzle. Whether it's got any bearing on who's behind the threats, isn't clear. But she's hiding something from me. And I can't help but worry it's going to rear up and bite my ass."

"Can't have that…not when I suspect you're saving that it for someone else to bite."

"Has anyone ever told you that *you're* an ass?"

"Every day. I'll call you when I have something to share."

Sam slipped his phone back into his pocket then went inside. He really hoped he was wrong—that their history was coloring his perceptions. That he simply didn't want to admit that he'd hurt her far worse than he'd ever imagined all those years ago. That he was the one that needed to atone. But he had a bad feeling his hunch was accurate.

Questions rattled around inside his head as he moved through each room, setting up the system he'd brought with him. When he'd learned that his assignment involved Bridgette—and that she could have anyone from gang members to paid professionals gunning for her—he'd come prepared. While he'd hoped she'd already have something in place, he wanted to be able to upgrade to a level he felt more comfortable with. Discovering she still used a set of dime-store push locks had nearly set him off. No wonder her father was scared. He wasn't the only one.

Sam took a calming breath. Regardless of the lack of adequate countermeasures, Bridg had managed to dodge any life-threatening attempts—and he was pretty damn sure there had been at least one after her slip with the word 'still' during their conversation. Now that her father had hired Sam—he'd personally see that her adorable ass stayed in one piece.

He pushed down the riotous strum of his pulse. She'd made it more than obvious she didn't want to have anything to do with him. Hell, she'd wanted to boot him out. Playing the part of her protector was about as close as he was going to get. And the sooner he got any traitorous thoughts out of his head, the better.

Indecision weighed on his mind as he made his way down the hallway. It wasn't as if he and Bridgette had been dating for years—had envisioned a life together. It had only been about eight months before everything had imploded and he'd walked—ran—away from her. From his life in Livingston. Not that he regretted joining the Army—making it through Ranger training. And if things had turned out differently, he would have happily spent his life in the service.

But things hadn't worked out, and Sam was faced with the cold reality that he needed to find a way to make civilian life his new goal. Joining Brotherhood

Protectors had been a great first step. The work he'd performed over the past ten months had managed to ease some of the worry that he'd never find another way to matter like he had as a soldier. A way to help people. But that was only one part of his new life.

He couldn't hide behind duty anymore. Couldn't spend every waking moment immersed in his job. Now that he'd gotten comfortable with living beyond his unit, he needed to make other aspects of his life an equal priority. Christ, he needed…someone.

He hadn't been lying to Bridgette. He couldn't remember the last time he'd been with a woman and had it be more than a way to blow off steam. A mutual ride that ended with the rising sun. It hadn't seemed to matter before, but as he'd walked around her house, it had been impossible not to imagine two generations of her family living their lives inside those four walls. Watching children grow and move on. Passing on their legacy. And it had made Sam realize he really had nothing to show for his thirty years. A few medals. More scars than he cared to admit to. A laundry list of regrets. But nothing—concrete.

You're slipping, Sammy. Getting soft.

Sam mentally flipped off the voice in his head. The one that hadn't quite come to terms with leaving his old life behind. Getting shoved out, actually. The part of him that still heard Gray whispering in the night, or saw reflections of the man in the shadows on the wall. Knowing his buddy wouldn't get a chance to make a life still burned hot in Sam's gut. Still ate at his soul until he wondered if living was really his punishment for letting Gray down. For failing.

The steady thrum of music pulled Sam out of his thoughts as he stopped outside Bridgette's office. A series of dull thuds sounded beyond the door, and he opened it, only to stop and stare. She was punching the bag he'd noticed hanging in one corner earlier when he'd installed the detector, the hollow echo of each hit bouncing off the walls. She seemed completely focused on the rhythmic strikes, not even glancing at him as he entered, moving to stand a few feet behind her.

Her increased breath panted through the room, her movements making him smile. She'd obviously been taking lessons for a few years, and Sam didn't doubt she could knock the average guy on his ass if need be. Not that he'd admit that to her—give her an excuse to try and kick him out the door, again.

Bridgette kneed the bag, lining up another strike when she must have felt his presence. She spun, landing a hook to his ribs before he'd managed to duck. The hit sent a jolt of pain through his torso, the old injury flaring to life. He blocked her second punch, shouting her name as he backed away.

She stopped, chest heaving, sweat dripping off her jaw as her eyes widened. She immediately pulled back, dropping her hands as her mouth gaped open. "Shit, Sam. I'm so sorry. I got so caught up in the workout, I forgot you were here, and then you startled me, and I just…reacted. Are you okay?"

He rubbed his side, trying not to focus on the raised scar that passed beneath his fingers, even through his sweater. "You do pack quite the punch for someone of your size, but…I've been hit by guys twice mine, so, yeah. I'm fine. You might want to try and twist your hips a bit more as you extend your arm next time. It'll make those strikes even more effective."

"Thanks. I'll remember that. Are you finished with the alarm?"

Sam held up his phone. "All set. The code is zero, two, one, four."

Bridgette nodded, mouthing the numbers a few times before pausing. "Wait, that's Valentine's day."

"It's usually easier to remember codes if they have some kind of personal meaning."

She arched her brow. "Call me crazy, but I didn't picture a bunch of Army Rangers celebrating Valentine's Day with roses and chocolate."

"Think farther back."

"Farther? No."

He smiled.

"Are you telling me that the date of our six-month anniversary has personal meaning to you?"

"As I recall, it had a pretty spectacular ending. The first of many over the next few months. And you always were a hard benchmark to meet, darling. Though, I'm a bit surprised you remembered. I would have thought you'd purged every last memory of us out of that pretty head of yours."

She tsked him. "You know, for some highly trained super soldier, who parachutes from thirty-thousand feet and infiltrates enemy territory as if it was a walk in the park, you know nothing about women."

"Is that so?"

"I'd just turned eighteen. You were my first serious boyfriend. I lost my virginity to you—that very night, as you implied. Of course I remember everything—every date, every kiss, every other time we..." She cleared her throat then gave him a sweet smile. "It's a girl thing."

His stomach tensed as desire hit him hard. While he might not have spent every waking moment fantasizing about her or their time together—agonizing over how it had all fallen apart—he'd thought about her often— more than had probably been wise. A fact he'd managed to ignore, until now.

Uncertainty weighed down his shoulders. He didn't like feeling this way—being out of control. Especially, where she was concerned. He had a job, and it wasn't shoving her against the wall and making her scream out a release.

He drew himself up, hoping to lighten the mood. "Like never dressing for the weather and always stealing the guy's jacket? That kind of girl thing?"

"I only ever did that once. And I'll have you know that I haven't asked for another guy's jacket since." She wiped at the sweat beading her forehead. "And for the record, when women borrow men's clothes, it's not just about being cold."

"Really? Then why?"

"Usually, because it's big and comfy and it smells like the guy. It's kind of like being hugged, I guess. It makes us feel safe. At least, that's my experience."

Sam edged closer. "Your experience? From the one time you wore my jacket?"

"You used to lend me your sweaters, too. But, yes, from that one time. I don't need fifty other references to know why I liked wearing your stuff."

He moved with her when she went to dart past him.

"So, why haven't you borrowed other boyfriend's jackets?"

Her smile fell as some of the color drained from her face. She fumbled with the sparring gloves on her hands, shrugging as she pulled them off. "Never needed to. I own a phone. I can check the weather, now."

Fuck. If Sam needed more proof that someone had hurt her, it was staring back at him.

He shifted enough to let her walk past, following her out. "I thought it wasn't just about being cold?"

Her pace increased as she headed for the stairs. "Is there anything else you need to tell me? About the alarm? Is it going to go off at night if I decide to get up and work, or get thirsty?"

He sighed. Obviously, her previous relationships were off limits where he was concerned. "It'll be fine. But it will sound if you leave without disarming it." He smiled when she stopped on the first step and glanced back at him over her shoulder. "And I'll get notified whenever you do that. Just so you know."

A hint of a smile lifted her lips. "So, I'm a prisoner, now."

"Prisoner is such a harsh term, Counselor. I prefer to think of it as temporary isolation."

"Men. I'm going to shower then maybe get some dinner. I assume you're locked in here with me?" She shook her head at his nod. "I'll make up some wraps after. You can cook tomorrow."

"Bridgette."

She paused, again, a few stairs up. "Yes?"

He climbed up until his face was even with hers.

"You know you can tell me anything, right? That I won't judge you or criticize your past decisions?"

"Just like you didn't criticize my lack of a bodyguard, earlier?"

He groaned. *Fuck.* "Fair, even if I was doing it to make a point. Regardless... Let me rephrase my statement, then. I promise I won't judge anything *else* you say to me."

The muscle in her jaw flexed as she seemed to force air in and out through her nose. She broke eye contact, furrowing her brow before finally looking at him. "Is that your subtle way of asking me if I'm hiding something?"

"We both know you are. I just wanted you to know that I'm not the same guy I was at eighteen. Not that I'm trying to make excuses for being an utter prick to you back then, but..." He lifted one hand and brushed some stray wisps of hair out of her face, cursing under his breath when she flinched slightly before quickly recovering. "If there's something I should know—someone else who might want to hurt you. Get back at you for something that's not related to this case—to any case—you can tell me. We've all got regrets and unfortunate decisions in our past."

"Unfortunate decisions? That's one way of putting it. I would have called it an epic fuck up, but..."

"But..."

"But nothing. I'm sure this is just one of Stevens' men trying to scare me."

He sighed. "I have all the non-sensitive files on Alexander Stevens and his drug cartel. But Hank didn't have time to gather any background information on your previous cases. I'll need a list of all the people you've helped get convicted since you started at the U.S. Attorney's office."

"Since I started? I've been involved in nearly thirty cases."

"And we'll have to go through each one. Rank the offenders according to how much we think they'd like to see you dead. While Stevens is the logical choice, I've discovered it's better if I don't make assumptions. Less likely something will crop up I'm not prepared for."

"Killing me won't stop the case from going to trial. You know that, right? They'll just give it to someone else. Which is why this has got to be posturing."

"I hope you're right. But it's my job to make sure we're prepared in case it isn't."

"Can I have a shower, first?"

He smiled. "I'd insist that you do."

"Ass."

"I'll go over the photos you just got. See if I can use them to trace back to the photographer. I don't suppose you kept a record of your previous threats?"

She pursed her lips, looking as if she was deciding how to answer, before releasing a weary breath. "There's a key in the left drawer of my desk. It opens the locked cabinet beneath the window. There's a folder with anything anyone has ever sent me that was... disturbing. Though, I might not have all the photographs here. But I can call the office and have them sent over."

"An entire folder? I know you said you'd been getting threats the past couple of years, but... How many times, exactly, have you been threatened to this extent?"

She paused, again, and he had an eerie suspicious that she was resisting saying the word never. That this time was so much worse than the threats she'd received before. But he knew she'd never admit to that. At least, not yet.

Bridgette sighed. "You'll just get angry if I tell you that."

"Five?" He narrowed his eyes when she simply stared back at him. "Ten? Christ, it's more than ten?"

"See? Angry."

"Of course, I'm angry, Bridg. You act as if it's no big deal." He held up his hand. "And I swear, if you tell me one more time that it's part of your job…"

"Sam."

"Your job is to see justice is served. Not to have people trying to kill you."

Her smile reached all the way to her eyes this time as she returned the favor and brushed a lock of hair out of his face. "How about we focus on the fact that nothing happened those…twelve other times."

"Twelve? Seriously?"

"I'm fine. And this time…I have you. So…" She pulled back her hand, staring at him with an odd expression before climbing up another step. "Go have a look. I'll join you when I'm done."

"Bridgette."

She chuckled as she glanced at him one more time. "Getting pretty chilly here."

"I meant what I said before. You can tell me anything."

Her chin quivered for a moment before she waved

him off. "I'm cold. And I stink, so...I'll be down in a bit."

He watched her round the landing then continue to the top, disappearing down the hallway. He stared at his hand, the lingering soft brush of her hair still tingling his skin. This was far more than he'd bargained on. How had he thought any residual feelings for her had withered and died? That he'd be able to be around her every minute of every day for the next few weeks and not want to do so much more than simply keep her safe? He just wasn't sure if it was temporary lust or something more.

CHAPTER FIVE

"This is crazy."

Bridgette glanced up from her laptop as Sam's voice sounded in the room, watching him spear his fingers through his hair until he'd fisted the strands at the back of his head. His blue eyes looked far more captivating than she remembered, though she had a feeling it wasn't just his eyes—it was him. All of him. From his shaggy locks to every hard inch of muscle, and god, was there a lot of muscle.

He'd volunteered to work with her on her kick boxing the past few days, and after a couple of hours of kicks and strikes, he'd stripped off his shirt. The sheer expanse of rippled flesh had stolen what little breath she'd had, and had left her feeling weak-kneed. And from much more than just fatigue.

Though, she hadn't missed the collection of scars crisscrossing his body—testament to everything he'd endured during his time in the service. Something he'd made clear was off limits, even if she hadn't come right out and questioned him on it. But it had been obvious by the shift in his eyes and the way he'd studied her that he'd been waiting for her to ask. And she'd felt certain he would have stopped the discussion before it had begun.

It seemed she wasn't the only one harboring secrets. Or who had changed over the past decade. But if she were honest, it wasn't his body that impressed her the most. The man was funny and sincere, with an intelligence that rivaled any scholar she'd encountered. His years in the service had brought out qualities in him she hadn't known he possessed, and the more time she spent with him, the harder it was to remember why she'd held a grudge for so long. Hell, it wasn't as if she hadn't made some horrible mistakes.

She brushed her fingers along her side, cursing silently when she realized Sam was following the movement. She had a bad feeling he'd guessed far more than she wanted him to know about the parts of her past she'd been keeping from him. But so far, in the week they'd been unlikely roommates, he hadn't pushed her for more information. In fact, he'd been the perfect guest—if having him shadow her every move, from work, to exercising, to getting groceries—classified him as a guest.

Either way, he'd definitely taken keeping her safe to a whole new level. He'd gone ballistic when she'd received a series of ominous calls on her new cell a couple days ago, especially when all his high-tech gear deduced was that the calls had come from a burner phone with a Seattle number. Nothing new, there. But since then, he'd increased his vigilance, not that she'd thought that was possible. But somehow, he'd gotten closer. He'd insisted on sleeping on a mattress on the floor in her room—a fact that had unnerved her the most. She'd been worried she'd have a nightmare, and end up telling him everything. But so far, she'd managed to hold it together.

Though, she'd heard him mumbling the past two nights and was curious what he'd been dreaming about. What missions still haunted him. Who the person was he'd called for a few times—not that she'd ask without provocation. The last thing she needed was to start that conversation. Give him a reason to question her.

Bridgette worked up a smile, nodding at the papers spread around the table. "Is there a problem?"

He narrowed his eyes, still focusing on her side before dragging his gaze up to meet hers. "Do you have any idea how many of your previous cases have suspects that are both capable and likely to be the person threatening to kill you?"

"Most of the offenders are still incarcerated. I'd say seven. Maybe eight."

"Seventeen, darling. Seventeen highly unstable, morbidly violent assholes have the means to either come after you themselves, or hire someone to do it. Being in jail doesn't seem to slow these guys down. At least three of them are still running their gangs from the inside."

She leaned back in her chair, resting her arms on the table. "It's a daunting task. Just getting enough evidence to make a trial possible is often years in the making. The police are overtasked and underfunded. And once we do manage to incarcerate someone…it's frustrating to try and gather more intel. The rules change once you're inside. All we can do is keep monitoring the gangs. Hope we can put more of them away."

She scrunched up her nose. "Though, seventeen sounds a bit high. Are you sure?"

He arched his brow.

"Fine. You're sure. I didn't realize they'd added up to that many over the past few years. Once I'm finished with a case, I move on to the next. Even now, I have three more I'm working on while I'm waiting for this trial to start. It's endless."

"In other words, there's a new list of people who will have your name on the top of their shit list."

"Only if I win."

"That doesn't seem to be a problem." Sam stood then made his way over to her desk. "And that's not even considering the felons you made deals with."

"I doubt you have to include them. The people who makes deals want to do their time and move on. Repent, I guess. Besides, I don't deal on the big cases. Period. Never have. Never will."

Sam palmed the table. "You know, if someone had bet me back when we were teenagers that you'd become this ball-busting lawyer, I'd have taken that bet. Whatever happened to becoming a psychologist? I thought you wanted to probe into people's psyches? Figure out what made them tick then help them put all their shit back together?"

A ghostly voice echoed in the back of her mind, followed by flashes of that night. The one she couldn't quite remember but could never forget. The disgust that had resonated in his words. The feel of his boot against her ribs. The cold slide of the knife…

She pushed to her feet, ignoring the way the chair scraped along the wood, making the hairs on the back of her neck stand up. "I started down that road. Got my bachelor's in psychology with a minor in law. Even managed to get my Master's in Forensic Psychology over the past few years from an online university." She smiled. "Between cases, when I had time."

"So, why go to law school, at all, instead of pursuing that straight off? It's obviously still a passion if you squeezed in enough time to get your Master's when you were already working your butt off as a lawyer. Looking at all of your past cases, there's no question you're kick ass in the courtroom. I'm sure you would have been just as great working the other side of things as a psychologist."

"People change. Take different paths. And I'd like to think I've done my part in making Seattle a bit safer for everyone. That I haven't sat idly by and prayed for a solution. I've made my own."

"Of course, you have. It's just…"

She cursed under her breath at the way he stared at her, and she knew she'd just given him more proof that she had demons lurking beneath her skin. She sighed. "I'm not the only mystery, you know. I never would have dreamed that you'd join the Army Rangers. Make it all the way through that training. Not many do. And you made lieutenant. That's impressive, Sam. You're a hero."

Shadows crossed his expression as he drew himself up. "Not a hero. Definitely not that." He narrowed his eyes then crossed his arms over his chest. "How long are we going to do this?"

A hint of panic cooled her skin, beading it with bumps. "Do what?"

"Are you really going to stand there and treat me like a fool? I realize I still have some groveling to do from before—if you ever let me explain—but you just said it, yourself. I'm not who I was before."

He moved around the table, gently taking one of her hands in his as he gave her an encouraging smile. "I thought you should know. I called Hank that day I arrived. I asked him to have his contacts look into something for me."

Bile burned the back of her throat. "Do I want to know what that was?"

He pursed his lips then released her hand, bracing one hip against her desk. "I wanted to know if you'd ever been involved in any personal lawsuits or criminal cases. If there were other factors that could impact this assignment."

"Personal?" She swallowed against the hard punch of fear, taking a quick step backwards. God, if he'd unearthed…

She wrapped her arms around her waist, doing her best to hold herself together. "I've never filed a personal lawsuit. Or been in a criminal case other than as a lawyer. A fact you could have just asked me about instead of going behind my back."

"Hank confirmed you hadn't. But you're only lying to yourself if you think you would have told me if you had."

"That's not fair. I've been very cooperative, especially

since I didn't want you here in the first place. Yet, you're still here."

"With respect to my presence and your work, absolutely. In fact, you've been a model client. But where your private life is concerned—"

"That's because it's just that. Private. And it has no bearing on someone sending me photos in the mail or calling my cell. I'm trying to put the head of the Stevens' family in jail for one of the largest drug smuggling rings we've uncovered to date. That's who's behind the threats."

"While I agree that's the logical answer, I can't rule out that someone might be using this case—a very high profile, publicly broadcast case—as a way of getting to you while keeping the focus on Stevens and the people under him. It would be the perfect cover."

"That seems like a bit of a stretch to me. This isn't some covert mission, Sam. Where real life is concerned, the obvious answer is generally the correct one. Like the saying goes…when you hear thundering hooves, think horses, not zebras."

"Assumptions are dangerous, and I won't allow you to get injured on my watch because I was too damn lazy or stupid to look beyond the obvious." He straightened, taking a step toward her. "I'm not prying just so you can think I'm an ass. I'm worried that whatever you're keeping from me might be tied to the threats against you. And I can't protect you if I don't have all the facts."

"It's not."

Sam broke eye contact, looking as if he was searching for patience, before releasing a long, slow breath. "I'm not saying this to piss you off, but seeing as it's my job to keep you safe, I should be the one to judge what's a threat and what isn't."

"Do you think I want someone to hurt me?"

He snapped his head up. "Of course not—"

"Then, I'm serious when I say, this is about work. Not my personal life."

"Bridgette..."

"Why did you leave the military?"

Sam inhaled, clenching his jaw then retreating a step. "Excuse me?"

"You want me to tell you what I'm hiding, then I think you should have to do the same. So...why did you leave the military?"

"You already know why."

"As I recall, all you said was that you weren't in the service anymore. That's not a reason."

He copied her stance, crossing his arms over his massive chest—making the muscles in his biceps flex, even through his sweater. "I got injured on a mission and was medically discharged. Your turn."

She scoffed. "Oh no. That's the easy, non-disclosure response you give everyone. Not the real one. And I'd know. I have a practiced answer, too. Want to hear it? I dated a guy who turned out to be a bit of a dick. But who hasn't?"

"This dick have a name?"

"If we're talking names, then who's Gray?"

Sam's nostrils flared, and he took another step back, bumping into the table. The thing slid sideways a bit, nearly tipping him onto his ass before he regained his balance by palming the surface. She didn't miss his increased breath, or the extra white in his eyes.

He closed them for a moment, then wet his lips before focusing on her, again. "How…"

She did her best to stay rooted to the spot, despite her innate desire to wrap her arms around him and shelter him from whatever memories haunted him. "You called out his name a few times the past couple of nights. I assume it's a him. A fellow Army Ranger."

The muscle in his temple pulsed. "I… He…"

She couldn't stop herself from moving forward this time. "You don't have to tell me. I was trying to make a point, but… I shouldn't have gone there. That was a low blow, and I'm sorry."

She kicked at the floor, sighing. "I know you're only trying to keep me safe, but… Shit. I'm not quite there. Not ready to talk about it. Some memories are better left buried. So for now, just please, trust me."

His chest heaved as he drew in a few deep breaths, the wild look in his eyes finally easing. He gave her a curt nod then walked back to his desk, not making eye contact as he lowered into the chair then started digging through the papers, again. She returned to her spot, cursing at the uncomfortable silence that stretched out between them. The tension in the room grew until doing anything other than breathing seemed impossible.

Bridgette closed her laptop then stood, making her way over to Sam. It took a few moments of standing in front of his work area before he finally looked up at her. Not even a hint of a smile curved his lips as he leaned back in his chair and stared at her as if she might lash out at him.

"Look, it's been a long few weeks." She sighed and let her shoulders slump a bit. "Honestly, it's been a long few years. And I tend to forget that I'm not in the courtroom all the time. That I need to pull back and not treat everything—*everyone*—with the same...intensity. I have a bad habit of going straight for the jugular, which explains why the few friends I have are either other lawyers, cops, or feds. I'm just not that great around other people. I have a hard time turning it all off."

Sam arched a brow. "Like I said before. Winning doesn't seem to be an issue for you."

"I'll assume that's your polite way of saying I'm cutthroat."

"You're a lawyer. That's to be expected."

"Right." She glanced away. While she suspected he'd meant it in a positive way, she couldn't quite crush the feeling that he viewed her like most people did—heartless. Cold. Dare she say unlovable?

"Bridg."

She forced herself to make eye contact, again.

He gave her a smile. "I didn't mean to imply—"

"Forget it. It's fine."

"Darling—"

She cursed the way the word rolled over her. He'd been using it since he'd breezed into her life, again, and it still affected her far too much. Made her long to hear him say it in more intimate surroundings.

"No. Really. I'm not really fond of lawyers, either. But... What I came over to say was, I'm beat. I think I just read the same paragraph seven times, which is a pretty good indication it's time to close the laptop. But, seeing as it's not that late, yet, I thought I'd make some popcorn. Put on a movie and wrap myself in a blanket on the couch. Care to join me?"

He tilted his head to the side as if trying to read whether she had ulterior motives before waving at the papers. "I still haven't narrowed down this long list of suspects."

"And I doubt you'll have it all figured out in the next couple of hours. Not because you're incapable, but because I'm betting there isn't any way to narrow it down. Come on, Sam. It's just a couple of hours. Didn't you say you had to stay close to me?"

He chuckled. "Using my own words against me. That's shrewd, Counselor."

"How about I sweeten the deal? You kick back and join me for a movie, and I'll let you pick what we watch. And…" She held up her hand when he went to interrupt here. "I have a case of beer in the fridge. Smithwicks. Nice and thick the way you like it."

"I get to pick, and you're plying me with alcohol. This sounds serious. I'll take your offer, but I'll just have a pop."

"A pop? What are you, twelve?"

"I'm working."

It was her turn to laugh. "Are you seriously telling me that the mighty Sam Montgomery can no longer hold his liquor? That you'll be impaired after one beer? Because the guy I knew could handle six when he was eighteen and still kick ass with the best of them."

He pushed to his feet. "Goading me, now?"

"I'm talking one beer. One. I don't drink often, either."

"You drive a hard bargain, but all right. We'll each have one beer, and you have to promise to watch the entire movie. No running off because you don't like what I choose."

"Deal. Just...no horror movies, okay? Or anything that's going to make me cry."

"But horror movies are the best. And I'd get the benefit of you begging me to hold you and keep you safe."

"In your dreams, Montgomery." She huffed, then headed for the doorway. "Fine. Pick whatever you want. Horror. Some sad flick that will have me questioning my life choices. I'm a big girl. I can handle it."

She stopped and glanced at him over her shoulder. "But when I wake up screaming in the night and freak you out, no crying foul."

She left, palming her stomach as butterflies fluttered to life, followed by a wave of heat just beneath her skin. Sensations she hadn't felt in...well, since she'd dated Sam back in high school. Though, considering her past, it wasn't much of a surprise that he was her benchmark of men. Not when the only other guy she'd gotten serious with had turned out to be an abusive prick. Still...she couldn't quite deny that her mandatory prison stay was turning out to be far more enjoyable than she'd imagined. And it wasn't close to being over.

CHAPTER SIX

Sam relaxed on the couch, watching Bridgette walk in from the kitchen balancing a bowl of popcorn and a couple bottles of beer. She held one out to him, smiling when he took it, then placed the bowl on the coffee table along with her drink. The cushion next to him dipped as she sank into it, tucking her feet to the side before tugging a soft, thick blanket over top of her.

He didn't miss the way she inhaled when her feet brushed against his thigh—as if even that contact made her wary. Anger burned beneath his skin, but he did his best to let it go. While he wanted to know who the guy was she'd described as "a bit of a dick", Sam wasn't quite ready to talk about Gray. And he knew Bridgette well enough to know she'd never willingly tell him what she was hiding without demanding the same from him. Just thinking that she'd heard him call out Gray's name made him sweat. His best bet was to give her some more time. Maybe then she'd confide in him without grilling him about why he'd left the service.

Bridgette took a pull of her beer, and the tension bled from her shoulders. She let her head fall against the sofa as she turned enough to stare at him. "Well? Do I want to know what you've picked?"

He grinned. "You say that as if you have no faith in me."

"Damn, it's a horror movie, isn't it? I knew I never should have told you they creep me out."

"I don't recall you using those words. You just said not to pick one, which of course meant I should absolutely pick one."

She rolled her eyes. "Thirty years old and you're still basically just a big kid. All right, put it on."

"Are you sure? It's not too late to admit you're scared...ask me to go easy on you."

"And have to put up with you teasing me for the foreseeable future? That's not the kind of deal I'd ever take, so..."

"Whatever you say."

Sam started the movie, then sat back, munching on popcorn as he slowly nursed his beer. Every few moments he glanced at Bridgette, noting the tight press of her lips and the way she fisted the blanket until her knuckles turned white. She obviously didn't enjoy being scared. Though, watching her try to keep from screaming every time something jumped out on the screen was priceless.

He resisted the smile twitching his lips. He'd already planned on stopping it partway through and putting on an action film. One he suspected she'd enjoy, but the chance to tease her had been too good to pass up. Instead, he sat there, chuckling whenever she startled, until she tossed a handful of popcorn at him.

He placed his hand over his chest. "That wasn't nice, darling."

"Don't you darling me, you traitor. I just hope you think this is all still funny when neither of us gets any sleep for the next week. Because I'll be seeing these freaking apparitions whenever I close my eyes for days."

"Guess it's a good thing I'm just a few feet away, then."

"Means I won't miss when I launch things at your head."

He laughed, and she threw more popcorn at him before purposely turning toward the television. She jumped a moment later, cursing under her breath as she drew the edge of the blanket up to her chin.

Sam glanced away, trying hard not to smile. Just a few more minutes and he'd end her torture. He turned back to the screen just as one of the creepy ghosts picked up a knife and headed down a long hallway—the creature's progress marked by a series of light flashes from the flickering lamps. He had a bad feeling this kill was going to be even bloodier than the last.

He sighed when a door flung open on its own, the blood-curling scream of the woman trapped in the bathroom echoing around them. No sense putting Bridgette through another gory scene. "Okay, Bridg. You've been more than game. I'll change…"

His voice trailed off as he looked over at her. All the color had drained from her face, as her chest heaved—the wheezy sound too fast to be effective. The beautiful blue hue of her eyes had been overshadowed by white, and her hands shook as she held the blanket just below her nose, the fluffy material knotted amidst her fists.

He leaned over. "Bridgette? Are you okay?"

His answer was another series of gasping pants.

He reached for her hand, the brief caress making her scream. She scrambled to her feet, dropping the blanket in a pool of gray around her ankles before taking a few stumbling steps back. One of her heels kicked a leg of the coffee table, tumbling her onto her ass. But she managed to bolt up, again, retreating to the wall on the far side of the room, all the while staring at Sam as if she'd never seen him before.

He stopped the movie, then stood, keeping his movements slow. She flinched when he took a step toward her, before she raised her hands into her boxing stance.

"Easy. I'm not going to attack you."

She glanced at the television, then back to him, hands still held up in front of her.

"Bridgette. Whatever it is you think you see isn't real. It's just you and me, here. And you know in your heart I'd never hurt her. Just try to slow your breathing. Break through those other images and find your way back."

He inched forward, stopping for a few minutes whenever she reacted to his motion. It took a while, but he finally got to within arm's length of her. A blue tinge colored her lips, her frantic breath still sounding around them.

"Slow your breathing. You're not getting enough oxygen. I don't want you to pass out."

Tears glistened in her eyes, a few slipping free before

she closed them, then dropped her head until she could palm her face. Her shoulders shook, but she managed to slow her breath a bit.

"That's it. In and out. Nice and even."

He closed the distance, tugging her into his arms. She stiffened, pushing against his hold as she shouted mumbled words at him. But he stood his ground, grunting when she landed a few strikes to his ribs before her muscles eased. A hushed sob tightened his chest, the warm evidence of her tears seeping through his shirt and against his skin.

He gathered her closer, letting one hand fall to the small of her back as the other carded through the hairs on the back of her neck. He pressed her head against his shoulder then waited.

Time faded into the sound of her breath and the feel of her chest heaving against his. He didn't move, didn't speak, just stood there holding her until most of the trembling had subsided and she wasn't gasping for air.

He gave her a small smile, tucking some hair behind her ear when she finally pulled back, alternating her gaze between him and some spot off to her right. "Better?"

She snorted, clenching her jaw as a few more tears dotted her cheeks. "Not unless the floor decides to open up and swallow me."

"Hey. It wasn't that bad."

"Says the guy who didn't just have a meltdown in front of someone."

"I'm not someone. You've known me since you were twelve. And that wasn't a meltdown."

"You're right. It was far worse." She wiped her cheeks. "I'm sorry you had to see that."

He cupped her chin, waiting until she looked directly up at him. "Stop. You don't have anything to be sorry about. Or ashamed of. I shouldn't have picked that stupid movie. It was supposed to be a joke. Had I known it would trigger something..."

She shook her head, easing free of his arms then backing up until she could brace her ass against the wall. "Trust me. This isn't your fault. And I've watched plenty of stupid movies like that and been just fine. I'm not sure why that scene triggered me the way it did."

"Maybe because you've been getting death threats, and you're so damn stressed it's taking all your strength just to get through each day. You can only deal with so much at a time, before something's gotta give." He moved closer, relieved that she didn't try to back away from him. "I assume this has something to do with the guy you dated who was a bit of a dick?"

"You could say that."

"Was he more than just a bit?"

"He was an abusive son of a bitch, is what he was, but..." She blew out an exasperated breath, staring up at him. "Don't look at me like that. I wasn't blinded by love. I didn't stay in some fucked-up relationship, believing a bunch of empty promises that it wouldn't ever happen, again. It only happened once."

"I never assumed that you had, and the only look I gave you was one of concern. Because I get the feeling that the one time was exceedingly bad."

She closed her eyes and let her chin drop to her chest.

Fuck. He'd known something had happened to push her down a different path. Had suspected some asshole had hurt more than just her heart, but standing there, watching her retreat into herself, spiked fear in his gut he hadn't felt since he'd been trapped on the side of that cliff.

"Bridgette. Please talk to me."

She shook her head, bouncing her hair wildly about her shoulders. "I... I can't—"

"Keep running from this. Keep burying it on the hopes it'll fade because it never does. It festers until it explodes when you least expect it. I promise, I won't judge you."

Her head snapped up. "Judge me? I'm not afraid you'll judge me. I already judge myself. For not seeing the signs for what they were. For putting myself in that position. For letting it happen... God."

He inched closer then reached for one of her hands, holding it in both of his. "Nothing you say is going to shock me. I knew a few female soldiers who were abused by their commanding officers. It's unthinkable, and no one should have to face it. And if it makes it any easier to talk about, this isn't news to me. I knew someone had hurt you from the first day."

Her mouth gaped open, but all she did was stare at him.

He gave her hand a squeeze. "Your body language. The way you shied away from any contact. Landing a few punches before you realized it was me. Your drastic change in career. You can talk to me. Trust me."

Her eyes narrowed before she looked away, again.

"Shit. It all comes back to that night, doesn't it? Prom. Fine. Let's talk about Jenny Stinson."

He took a deep breath. "Condensed version—I didn't sleep with her that night. Not saying I never did. I'm not exactly proud of those teenage years, but I've never cheated. And I stopped having sex with her the moment you agreed to go out with me. True, it was pretty shitty of me to use her like that then drop her because I finally got you to notice me. And a douche-move not to tell you I'd been fucking her for a few months. But... Shit, you were my dream girlfriend, Bridg. I can't believe you thought I'd screwed around on you."

He pressed a finger across her lips, preventing her from interrupting. "It turns out that Jenny started seeing Brad Porter after me."

She frowned, waiting until he'd removed his finger. "Wasn't he your good friend?"

"Good and friend are subjective, and it turned out he was neither. But...that night, Brad came racing up to me in the gym and said he had an emergency. That a mutual friend was hurt, and he needed my help. You were in the washroom, so I darted out, thinking I'd only be a moment or two. It was Jenny. She was writhing on the ground with blood dripping down her legs. That's when Brad informed me she was pregnant and had tried to terminate the pregnancy by herself."

"Damn."

"Yeah. So, I loaded her in my truck and took her to the hospital. Brad gave some bullshit story about why he couldn't come, so I told him to tell you there had been an emergency, and that I'd make it up to you. Of course, he decided to tell you I'd run off to sleep with

Jenny, instead. By the time I clued in to what had gone down...well, no one was talking to me."

She frowned. "Why didn't you try to explain all of this instead of just disappearing?"

"Like you would have believed my version back then."

"God, I was right before. You really don't understand women at all, do you? They should teach you guys a bit about that between all the weapon and hand-to-hand combat classes."

"So, you're saying you would have listened to me?"

"I was in love with you, Sam. And I was eighteen. Yes, I would have believed you. I would have talked myself into if need be. I kept waiting for some kind of explanation. Then, you left, and I figured it was because everything was true, and you didn't want to face me."

Shit. All this time, and he'd left for the wrong reasons.

He sighed. "You're right about not wanting to face you, and while I'm sorry I hurt you, I can't change the past. Probably wouldn't even if I could because that one act is why I ended up in that recruitment center. Why I signed on to have a chance at the Army Rangers, and it made me a far better man than I would have been otherwise. So... Now that we have that straightened out, I'd like to know how bad that asshole hurt you."

She crossed her arms over her chest in a clearly defensive stance as she continued to kick at the floor.

"Bridgette."

"He put me in the hospital, okay? Almost killed me."

"Do you think you could start closer to the beginning?"

She scrubbed her hands down her face, her fingers still trembling, before finally meeting his gaze. "It was near the beginning of my third year at college. We'd gone out to our favorite pub to celebrate our one-year anniversary. Up until that night, Brock had been the perfect boyfriend. He didn't yell. We'd never really fought. I'd noticed that he got…possessive at times. Especially if other men talked to me. And there had been a few instances when he hadn't passed on messages because he didn't want me to go out without him."

She nodded. "I know. Those were huge red flags, and I should have listened to the voice in my head telling me he wasn't all that he seemed. But all my girlfriends kept insisting it was a good thing. That I was so lucky to have found someone so invested in me. Someone who worshipped me."

She huffed. "Satanic worship, maybe. Because it turned out that he wasn't invested in me. He thought he owned me. That he could control every aspect of my life. That night, a friend came over to talk to me while Brock was off getting us drinks. He went crazy when he got back, practically starting a fight. I told him I wanted him to take me home. That I was done with him acting like a child."

Sam nodded. "What happened next?"

"He didn't speak to me the entire ride home. I was convinced it was over. Then, he said he wouldn't feel right if he didn't see me to the door. That it was his duty to make sure I stayed safe, and that he was sorry. I should have just gotten out of his car and gone up on my own. But it was dark, and I didn't exactly live in the best neighborhood, so I agreed. I said goodbye on the porch and told him we could talk about it the next day. But as soon as I opened the door..."

Sam clenched his fists, images of her story playing out in his mind. And he had no trouble picturing how it ended. "He hit you."

She pursed her lips, giving him a shaky nod. "He's big, like you, and that one punch knocked me into the wall. I hit my head on a shelf then fell on the floor. That's the last clear memory I have. The rest are just flashes, like when lightning gives you a glimpse of a room. He was yelling. Something about me being a slut. That I wasn't worthy of him. I remember him kicking me a few times, then..."

She closed her eyes as shivers shook through her, beading her skin with bumps. Another round of tears washed down her face, falling silently to the floor.

Sam brushed his thumb across one cheek, wiping away the moisture before lifting her chin enough to make eye contact "He can't hurt you, now. Anyone who tries to, has to go through me, first. And I promise you, they won't make it."

She swallowed, nodding too fast to be believable. "I remember looking up and seeing a knife. He was still screaming at me, then there was this burning pain in my side. I must have blacked out for a bit before waking, again. I saw all the blood, and I managed to crawl over to my phone—call for help. There were sirens and disjointed voices, then I woke up in the hospital a few days later."

"The fucker stabbed you?"

"Sam—"

"Please tell me you put his ass in jail for the next twenty-five years."

"I tried. I know the knife was still in my side when they took me to the hospital, but it disappeared from evidence. And when the cops went to question him, suddenly, he had all these guys swear we'd gone to his house, and I'd left alone."

Sam leaned in close. "What's Brock's last name?"

"Worthington."

Pieces fell into place as he hissed out his next breath. "As in Senator Dwayne Worthington's son?"

"That was the day I learned that money could buy you any version of the truth you wanted. Without the knife, it was my word against his. The smattering of other evidence wasn't enough to attempt to prosecute someone with his connections. I was basically told I could pursue a civil suit if I wanted, but my time and money would be better spent on therapy."

"That's why you became a lawyer."

"The courses I'd taken hadn't prepared me for anything like that. So, I switched gears. I worked even harder, studied for the LSAT, passed it, and applied to a few law programs. I guess it paid off because I got accepted that year. After that, I never looked back, and I swore I wouldn't let anyone else feel helpless the way I had. All those years as a public defender was a desperate attempt to give that singular moment some sort of meaning. Then, I realized that I could go after bigger assholes if I joined the U.S. Attorney's office. And now...now I'm back to hiding because there're monsters under my bed, again."

"Hey." He shook his head. "We're not hiding. We're

making wise choices based on the information we have."

"Feels the same from where I'm standing."

"That's because you're too hard on yourself. You seem to think you have something to prove. Which you don't. Though, I will be taking a good long look into Mr. Brock Worthington."

"There's no reason for him to come after me. He won."

"So far. But we both know that situations change over time. Maybe something changed that's got him worried."

"They did just extend the time to press charges for attempted murder up to ten years in Washington state, so theoretically, he's liable, again, for a few years should I want to try and make a case against him."

"Bingo."

"Having a few more years doesn't do me any good if I don't have new evidence to make a case."

Her shoulders slumped, and she braced more of her weight against the wall. Another round of shivers rose more goosebumps along her skin, and she released his hand to rub hers along her arms. If he'd thought he'd felt protective of her before, seeing her vulnerability exposed like this escalated his feelings to a new level.

He moved slowly, watching for any sign he was crowding her as he gently reached for her hands, again, and cupped them in his. "Come on. I have an idea."

She furrowed her brow but followed him back to the couch. He motioned for her to sit then took his place beside her. He found an old movie he knew they'd both watched before and put it on then turned to face her, lifting his arm so she could tuck herself against his side. Bridgette stared at the space, eyes wide.

He sighed. "I know it's hard to trust. But I swear I'd never hurt you like that."

The creases over her nose deepened. "What if I made you angry? Really, *really* angry?"

"Violence doesn't belong in a relationship. Ever. There's nothing you could do to make me raise a hand to you. What happened wasn't because of anything you did. It was all him."

She nodded, though he suspected a part of her didn't quite believe him. Not that he was surprised. It took more than pretty words to vanquish that kind of trauma. And it was obvious she hadn't come close to putting those demons to rest.

"Come on. You're exhausted, and I know it would be too much to have me hold you on the bed so...snuggle in. We'll watch an old movie, and if you fall asleep, then we'll just stay here. Where you hopefully won't feel trapped. Okay?"

She didn't move for a few moments, still staring at his side, then inched closer. He smiled as he laid his arm behind her shoulders and drew her against him, reclining both of them until her head was tucked into his shoulder while her body was next to his.

He dropped a kiss on her forehead, giving her a light squeeze. "Comfortable?"

Brilliant blue eyes looked up at him. "Yeah. Are you sure this is okay?"

He chuckled. "A beautiful woman in my arms? What wouldn't be okay about that?"

"Sam."

"It's perfect. Now, relax. I'll keep you safe tonight."

And a hell of a lot more if she'd let him. Because as she placed her hand on his chest, her soft breath caressing his neck, he realized he'd been fooling himself all these years if he'd thought he was remotely over her. He just needed to prove he was worth the risk.

CHAPTER SEVEN

"No, Gray."

Bridgette startled awake, the distinctly male voice rousing her from sleep. She blinked, trying to clear the hazy images, before freezing. Memories of the previous night slammed into her, making her acutely aware that not only had she told Sam everything, she'd agreed to cuddle with him on the couch—the same one she was still curled next to him on, with her head nestled into the crook of his shoulder while half of her body splayed across his. He had one arm wrapped around her back, and the other resting across his hip with his hand palming her waist.

She cringed inwardly. She was practically sleeping on top of the guy. And not just any guy—Sam-freaking-Montgomery. She hadn't been lying to her father. Sam was the only man who'd ever truly broken her heart, and who she'd wanted to stab through his on more than one occasion—make him feel even a fraction of the pain she'd felt when he'd left. When she'd thought he'd cheated on her.

Brock had never gotten to her like that. Sure, she'd fantasized about killing the bastard. But that was different. And she'd never loved him the way she had Sam. In fact, she'd never really loved anyone other than Sam. And it seemed she hadn't crushed that desire nearly as much as she'd thought.

She looked up at him as he twitched in his sleep. While she'd already been on her way to burying the past, learning the truth about it had shifted something inside her. Whether it had opened a door or closed one, she wasn't sure. All she knew was that he was the first person she'd trusted since she'd woken up in the hospital. And that lying in his arms all night had been more intimate than any sexual encounter she'd had in the past several years.

He whispered something she couldn't make out, grunting as if he'd been hurt. Bridgette shifted slightly, rubbing her hand on his chest in the hopes of calming him down without waking him. Sam called Gray's name, again, then settled, tightening his hold on her.

She inhaled, waiting for the panic that usually followed any kind of firm, physical contact, but the telltale flash of sweat didn't bead her skin or slither down her spine. All his embrace did was make her feel safe. She frowned. She wanted to offer him the same sense of peace he'd given her, but she still didn't know what ghosts haunted him. Who Gray was or why Sam felt guilty over whatever had happened. And she knew he felt guilty. He had the same tightness around his eyes, the same uneasy smile she'd been faking since that night with Brock. She just didn't know how to break through to Sam—convince him she could be his safe place to fall.

Bridgette groaned inwardly. Obviously, the stress of the upcoming trial and the threats she'd been receiving were getting to her. She wasn't anyone's "safe place to fall" least of all Sam's. He wasn't looking to reconnect with her. He'd simply been doing his job, and being a decent human being—proof that such a thing still existed. Getting her to talk about Brock had been a means to an end—a way to garner the information Sam had been worried about. And holding her all night had simplified his job. Stopped her from screaming awake and giving him a chance to sleep, too. It didn't mean anything else, and she needed to get any other idea out of her head. He'd be gone the moment the trial started, or they caught the creep.

Of course, her next case would likely start the cycle all over, again. More photos. More violent threats left on her cell. More days and nights spent looking over her shoulder. Just more emptiness.

Part of the job, she reminded herself. If she was going to seek this level of justice, she had to make peace with the ugly parts that accompanied it. The ones that hadn't seemed to bother her that much until Sam had shown up and made her feel...

She shook her head, stopping that train of thought. She prided herself in not *feeling* much of anything, other than her desire to win. That's how she kept her life uncluttered. Feeling led falling, which led to trusting that person never to hurt you. And that was one lesson she didn't need to learn twice. Simple, non-committal encounters were the only way she'd stay safe. Stay sane. Not everyone's happily ever after included a partner—a life outside of work. Hers would be found in the courtroom, putting men like Brock behind bars for the rest of their lives.

Sam groaned in his sleep, repositioning himself until he had her pressed tightly against him, his one hand slipping up from her waist to settle in the middle of her back. He smiled, dropping a kiss on her forehead before drifting off. The brief contact burned its way to her core, making her acutely aware of every inch of the man beneath her, including the hard ridge pressed against her thigh.

God, she remembered how large he'd been. How he'd taken his time, brought her orgasm multiple times before finally trying to slide inside her. Even then, their first time had been a fine line between pleasure and pain. But after that... She hadn't been with another guy, yet, who'd been able to set her off like Sam had. Who'd been as invested in her pleasure as much as their own. And she doubted she ever would.

Bridgette sighed, relaxing against him, again. Now wasn't the time to think about sex, especially when she wouldn't be in a position to have any for the foreseeable future. Even then, it would most likely be another empty encounter. Another failed attempt at pretending she was fine. That Brock hadn't broken her beyond repair. That he hadn't won despite what she'd told Sam the night before.

She closed her eyes, wondering if she'd be able to fall back to sleep with a thousand questions tumbling around in her head, only to wake when Sam moved. She blinked, again, this time squinting at the sun filtering through the windows. Large, square shadows covered the floor off to their left, suggesting they'd slept later than usual.

Sam sighed when she glanced up at him. "Sorry, Bridg. I was trying not to wake you."

She rubbed her eyes as she sat up, giving him room to move out from under her. "It's okay. Looks like it's already late. I never sleep in."

His smile made her stomach flutter. "Maybe that's your problem. You never let yourself shut down long enough to properly recharge. You can't keep pushing forward when you've got nothing in the tank. When's the last time you took a vacation?"

She laughed. "Vacation. Right. Good one."

"I'm serious. You obviously get time off. Surely you've taken advantage of that, even if it was just chilling in your apartment."

"I spent six years in school working my ass off to get the highest GPA I could, then went straight to work as a public defender. Taking time off wouldn't have gotten me a shot at the U.S. Attorney's office before the age of thirty. I had to earn that, and earning it meant working eighty-hour weeks, every week. Even now, it's a constant balancing act between work and breathing. I don't want to give them a reason to think they made a mistake when they took a chance on me."

Sam stared at her. "Taking time to ensure you stay physically and mentally sane isn't showing weakness. It's called being human."

"You say that as if you think I'm missing out on something."

"You are. Christ, even I've taken furloughs. Gone to Vegas or spent a week in Paris. Something other than a tent and endless desert landscape."

"That's different. You risked your life every day. You deserved some time to quiet all of that."

"And you don't? Just because you don't carry a gun doesn't mean you don't take risks. Why do you think I'm here?"

"Because my father is over-protective." She sighed at his huff of frustration. "Fine. I'm here, now. I can count this as my vacation."

"It's not a vacation when you spend twelve hours a day in your office working. A vacation means you don't do work. Period."

"If I don't work, all those cases—"

"Will still be there in a few days. They aren't going anywhere. I know people depend on your assessment of whether a charge is viable or not. Whether they've done their job well enough to have you prosecute. But a few days here and there won't change that outcome." He knelt in front of her, tucking her hair behind her ear. "You need to take better care of yourself. And I don't mean working out more hours a day. I mean you." He tapped her chest. "In here. And inside that pretty head of yours. You need to have fun."

She pushed down the traitorous leap of her heart when his finger brushed against her before falling back to his side. God, one innocent touch and she felt wired.

He arched a brow. "What's wrong, Counselor? Afraid you might actually discover you can have a life outside the courtroom?"

"I'm not afraid. I already know that isn't how my future plays out."

"Then you won't mind me trying to prove you wrong. How about a bet?"

She narrowed her eyes. "A bet?"

"You give me one day—today—and if by the end of it you haven't had any fun—if you still think it's a waste of your time—I won't bring the subject up, again."

"So, I'm just supposed to not work? At all?"

"It's Saturday. No one's working."

"You are."

He chuckled. "Damn, there's just no reasoning with you, is there? And I'll have you know that I had a week off between this assignment and my last one. I spent it in Eagle Rock, helping out at a friend's ranch. Communing with Mother Nature, you could say."

"You helped out at a ranch? Do you even know how to ride a horse?"

"Of course I do, but you're missing the point."

"Okay. Say I take this bet. What happens if you do win? If you magically make me see the light?"

"Then you give me tomorrow, as well."

It was her turn to laugh. "Two days off. In a row. That's madness. But...I'll take that bet because seeing as we're prisoners in here, I don't see how there's much fun to be had."

"I never said we couldn't go out. We just have to do it responsibly. Though, I can work my *magic*, as you called it, right here."

"Really?"

"Oh, I love the underlying tone of disbelief. You're going to have to eat crow tonight. Okay, first off, breakfast. And I'll cook. You can freshen up and put on comfortable clothes. Nothing fancy and nothing you wouldn't want to get dirty."

"Dirty?"

He smiled, tumbling her stomach, again. "Not knowing is half the fun. Go on. I'll be in the kitchen when you're ready. But don't keep me waiting."

Bridgette rolled her eyes then headed for the stairs. She washed up, deciding to shower after they'd done whatever might get her dirty then made her way back downstairs. She smiled as she walked into the kitchen, laughing at Sam's ensemble. "You know, that apron matches your eyes."

He grinned. It had the same effect as earlier, and made her wish she'd eaten, first, so she wouldn't have to mix food with the butterflies rioting in her stomach. "I was worried you wouldn't notice. Hungry?"

Her stomach growled, betraying the lie she'd been about to pass off.

Sam chuckled. "I'll take that as a yes. I noticed you're pretty much a vegetarian, but figured since you had eggs, they weren't taboo or something."

"Not taboo." She inhaled as he set down a plate in front of her. "Jesus, if that omelet tastes half as good as it smells I might hire you as my cook."

"Sorry, darling. I only hire myself out as a bodyguard of sorts. The omelet's just gravy."

"Special treatment. I like the sound of that." She took a bite, moaning at the mix of tomato, cheese and egg. "Oh my god. This is…"

"Pretty damn good?"

"Way better than that. Almost as good as chocolate. Thank you."

Sam arched a brow as he set a mug of coffee in front of her then took his seat. "Don't women equate chocolate to sex or something?" He grinned smugly. "Are you saying my cooking is as good as sex?"

"That's not what I said."

"Oh, but I think it is. Which means you haven't been getting anything decent in a while."

She glared at him. "How do you go from charming cook to asshole bodyguard so quickly? Is it a gift?"

"I think you like the touch of asshole in me. It reminds you that you're the only woman in this relationship."

Her breathing hitched at his choice of words. Though she was sure he'd meant their *business* relationship, a part of her reveled in the thought of something personal. Something dangerously intimate.

She wet her bottom lip, staring for a moment as he followed the path of her tongue before dragging his gaze up to her eyes. "Are you suggesting women can't be assholes?"

"How often do you describe a woman that way?"

"Well, I guess, never, but—"

"Point and match."

"Is everything we do today going to be a competition?"

He laughed—hard. "Oh, Bridg. You even said that with a straight face."

"What?"

"You mean besides the fact that you're the most competitive woman I know? Actually, I'll amend that.

You're the most competitive *person* I know outside of my old Ranger squad. Thinking you missed your true calling. You should have signed up for JAG."

"The Judge Advocate General? Seriously? Do you really see me as someone who'd be happy following all those rules?"

If it was possible, Sam laughed even harder, a few tears leaking out of the corner of his eyes as he grabbed his stomach. "Stop, please. God, it hurts."

"Not funny, Sam."

He wiped away the moisture, doing his best to calm down. "I'm sorry. I couldn't help it. It's just...are we talking about you or someone else? Because not only are you competitive, you're the strictest person I know. Your entire life is rules. What's admissible in court. What clothes to wear for each phase of your trial. Hell, what constitutes a safe fuck for you. It's nothing but rules."

"I don't recall telling you anything about the guys I fuck."

"You don't have to. It's written all over your face. You already told me your friends are mostly lawyers, cops, and feds. All of which are safer choices for no-strings encounters. That, based with other bits of conversation and how you reacted last night tells me everything you won't."

Pain tightened her chest as she put down her fork and stood. "You make me sound cold. But I'm not. I'm careful. If that makes me distant and a rule-follower, then so be it."

Sam shot to his feet, stopping her from walking off. "Hey. I didn't mean to upset you. And I don't think you're cold. I think you're scared. Afraid to trust anyone because of one asshole. Though, based on what he did, I don't blame you." He scrubbed a hand down his face. "This isn't going quite how I'd envisioned. Please, sit down. Eat. I'll try to be more of the charming cook and less of the asshole bodyguard."

She glanced at the food. She'd barely eaten any of it despite the gnawing hunger in the pit of her stomach. But sitting there made her feel on display. As if he was constantly judging her, or at least her reactions.

Sam moved closer. "I'm sorry, Bridgette. Really sorry. I have a bad habit of not thinking shit through before saying it. Something I haven't lost from my time in the service. Being around mostly men twenty-four seven has obviously done a number on my manners."

He didn't move until she'd allowed him to help her back into her seat. Even then, he looked as if he was ready to pounce across the table at a moment's notice. She did her best to let the conversation go, focusing on eating. But what had been delicious before felt like rock in her gut.

After another fifteen minutes of agonizing silence, she grabbed her plate and moved over to the sink. She emptied any leftovers then put the dish in the dishwasher. Sam followed her, putting the rest of the dirty dishes next to hers. She spun, expecting him to step aside, but he just stood there, extremely close as he stared at her.

She shifted under his intense gaze, finally palming her hips. "Is there something in my teeth?"

The skin over his nose bunched. "No. Why?"

"Because you're staring at me as if I've sprouted an extra ear or something."

He sighed. "I just wanted to make sure you're not still mad. I mean, I'm sure you are, but I wanted to gauge how mad you still were."

She snorted. "Are you going to talk in riddle speak all day? I'm fine. Besides, from where I'm standing, I'm already winning."

A hint of a smile twitched his lips. "Fair. But you won't be after our next round."

"Round? So, this is like a boxing match, now?"

"Yup. And I'm coming out swinging. Are you ready to start your slow descent into the loser's corner?"

Some of the tension eased, and she cursed that he knew her so well. That he was able to get her to live in the moment better than anyone else she'd known. Or maybe she just had a hard time staying mad at him when he'd spent the night holding her. Keeping her demons at bay with nothing more than his arms around her.

She cocked an eyebrow. "Fine. What's this amazing combination you think will edge the points in your direction?"

"Simple. We're going to play a game."

She laughed this time. "A game? Like what? Red Rover?"

"Close, but not quite. Hide and seek."

Her mouth gaped open before she could keep it snapped shut. Surely, she'd heard him wrong. "Did you just say, hide and seek?"

He maneuvered closer, heating the air around her

until she found it hard to breathe. "What's wrong? Have you forgotten how to play?"

She swallowed, coughing at the dry rasp in her throat. She hadn't forgotten. In fact, she'd played a deadly version of it a couple weeks ago. "I know how to play. It's just…"

"Just what? Afraid I'll find you, but you won't find me?"

The smug tone ignited the competitive side of her Sam was all too right about. And after surviving against an armed assailant, this should be tame in comparison. "Fine. Hide and seek it is."

"I'll count, first. You hide. There's only one rule." He leaned in even closer. "You have to stay in the house. Deal?"

"Oh, baby. I don't need to cheat to win. I hope you ate enough because you're going to spend the next hour looking for me."

"We'll see. Now, go. I'm already counting in my head."

CHAPTER EIGHT

Sam smiled at the playful grin on Bridgette's face as she turned and darted out of the kitchen. Especially after he'd royally fucked up during breakfast. He hadn't meant to make her feel as if he thought she didn't care. In fact, he was pretty sure the problem was that she cared too much. About everyone and everything else. Everything except her own happiness.

He glanced at the knives sitting in the butcher block, tamping down the resulting surge of anger. He still couldn't believe she'd nearly died at the hands of Brock Worthington. Sam had actually met the bastard's father, once, when the senator had toured Sam's Ranger Regiment in Fort Lewis just before he'd left on his first deployment overseas. Had he known, then, that the man had bought his son's freedom and that Bridgette had been the victim...

There were a few ways Sam could have gotten some form of retribution. Not that revenge would have helped Bridgette. But, damn, it would have felt good. As it stood, there wasn't much he could do without putting Bridgette at risk, either personally or professionally. And after all she'd endured—how she'd managed to turn the horrifying incident into something worthy—he'd never chance ruining her career.

A voice whispered in his head that he had the means to dispose of Brock without leaving a trace. That he'd spent years training for such a mission. But this wasn't a war zone, and Sam couldn't guarantee that Brock and Bridgette's history wouldn't somehow put her in the limelight. But fuck how Sam wanted to. Wanted to watch the asshole's face as he returned the favor—right down to the knife wound. Only...Sam wouldn't leave any evidence or victims alive.

Shit. Get a grip, buddy. Move forward, like she has.

Sam closed his eyes as Gray's voice echoed inside his head. Just Sam's luck, his buddy had become his inner voice of reason. Sam's own fucked up version of Jimmy Cricket. Which was better than seeing Gray's ghost at every turn. But what pissed Sam off even more was that Gray was seldom wrong. Sam wasn't a cold-blooded killer any more than Bridgette was. If she could find a way to rise above the atrocity, surely Sam could find a way to help her. She needed to be his focus, which was what today was all about. Though, should Brock turn out to be the creep stalking her—threatening her—Sam wasn't above using whatever force was necessary to keep her alive.

Not helping. Weren't you supposed to go find her?

Sam mentally flipped off the voice then moved to the doorway. "Ready or not, Bridg, here I come."

He snickered at the choice of words. What he

wouldn't give to be *coming* in a difference sense. When he'd first gathered her in his arms last night, all his thoughts had been focused on making her feel safe. Showing her that not every man was out to hurt her or use her. That *he* wasn't out to hurt or use her. While he'd hoped that clearing up the past had eliminated any doubts she'd been harboring about trusting him, he wasn't naive. Suffering that kind of trauma—he considered it a miracle that she hadn't found a way to kick him out, after all. That she hadn't lost it when he'd insisted on sleeping on the floor in her bedroom. The woman never ceased to impress him.

But once she'd given in to sleep last night, holding her had shifted from an act of chivalry to one of pure need. He'd forgotten how perfectly she fit against him. How good she smelled—an intoxicating combination of womanly sweetness and fruity fragrance mixed with a hint of roses. It was the same essence he'd associated with her from when they were teens. He just hadn't realized how ingrained it was in his senses until she'd pressed her body against his.

Then, she'd burrowed into him, laying one leg over his thigh before wrapping it around his calf. And her hand had crept onto his chest, her thumb twitching against his shirt as she'd mumbled in her sleep. He'd spent most of the night lying there, watching her— wondering if it was all some kind of weird dream, only to hear her whisper his name.

That had made everything real. Had made him acknowledge that—like it or not—he needed to explore his latent feelings for her. See if she still had any feelings left for him. She'd told him, outright, that she'd loved him back when they were eighteen. He only hoped that translated into something more than idle curiosity, now. That maybe she hadn't gotten over him anymore than he had her.

Of course, convincing her to snuggle against him when her world was falling apart and having her agree to resurrect their intimate relationship were distinctly different. But he wasn't the kind of man to back down once he'd accepted a challenge. And Bridgette Hayward was definitely going to be one of his toughest challenges since joining the Rangers—one he couldn't afford to fail.

And it all started by getting her to relax. He really was worried the constant level of stress was taking far more of a mental toll on her than she realized. If she didn't learn how to shut off that part of her life, she'd end up having a breakdown. And he wouldn't be the only one witnessing it next time.

So, here they were, playing hide and seek. It might have seemed silly, but there was something inherently exciting about trying to outsmart an opponent without it being life-or-death. And he knew the game would engage both her mental and physical prowess. That, and she hated to lose.

He smiled as he slowly picked his way through the rooms. He'd made a point of listening to her fading footsteps and judging which direction she'd headed in. Now, all he had to do was look for other clues. Disturbed dust, or a curtain that was still swaying. Something would lead him straight to her.

He stopped in the parlor, noting the subtle

indentation on the throw rug—as if someone had stood there for a few moments before moving on. He headed that way, stopping at the small hallway off to the right. It led to a modest, three-piece washroom and the laundry room.

Sam cocked his head to one side, smiling at the hushed squeak that drifted to him. He walked to the second door, wondering what seemed different, when he realized the door was opened. And he knew he'd closed them all, earlier.

He tsked, taking one step in then jerking the door aside. "Really, darling, you're going to have to do better than this if you want to win any of these matches."

Bridgette jumped then glared at him. "You know, it's cheating if you use your Army Ranger skills to find me."

"I can't help it if I'm a skilled tracker." He shrugged, allowing his lips to curl into a smug grin. "You can just admit defeat, now, if you'd like. Move on to something new."

"Fat chance, *Ranger*. Two can play the tracking game." She pushed past him. "I'll be counting in the kitchen."

Sam managed not to laugh until she'd cleared the doorway. Damn, he didn't know why sparring with her was so fucking hot, but he wasn't going to question it too deeply. And he had a feeling she wasn't quite as pissed as she pretended to be. That she enjoyed the challenge, too.

He heard her yell out the first few numbers and headed out. He'd make the initial round fairly straight forward. Not that he'd make it easy for her, but he wouldn't use all his tricks to avoid detection. The ones he planned on using later.

Sam headed for the stairs. There was a small nook behind them where she'd stored some old paintings, and he was pretty sure it was just big enough to fit him. He took his time, careful not to scrape anything across the floor, before settling into the shadows. Bridgette called out the telltale phrase, followed by her footsteps across the hardwood floors. He smiled when she walked past him, heading for her office. He wondered how long it would take for her to find him when a small beam of light illuminated his face.

"You know, Sam, if you're not going to take this seriously, then why bother?"

His mouth gaped open before he had the sense to close it. "How the fuck did you find me so fast?"

"Now, now. I wouldn't want to give away my secrets." She offered him her hand, helping him untangle himself from the small space. "Though, I figured you wouldn't hide anywhere too hard this first round. That way you could spring all your fancy moves on me later." She laughed when he furrowed his brow. "Oh, and you can see this spot from the mirror by the door. Your foot was sticking out just enough to show in the reflection."

He glanced at the mirror in question. "Well, I'll be damned. Good job. Which means it's a tie so far. I hope your next spot is better than the last."

Bridgette's eyes lit up, and she motioned to the kitchen. He made his way back, once again giving her a chance to hide. It took him nearly fifteen minutes to find her this time. The crafty girl had curled up in his bed in place of his pillows, and he'd missed her the first time he'd looked into his room. She'd laughed when he'd finally uncovered her, the lilting sound easing the tension in his shoulders.

This is what he'd been hoping for. A day of unfettered happiness. And so far, his plan was a shining success. Which he hoped meant she'd hold true to her word and give him tomorrow, as well.

Sam choose to conceal himself in a closet, next, until she'd walked by. Then he'd snuck out and shadowed her every move, ducking behind anything handy when she backtracked. He lasted ten minutes before he must have made a sound and she'd spun around to catch him diving onto the couch. She'd jumped on top of him, pretending she didn't see him until he'd confessed she'd won that round. Then she'd taken off, again.

They'd continued the game for over an hour before they'd started to run out of places to hide. Not wanting to drag the game out until it had lost its appeal, he declared one final round. Of course, he intended on using every trick to beat her, this time. But she didn't have to know that.

Bridgette nodded, motioning him to turn around, before she raced off, her sock feet barely making a sound. He gave her a bit more time, then struck off, methodically checking each room. He had to hand it to her. She'd adapted quickly to the methods he'd been using to track her, and he started to think that maybe he shouldn't have told her some of his secrets, when his watch buzzed.

Sam glanced down, frowning at the alarm message

flashing on the face. The side door on the opposite side of the kitchen had been opened. He had a momentary thought that maybe she'd chosen to break his only rule then decided against it. Bridgette wouldn't consider it a worthy win if she'd had to cheat.

Scenarios rolled through his head as he quickly retrieved one of the guns he'd holstered at his ankles, checking the chamber then clicking off the safety. He glanced at the stairs, but he was fairly certain she'd stayed on the main level. Regardless, he needed to clear each room—ensure no one ambushed him from behind, as he searched for Bridgette and any sign of an intruder.

He moved silently through the rooms, running every small noise he'd heard Bridgette make through his mind. He was certain she'd gone through the parlor, and then... Shit. He'd heard a small scuffing sound but had brushed it off. But it would have coincided with her doubling back to the kitchen after he'd walked past.

He quickly cleared her office then turned back to the kitchen, glancing up the stairs, again, before crossing them and heading to the next doorway. A cold breeze swirled around his legs, and he heard birds chirping in the distance. He tamped down the twinge of fear that burned beneath his skin. What if she'd been taken? What if he'd put her life in jeopardy because he'd been thinking with the wrong fucking head? What if he'd lost her?

Fear gripped his gut as he pressed his back into the wall beside the doorway. Nothing sounded beyond the threshold except his own heartbeat thrumming through his ears. Which wasn't helping. Now wasn't the time to be the charming cook.

Shoving his emotions down as far as he could, he took a quick peek inside the room. If Bridgette had ventured outside, he'd be able to tell by the footprints in the snow once he'd reached the door. He took a step toward the entrance, when the closet beside the door opened and Bridgette slipped out. She looked at the open door, the color draining from her face before she slowly backed away.

Sam darted in and grabbed her, covering her mouth with one hand as he tugged her body against his. "Don't scream, it's me."

The elbow she'd raised paused mid-strike, and she gazed back at him when he slowly released her. Her eyes widened before the tension in her muscles eased.

He motioned to the door then pushed her behind his back as he faced the way he'd come. "Stick to me like glue."

She nodded. "Do you have another gun?"

He frowned at the hushed words, stopping to look at her. "You know how to use one?"

"I was attacked in my own apartment. So, yeah, I know how to use one. Not saying I'm anywhere close to your skill, but I can hit a target."

He bent over, grabbing the gun from his other ankle then handing it over. Bridgette took it, checked the chamber, the magazine, then flicked off the safety before motioning him to continue.

Shit, was there nothing she couldn't do?

He'd question her about who'd taught her later. First, he wanted to clear the house. They moved together, checking every damn hiding spot they could think of before finally returning to the kitchen. Sam closed the door and reset the alarm.

Bridgette pressed against him, her gaze still sweeping the room. "Do you think it's okay?"

Sam sighed at the shiver that shook through her, laying one hand at the small of her back. "I think so. The locks are old. I suppose there's a chance that door didn't quite catch after I took out the garbage, and with the lock not fully engaged, the wind could have blown it open."

"But you don't think so."

"Hard to tell. The gusting conditions have swept away any good footprints. They look like mine, but someone could have used boots with a similar tread and just walked in my old footprints to trick us."

"God. How did you live like this for twelve years? Wait, you're still living like this."

He reached his other hand toward her, smiling when she moved into his embrace. "You get used to it."

"That's the practiced answer, again."

"Damn, but you're tough. Okay, maybe I don't want to admit that a part of me liked the adrenaline rush. That I got addicted to it. I won't deny that it's a pretty big high to infiltrate enemy territory and not even be seen. To rescue soldiers or civilians that have been captured. To be honest, I miss it. Though, the security work I've been doing is a close second, considering it's civilian."

She stared at him, then offered him back the gun. "I don't think I really understood what you did...until now. How stupid I was to think I was remotely as capable as you are. I'm sorry I ever doubted you."

Damn, he hadn't been prepared for that.

He took the gun, checking it over then shoving it back in his ankle holster. "The world would be a pretty horrible place if everyone was trained like that. And I prefer you just the way you are. Though, I am curious when you learned to shoot."

Her lips quirked. "It was shortly after I got my first job as a public defender. I was working in a pretty rough district, and a friend of mine, Jack Taylor, thought I should know how, in case I needed to defend myself. He wanted me to carry, but…" She shrugged. "He was kind enough to give me some lessons. He's a fed."

"A previous lover?"

She opened her mouth then closed it on a sigh. "We…hooked up a few times. Usually at conventions. He's—how did you put it? Safe? We're not…together or anything. Never were. In fact, he just married a very beautiful neural surgeon. They're sickeningly perfect for each other. But it was purely sex between us." She shook her head. "Which only proves your point more, I suppose."

"Bridgette, I—"

"I know. You didn't mean it the way it sounded earlier, but… That doesn't make it any less true. My life *is* about rules, and I *am* careful with who I sleep with. I do my best to keep it strictly physical."

He brushed his finger along her jaw. "It's completely understandable. What you went through…"

"Has turned me into an emotional hermit. Yeah, I'm aware." She glanced around the kitchen. "So, does this intrusion mean we're moving? Off to some crappy motel with shag carpeting?"

He grimaced. That was exactly what he'd been thinking. "I don't want you to think I'm overreacting, but—"

"I'll go."

He froze. "Say what?"

"I said, I'll go. Wherever you think is safe. While it pains me to admit this...you were right. This time is different. I've never been scared enough by the threats that I've had to escape Seattle. And no one's ever broken into my home before. If there's a chance someone can get past your security here..." She shivered. "This is way past my comfort zone—was before I got here. Not that I relish how you'll gloat over that fact now that I've admitted it. And I...I trust your judgment."

Sam had to stop his mouth from gaping open, again. Had she really just said she trusted him? "Let's pack a bag. We'll head to a motel for the rest of the day, but I'd prefer to take you somewhere safer. I'll call Hank. See if there's a place he recommends in Eagle Rock. I'll make sure you can still do your work, okay?"

Bridgette nodded. "Thanks, though I won't be doing any work until Monday."

"Monday?"

"I hold true to my word, Sam. And up until we were rudely interrupted, I'd had more fun than I can remember having in a long time. So...you won. You get tomorrow, too. Let's just leave the possible stalker out of it, though, okay?"

"Deal. Though...we're not done with today, yet. Just because we're moving locations doesn't mean I don't still have some plans in store for you."

She gave him a long, slow sweeping gaze. "I look forward to them. I'll grab some clothes and my laptop."

"We'll get them together."

Because he'd be damned if a hair on her head got damaged while she was under his care. And he had a bad feeling the situation had only just begun to escalate.

.

CHAPTER NINE

God, she'd been right—shag carpeting. *Mottled brown* shag carpeting to be exact. With patterned wallpaper that instantly made Bridgette's head ache. The only saving grace was that Sam had assured her they'd only be staying until nine or ten tonight. Overnight at the most. Not that she was going to complain. In this instance, ugly equated safe. And safe sounded pretty damn good in her book.

She shivered as she recalled the moment she'd realized something was off during their game. She'd been hiding in the closet—her feet shoved into an old pair of gumboots and her body concealed behind a couple of her long jackets. It'd been perfect. Even if Sam had opened the door, it would have taken moving the jackets in the far left corner out of the way to actually see her. Sure, he would have eventually found her, but it might have been enough to make her feel as if she stacked up to him. Because…damn.

She knew he'd been using his Army Ranger training

to figure out her hiding spots, not to mention as a means of evading her when she'd been hunting him. But she also wasn't vain enough to think she remotely measured up to his skillset. A fact that had made her view the past week in a new perspective. All the times he'd "checked" the perimeter, or said he was going to "stand watch" for a bit, meant something different, now. And she realized how difficult she'd made his job by resisting him, at first. And by keeping secrets from him. He'd willing put his life on the line, and she'd been too worried about her pride to confide in him.

Then she'd heard the door click open and felt the telltale swirl of cold air breeze through the cracks on the sides of the closet doors. At first, she'd thought Sam was breaking his own rule and had gone outside. She'd nearly jumped out of the closet to confront him when she'd realized there was another possibility. That there was a chance it wasn't Sam, but whoever was intent on keeping her from making it to the trial.

Him. The guy from the garage.

And she'd panicked. She'd waited until the weight of not knowing had nearly crushed her before opening the closet and slipping out. She'd turned to look at the open door when Sam had grabbed her from behind.

Since that moment, she'd been stumbling her way through. Watching him put his body in front of hers, intent of being her first line of defense, had hit her hard. And she knew she'd never look at him the same way, again.

Sure, he was getting paid to protector her, but the nagging voice in her head insisted that he would have ridden to the rescue, regardless. That if she'd called him up out-of-the-blue, he would have been standing in front of her door in record time in Seattle. No hesitation. No questions asked.

Because Sam Montgomery was one of the good guys. In every sense of the word. And she was quickly falling under his spell, again.

She laughed inwardly at the thought. She was only fooling herself if she thought she'd ever been free of his spell. The truth was, she'd only managed to hide from it all these years. But it had been there, waiting until the right moment to resurface. And it had. With sobering clarity.

Now, she was left dealing with the ever-present need slowly driving her insane. It was bad enough when she'd had an entire house to seek refuge in. The new arrangements meant she'd never be more than a few feet away from him. Ever. Even hiding in the bathroom wouldn't give her any peace—not when she knew there were only a few inches of compressed wood between them. That he'd be sitting on the bed…waiting.

Which made her acutely aware of another issue. There was only one bed. Apparently, there was some kind of winter festival in town. Who knew there were festivals in January? Weren't people still reeling from Christmas? Either way, there had only been one room with a king size bed.

Bridgette pushed away the thoughts. They might not even stay the night, so worrying if she was going to have to share a bed with Sam seemed pointless. And it wasn't as if they hadn't shared a bed before. Surely, she could lie on her half without losing it.

Or worse—pouncing on him.

Sam placed their bags beside the bed, twisting to face her. He sighed, motioning to the room. "I know. It's...pretty bad."

She plastered on a smile. "I've stayed in worse."

"I already told you that you have a tell, darling."

"I wasn't lying." She hitched out one hip. "Am I happy we left my nice, albeit old-fashioned, farm house for this seventies time warp? No, not really. But I'm not some prissy drama queen who needs five-star hotels. If staying here means we're safe..."

"It does. At least, for now. I'm working on alternate arrangements."

She nodded, testing out the bed with her hand before cautiously sitting. "The bed's decent."

Something flickered in Sam's eyes, but it was gone before she could decipher what it was. He nodded, then started digging through one of the bags he'd brought in. After a few moments, he pulled out a small elongated box. One she swore looked as if it held jewelry.

She arched a brow. "You know, Sam, just because I didn't pitch a fit coming here doesn't mean we're going steady."

He chuckled, sitting beside her before opening the box, revealing a beautiful silver necklace with a matching pendant. "You are tougher than most to charm in that way. I had Hank order this for me when I discovered you were my next assignment. Think of it as a Hail Mary."

"A necklace is a Hail Mary? And is that a gavel?"

"You're a lawyer. I wanted something that suited you. Something...pretty." He removed it from the box. "It has a

GPS locator inside the pendant, so, if the shit hit the fan and we got separated, I might still have a way to find you. Assuming it didn't get broken or lost. Hence, a Hail Mary."

She furrowed her brow, lifting her hair so he could clip it around her neck. "Call me crazy, but I'm a bit surprised you're only asking me to wear this, now."

"We were safely in your house before. It wasn't needed. Besides, you never would have agreed to wear it before."

"And it's needed, now? I'm not going to try and ditch you."

"While it's comforting to hear you say that, that's not the reason. Leaving your home means we're adapting from here on in. I just don't want to take any chances. And—once we're done—I can deactivate the GPS so you can keep it..." He cleared his throat. "If you'd like. Consider it my way of saying I'm sorry for being a prick at eighteen. For leaving instead of facing you."

She gazed down at it, wondering if the heat pulsing beneath her skin was from the necklace, or the brush of Sam's knuckles against her chest as he held the pendant in his hand for a few moments before finally letting go. "You already apologized. And explained." She smiled when he frowned at what he obviously thought was going to be a rejection of his gift. "Are you sure? You could use it for your next client."

"Did you miss the part where I said I had it made for you? If you don't want it—"

"It's beautiful, Sam. I love it. Thank you." She lifted the gavel with a couple of fingers. "And it's not that I didn't want it, I've just never had anyone give me jewelry, before. Other than my mom."

Sam brushed his thumb along her jaw, gaining her attention. "None of your other boyfriends ever gave you jewelry? Not even Brock before he became a raging monster?"

Other boyfriends. Christ, he'd said as if he were her boyfriend, now. And the thought shouldn't excite her—shouldn't feel as right as it did.

"Nope. Unless you count a ring pop. Though, it *was* cherry flavored, so that might have made it special."

"Oh, darling. You really have dated the wrong guys, haven't you? You should be showered with gifts."

"I'd be happy to start with a guy who doesn't try to kill me."

Though she'd meant it as a joke, there was no missing the instant change in Sam's demeanor. The way his lips pursed tight and his eyes narrowed. The slight slash of red on his cheeks.

He held her chin, leaning in close enough he could have kissed her. "Never. Again."

Then he backed away as he stood. "Okay, now that we're situated, time to continue our game."

She fought to draw in a breath around the tight press of her chest. Christ, she wasn't sure if she was more on edge because he hadn't kissed her or because she'd wanted him to.

She managed to clear her throat, only coughing once. "You already won. We don't have to keep playing if you have other stuff to do."

"Oh, no. You promised me the whole day—and

tomorrow, now, too—with no work, so I suggest you get comfortable."

Any tension that had crept into her muscles, eased. Games she could handle. They'd take her mind off the fact that Sam had gotten the pendant made—for her—before he'd even arrived on her doorstep. And knowing he'd taken the time to choose a design he hoped would have more meaning to her so she'd want to keep it, after, warmed her heart.

She groaned inwardly as the heat spread down her torso, settling hot and needy between her thighs. She muttered a curse, forcing a smile when Sam glanced her way. The last thing she wanted to do was show him exactly how far she'd fallen. That the only game she wanted to play involved them getting naked then rolling around on the bed for hours.

Instead, she pushed away the thoughts and smiled up at him. "Seeing as we can't roam around like our previous game, I'm guessing we're sidelined to Trivia Pursuit or something?"

Sam scoffed. "Oh ye of little imagination. Yes, I do plan on challenging that gray matter of yours, but I also found this at your place and brought it along."

He rummaged through another bag and removed a white, square box. His face lit up around a devious smile before he flipped it over.

Bridgette couldn't stem the laugh that bubbled free. "Twister? You found twister at my place and actually brought it along?"

"What can I say? I'm betting I'm nimbler than you are, Counselor."

"Really? You think all that muscly brawn you have can bend into a pretzel?"

"Guess we'll find out. But first..." He held up his phone. "I have this other game. You hold the phone to your head and the other person has to give you words to guess whatever's on the phone...I'm not really sure. But I thought we could start with that—save the twisting fun until the end. That way we can shower then get some dinner."

"We're going out for dinner?"

His lips quirked before he sighed. "Not quite. We'll have something delivered, but..." he added when he obviously noticed the slump in her shoulders, "...we are meeting up with some friends later tonight. Around nine at the Blue Moose tavern. All right?"

She chuckled. "The fact I'm excited to go to some hole-in-the-wall tavern just to get out shows exactly how far I've fallen from grace."

"It's a nice place. You'll like it."

"At this point, I'd like anywhere that's 'out'."

"Are you saying I haven't been enough company for you?"

"No. I'm sure it's no surprise that I don't go out with people like that very often. That I'm more of a loner. But, I *am* used to getting outside. I usually run four or five times a week. Stop for coffee on my way to work. Just...out. Staying inside the same four walls all the time makes me feel trapped."

Sam moved over to her. "I know. And if all goes well, it won't be for much longer."

"Until the next case. The next gang leader who thinks I should reconsider my career choice."

Bridgette regretted the words the moment they slipped free. This was exactly what she'd told herself *not* to do. Playing on Sam's inherent protective instincts would only erupt into another discussion about taking better care of herself.

As predicted, Sam clenched his jaw, making the muscle in his temple jump. He reached for her hand then changed his mind and let his arm fall to his side, again. "Let's just deal with one threat at a time, okay?"

Her mouth gaped open for a moment before she managed to shut it as she nodded her agreement. Though, the wild look in his eyes suggested his statement hadn't been what he'd really been feeling. Not that she was going to push her luck.

She extended her hand, wiggling her fingers toward her. "Hand it over. I'll guess, first."

Whatever else he'd been feeling faded into a smile as he launched the game then gave her his phone. She read the instructions aloud, then picked a category. Before long, they were laughing so hard her stomach hurt. She never would have guessed Sam had such a playful side to him. Being ex-military, she'd expected him to be focused. To never let his guard down. While she had no doubt he'd turn all of that on, again, in an instant should the situation warrant it, knowing he could let it go—even for just an hour or two—impressed her. The man was full of surprises.

After they'd gone through several rounds, each, they moved on to a trivia game. She'd hoped her knowledge of current affairs would give her the edge, but damn if Sam wasn't just as skilled. In fact, she had a disturbing feeling that he was intimately aware of more than he let on from the endless missions he'd performed overseas. Either way, she was quickly discovering he was a hard man to best.

In a last-ditch effort to win at something, she suggested they hit the twister board. It started off innocently, enough. Feet and hands going to various positions, which got harder with every spin. It wasn't until they were pretty far into it that she realized she'd wrapped herself around Sam's body with her face dangerously level with his groin. The fact his arm was pressed between her thighs didn't help matters any, either.

Her heart thrashed against her ribs, threatening to pound through as the next spin required her to somehow reach between his legs. And she knew she'd never achieve it without pressing part of her body against his crotch.

Sam laughed. "Rut roh, Shaggy. Looks like you might be stumped on this one." His smug tone ignited her competitive spirit.

She glanced over at him. "Oh, really?"

She sucked in a breath then slid her hand through his legs to the green circle behind him. There was a moment of rock-hard pressure against her shoulder before he attempted to shift. The slight change in position was all it took to tip her against him, and they landed on the floor in a tangle of limbs. Somehow, she ended up with her head notched in his groin and one of her thighs curled over his upper torso, placing his head squarely between her legs.

Their gazes clashed between a sea of denim, and she wasn't sure whether to scramble to her feet or simply lie there, staring at him. Drinking in the way his breathing kicked up, and how the blue in his eyes looked darker— more of a stormy gray, now. Even his skin seemed flushed, though it could have been from the game. But damn if she didn't hope it was from the same restless energy strumming through her, burning up her cheeks and no doubt, turning them a deep shade of red.

Sam recovered, first. He gave her a panty-melting smile, which didn't help considering his location, then somehow levered up. There were a couple of moments of being bent together before he gripped her shoulders, holding her up enough he slid out from beneath her as he moved over her, his hands cradling her head while his body hovered over her. On his elbows, they touched from the waist down, that hard, long ridge in his jeans pressing against her abdomen.

Bridgette stared into his eyes as her palms pressed against his chest. She instinctively fisted the material in her fingers, caught between wanting to shove him off and needing to draw him closer. She didn't allow herself to get in this position—allow any man to have absolute control over her. Even during her occasional sexual encounters, she insisted on either being on top or in front—any way that didn't trap her with no escape. Lying there beneath Sam, his massive body eclipsing her view of the room, should have frightened her. While a touch of panic quickened her breath and slicked her skin with a cold sweat, another part of her wanted more— wanted their clothes gone, his skin touching every inch of hers. Wanted to feel him hold her in his arms as he slowly moved inside her.

Wanted her to submit.

Sam's smile faded. "Bridgette? Are you okay? Did I hit your head or something?"

She couldn't answer. Couldn't get any words past the singular thought in her head. She never submitted. Had sworn it would be a cold day in Hell before she gave over control—trusted a man enough. Because the last time a guy had hovered over her like this, she'd been knifed and left to die.

"Darling?"

She should tell him to move. Explain why her heart thrashed against her chest. Why the room seemed to dissolve into flashes of that night—Brock's hatred glaring down at her as he waved the knife, making the blade glint from the hallway light. Instead, she whimpered as her hands flexed around his shirt.

Frozen. That's how she felt. Frozen between the past and the present. Stuck in some kind of limbo where she couldn't let go without falling but aware the fall, itself, might kill her.

Sam's face paled. "Shit."

He scrambled off her, then helped her up, doing his best to support her without crowding her. He planted her ass on the nearest chair then shoved her head down between her knees, all the while telling her to breathe. It was then she realized she'd been holding her breath. That the burning in her chest wasn't fear but the desperate need for oxygen. She tried to inhale, panicking when her throat tightened.

Sam leaned in close, rubbing one hand along her back in easy circles. "It's okay. You're safe, just try to relax. The rest will happen on its own."

She reached for his hand, clenching it in hers when

he threaded their fingers together. The hard grip grounded her, slowly forcing out the patchwork memories until her chest loosened, and she managed a few shaky breaths.

"That's my girl." He applied gentle pressure on her neck when she tried to look at him. "Not yet. Just stay there. Breathe. Give your body a chance to equalize or you'll just get lightheaded."

Shit. She knew that. What was it about Sam Montgomery that fried her intelligence and made her look as if she couldn't think straight—take care of herself? What made her want him to take care of her?

Thoughts tumbled through her head, as she stayed bent over in the chair, waiting for the room to stop spinning. Once it had stabilized, she slowly straightened. A few latent images teased her senses, but not enough to derail her efforts.

Sam moved in front of her, kneeling down to her level. "Are you still dizzy? Feel like you're gonna puke?"

She shook her head. "I'm fine, now."

"No, you're not. But at least some of the color is back in her cheeks. Was it something I did? Something I said?"

"It's not you, Sam. It's me. It's all in here..." She tapped her temple. "One minute, everything's fine, then the next, he's there. That fucking night is just looping inside my head, waiting for a chance to pounce."

She pointed at the twister mat. "You want to know what it was this time? It was lying on the floor beneath you, because the last time any man was on top of me that way..."

He clenched his jaw, those red slashes returning to his cheeks. "Brock stabbed you."

"It wasn't your fault. It's crazy." She palmed her face. "God, you must think *I'm* crazy."

He snorted, the odd sound drawing her attention, and she forced herself to look up at him. He skimmed his fingers down the length of her hair, toying with the ends as he sighed. "You're not crazy. And you're not the only one with ghosts that won't leave you alone."

Her breath stalled, again. "Is your ghost Gray?"

His mouth pinched tight, but he didn't look away. "His name was Rick Lawson, but everyone called him Gray because he already had gray hair. Some kind of genetic mishap. We were in basic training together and managed to stay that way for twelve years. He was the closest thing I ever had to a brother. But our last mission..."

Bridgette touched his cheek. "You don't have to tell me any of this."

He took her hand and held it in his. "I can't say too much. National security and all that bullshit. But...the jump went bad. Gray was unconscious, and I tried to help him, but we got caught under enemy fire and..." He swallowed, the sound tearing at her heart. "He died. Died because I wasn't good enough to save him."

"You got hurt on that mission, too, didn't you? That's why you were medically discharged. You injured something that prevented you from returning."

"Injuries heal. I get a second chance. Gray... *I* was his second chance, and I blew it."

"Sam—"

"It's true. All that training, and I couldn't save him."

"Do you know why I win as often as I do? It's because I'm pretty good at seeing through to the truth. Despite what people 'think' happened. And I can say with absolute certainty that you didn't fail. Sometimes, we lose, even when we do our best."

"I'm not sure it matters when the end result's the same."

She sighed. She couldn't fault him on his logic. It's why she hadn't been able to move past her own fears, yet. "Do you get flashes of that mission?"

"Not exactly." He stood, pacing to the other side of the room. "It's not that mission I see, it's him. Gray. At first, I swear I saw his ghost everywhere. Just standing there, mocking the fact I was still alive. The doctors told me it would fade. That it was just a by-product of guilt. An apparition caused by my own self-loathing."

She followed him over to the window by the door. "And did it?"

He made eye contact. "It…changed. Now, he's a voice inside my head, telling me whenever I've fucked something up. Like at breakfast this morning. When I made you feel like shit. My conscience, I guess."

A few tears slipped free, but she didn't bother wiping them away. "That doesn't sound too scary. In fact, it sounds as if you've found a way to make peace with it. With him."

"Peace? That doesn't exist, but… Let's just say we're sharing my head space better than we used to."

He turned to fully face her as he placed his hands on her shoulders. "So, no, Bridgette. I don't think you're crazy. Or cold. Or weak. Or anything else you've worked up in your head. You were hurt. Most people would have let that beat them, but you chose to turn it into something powerful. Something that benefits everyone else at your expense. So, you might want to cut yourself some slack. Because that's not a ghost haunting you, it's a demon. There's no making friends with it. And nothing but time will exorcize it."

His hands fell to his sides. "Thinking we should shower." He chuckled at her raised brow. "We should *each* take a shower. On our own. I don't know about you, but I'm starving. And we are going out tonight."

"A shower sounds good. I hope there's lots of hot water."

"I don't mind it cool, so...you go, first. Take as long as you need. I'll see if I can find a menu for that delivery place Hank mentioned. We can order once we've both cleaned up and had a chance to see if there's anything besides burgers available."

"All right." She turned then walked to her bag, removing the items she needed before heading to the bathroom. She paused at the threshold, looking back at Sam over her shoulder. "Thank you."

"For what? As I recall, you'd said it was only fair if I confessed my secrets if you had to. And I'm a bit late in that."

"You didn't have to tell me. I know how hard it must have been. If it helps, you're the first person I've ever told about Brock. About that night."

"Seriously? Didn't the hospital call your dad?"

"It hadn't been very long since my mom had died, so I'd changed my emergency contact information. I didn't want him worrying if anything happened to me when he was a few states away and couldn't do anything. I had my girlfriend swear she wouldn't call him unless I was actually dead. Thankfully, she followed my wishes. After I woke up, I guess I didn't want anyone else to know." She fiddled with her hair for a moment in an effort to control her emotions. "But I also meant for taking care of me. No one's done that in a very long time."

She cleared her throat. "I won't be long."

The door swirled air around her legs as she closed it then leaned against it. This was quickly becoming far more than a simple security assignment. And she had no idea whether to embrace it or run while she had the chance.

CHAPTER TEN

Fuck, he was in serious trouble.

And not the kind Sam's years of training would get him out of. This...this went far deeper than trying to outsmart an enemy. This involved his heart. The one Bridgette had somehow wormed her way back into, resurrecting the damn thing after he'd gone to great lengths to bury it. Hell, he'd burned the fucker into ashes, and yet—there it was, beating frantically inside his chest, and all because of the woman behind the flimsy wooden door.

He'd nearly blown it, again. When he'd first moved over her, he'd come damn close to kissing her. Those pretty pink lips had been so fucking close—slightly parted as if begging him to slide his mouth over top and delve inside. He'd actually leaned into her, pressed his erection against her hip, with every intention of lodging it in her cleft as he slipped his tongue inside her mouth—tasted the sweet essence that had been tempting him all week. Thank Christ, he'd had the

MIDNIGHT RANGER | 133

sense to gaze into her eyes, first. That was when he'd seen it.

Fear. Oddly mixed with arousal, but fear, nonetheless.

He should have considered the possibilities. That Bridgette might have lingering uncertainties about being in specific positions. But after she'd confessed she'd taken other lovers after Brock—even if only for brief, limited encounters—he'd just assumed…

Shit. What had he told her about assumptions? That they usually came back to bite him in the ass? And damn if he didn't have a set of marks burning a hole in his jeans right now. Bridgette-sized marks because Sam hadn't thought through every scenario.

He raked his hand through his hair, cursing the tremble in his fingers. Only it wasn't from fear. Being that close to her had him on edge. He'd been hard after only a few minutes of trying to bend his body around hers, the feel of her against him driving him mad. Her scent had been a combination of perfume and arousal, and he'd wanted to yank off her jeans and bury his face between her thighs. Drown in the taste of her. Even now, the aroma clung to his clothes like an ever-present itch he couldn't scratch.

He forced in a long, slow inhalation, using the techniques he'd learned to take control of his emotions. Just a few more breaths and he'd be able to think clearly. Ease the pounding in his chest and allow himself to focus.

He took a couple of steps away, when Bridgette screamed. The high-pitched sound rose every hair on the back of his neck as he grabbed his gun off the side table and darted to the bathroom door. He didn't bother trying it, choosing to kick it open, instead. The wood around the lock splintered, shooting chunks through both rooms as the frame gave-way, bouncing the door wildly against the wall. He barreled through, gun aimed in front of him, his shoulders braced to fire.

Bridgette screamed, again, as she spun to face him, her face bleached white, her hands fisted around the edge of the towel pressed against her chest. Her nostrils flared, accentuating the overly white look of her eyes. He motioned for her to move into the small space beside the toilet with a flick of his gun then stalked forward, glancing into the shower then out the window.

Nothing.

Sam turned, rechecking the shower before slowly lowering his gun. Blood pounded through his veins, the steady surge of it echoing in his ears. Adrenaline pumped through his system, making him hyperaware, every sense stretched to the limit. He took one last scan of the adjoining room then centered his attention on Bridgette. She'd wrapped the towel around her, the pale color a close match to the hue of her skin.

He took a few steps toward her, cutting their distance in half. "Are you okay?"

She nodded, the jerky motion tumbling her hair over her shoulders and across her face.

He sighed, getting close enough to brush the silky locks back. "Can you tell me what happened? You scared me half to death."

Her mouth gaped open for a few moments before she seemed able to shut it. "I scared you? What the hell,

Sam? You broke down the damn door then looked at me as if you were about to wage war."

"You screamed. I reacted. Appropriately. End of story. Now, why the fuck did you scream?"

Her brows drew together, before she broke eye contact. "Shit."

"Shit? What's 'shit' mean in this instance?"

"You're going to laugh. Or get angry. Maybe both."

"Try me."

Bridgette sucked her lower lip between her teeth, worrying it for a few moments before groaning. She drew a deep breath, then met his gaze. "I was ready to jump in the shower. All I had to do was get the water running so it could heat up a bit. But when I reached in to turn on the taps, this...hideous..." She snorted. "I swear it was fucking huge. Like something out of a horror movie. It landed on my arm, and...and...it caught me off-guard."

Sam arched a brow. "What, exactly, landed on your arm?"

She pursed her lips together, looking incredibly lethal and sexy at the same time. "A spider."

He stared at her, positive he'd heard her wrong. "A spider?"

"Don't take that tone with me. It was huge."

"You mentioned that. Hideous, too, right?"

"See? I told you that you'd laugh and get angry. But you didn't have to feel that...thing touch your skin. All those hairy legs. And the eyes! I swear they all looked at me at the same time."

She shuddered, rubbing her left hand over the patch of skin where the spider must have landed on her right arm. When Sam just stood there, staring at her, she swatted him in the chest.

"See for yourself. It's in the tub…somewhere."

He waited for a few more moments before reluctantly stepping sideways and glancing in the bathtub. A dark shadow tried to scurry up the side, slipping before it got to the top.

He looked back at her. "You're serious? You screamed over that thing?"

"It's. Huge."

"And yet, still a thousand times smaller than you."

Bridgette huffed as she crossed her arms over her chest. "If you're just going to stand there and criticize me, you can leave, now. But a real man would kill that fucker so I could get on with my shower."

He resisted the smile tugging at his lips. "A real man? You bitch at me for asking you why you don't have a boyfriend, claiming I'm being sexist, then you toss that comment my way? I'm sorry, but I object, Counselor."

Her eyelids fluttered a few times, giving him fleeting glimpses of blue, before she focused on him. "You're right. That wasn't fair. It's just…" Her chin quivered, but she seemed to gather herself. "How about as my bodyguard, you hold true to your oath and, you know, guard my body?"

"I hardly think the spider is the one who's been sending you death threats."

Red rose high on her cheeks. "Damn it, Sam, do you think this is easy for me? To ask you for help? But…" She shuddered. "I hate spiders. Like on an atomic level."

"All you have to do is wash it down the drain—"

"No! It'll just come back. Didn't you ever sing that annoying song as a kid? The Itsy Bitsy Spider? He climbs up the spout, again, which means I'll only be pissing it off. And considering we might have to spend the night here..."

She groaned, again, when he didn't move. "Please, Sam. I'll pay you back. Give you a massage later, or... whatever. Just please, get rid of that abomination in the bathtub."

"I'll take care of the spider. But my price is a kiss."

He stilled as the words slipped free. Shit. That wasn't what he'd planned on saying. In fact, he vividly remembered how incredible her massages had been. And he was pretty damn sure they'd only gotten better. But, somewhere between his brain and his dick, he'd lost connection, allowing his prick to answer for him—even if it wasn't the part of him she'd kiss.

Bridgette snorted. "You want a kiss? To kill a spider?"

"That's my counter offer. Take it or leave it."

"I would have agreed to a dozen kisses if it meant you'd kill that spider, so..." She held out her hand. "Deal."

"You said that just to try and up me. Don't think I don't know you, Bridg."

He shook her hand then turned, seeking out the spider. Bridgette fussed behind him, telling him not to touch it or he'd have to wash his hands before she'd consider kissing him. Instead, he removed a shoe, killing it with one hit.

He glanced back at her. "Can I wash it down the drain, now?"

"Are you sure it's dead."

"I'm a highly trained specialist in the art of combat. I'm pretty damn sure I can kill a spider. So, yeah, it's dead."

She continued to worry her lip as she nodded. He paused to stare at her. At the way she followed his every move. At how the golden cast of her hair made her skin gleam wherever it touched her shoulders. The woman was amazing, and he prayed he'd be able to control himself when he collected his payment.

Sam flicked on the shower and washed away the corpse. He adjusted the taps until the water was warm, but not so hot it would burn her before spinning to face her. She swept her gaze down his torso then up, staring at him with those beautiful blue eyes.

Then she arched a brow. "Guess it's my turn to hold true to the deal."

Sam pulled her into his chest before she could move, holding her body tight against his. He smiled at her gasp, searching her face for any signs of hesitation or that their position was freaking her out. Her lips were slightly parted, her pupils larger than just a few moments ago. He didn't miss the wild strum of her pulse near the base of her neck, her skin fluttering with every frantic beat.

Good. He didn't want to be the only one insanely aroused. Fighting to bury his attraction. Though, seeing her reaction made him press more fully against her. She definitely felt the hard line of his cock nudging her abdomen, but if it scared her, she didn't show it. In fact, her pupils dilated further, and her breathing kicked up.

Sam placed his gun behind them on the counter then

lifted his hand, brushing his thumb along her cheek as he gently palmed her jaw. After dreaming about this since the day he'd left, he wasn't about to rush it. He might not get another chance to taste her lips or feel her wrapped in his arms, and he'd be damned if he was going to mess it up. Moments like these needed to last a lifetime, and he planned on making it one hell of a memory.

Bridgette pressed into his touch. Whether actively or instinctually, Sam didn't know. But that simple action was all the consent he needed. He dipped down, teasing her lips with a hint of contact, then pausing with his mouth a breath away. Bridgette whimpered just loud enough to make his dick impossibly harder as his balls drew up against his skin. One more sound like that, and he might just come in his pants.

Fuck that.

He moved, claiming her mouth in one swift tilt of his head. She responded instantly, tiptoeing up as her hands landed on his shoulders. One traveled higher, carding into his hair then fisting around the strands. For the first time since he'd left the army, he praised his decision to grow out his hair. He'd been tempted to cut it a thousand times but had wanted to rid himself of any visible memory of his time in the military. His pathetic attempt to start over. But standing there, his arms wrapped around Bridgette as she tugged on the strands made it seem possible. That with her, he could find what he'd been missing. Fill the void inside him that had plagued since he'd held Gray's lifeless body before passing out.

Bridgette hummed, opening when he slid his tongue

along the seam of her lips. Fruity sweetness filled his senses, and Sam knew he'd never be able to stop at one kiss. Hell, one round of mind-blowing sex wouldn't be enough to douse the fire raging beneath his skin.

Bridgette didn't move once he'd eased back, her pretty gaze locked on him. She licked her lips, and he lost it. He dipped down, again, twisted her mouth open then plunged inside. She battled him for control, finally allowing him to dominate the kiss.

That one surrender had him lifting her in his arms. He glanced at the wall but decided against it. If she'd spiraled by having him over her, pinning her to the wall wouldn't be any better. And the last thing he wanted was to give her a reason to ask him to stop. To let her go because he swore his fingers wouldn't release their death grip on her towel.

A breathy moan caressed his ear as he planted her ass on the counter then stepped between her thighs, hoping it wasn't too confining for her. He nuzzled her nose, their breath mixing. Indecision clouded her gaze, and he nearly pulled back, then it vanished, replaced by lust.

She toyed with his hair. "This is probably a terrible idea."

He smiled, dipping down to lave her neck—lick her pulse still beating wildly beneath her flesh. "The worst."

"It'll screw up our working relationship."

He nodded, mouthing her nape then nipping her earlobe. "Probably, but..." He lifted his head until they made eye contact. "I've got plenty of colleagues."

Her eyelids fluttered closed, and he took that as a sign to continue. He kissed her, again, taking his time to trace every contour before releasing her and working his way to the edge of the towel. He inched back just enough to yank the edges apart, allowing the terry to drop to the countertop.

Sam took a moment to admire the creamy expanse of skin. The splash of pink on her nipples, and the line of trimmed hair along her mound—like a damn arrow pointing to where he planned on spending the next hour joined to her. He wet his lips, groaning at the shiny evidence of her desire coating her pussy before finally looking her in the eyes.

"Christ, you're even more beautiful than I remember. And I'd memorized every inch of you. Pictured you countless times in the past dozen years. But, damn…my imagination didn't do you justice." He leaned in. "Tell me you want this. I need to know for sure."

She swallowed, never breaking eye contact. "I want this. It's just…"

He smiled, thumbing the corner of her mouth. "No trapping you. Got it. Do you feel trapped, now?"

She shook her head, bouncing her hair around her shoulders.

"Good. Because there are countless naughty things I can do to you on this crappy old counter."

Her eyes widened right before he captured her mouth. He palmed her back, moaning at the soft press of her skin beneath his hands. Bridgette fisted his shirt behind his neck, tugging at it in what he assumed was a desperate attempt to pull it over his head. He made her wait until his lungs burned before easing back and dropping his chin.

The blue cotton slipped over his shoulders, falling to

the floor at his feet. He straightened, intent on pressing every inch of her skin against his, when her palms landed on his chest, anchoring him to the spot. Her eyes rounded as her lips parted to form a lopsided O. She made that same throaty noise as she traced her fingers along his pecs then down his ribs. A frown marred her pretty face when she skimmed her fingertips across his collection of scars, finally raising her gaze to his.

Sam covered her hands with his, holding them firmly against him. "Ancient history."

She opened her mouth, but he leaned forward and claimed it, allowing her hands to slip free from his grasp. They slid down to his jeans, her fingers working to pop open the button and lower the zipper, which he knew wouldn't be easy with his dick stretching the fabric to the limit.

Bridgette moaned when she finally opened his fly, cupping his cock through his briefs. The firm contact nearly sent him over, and he had to press his fists against the counter to stop from spilling against her palm.

"Hold that thought."

She stilled as he grabbed his jeans and shoved them over his hips, taking his briefs with them. His dick sprang forward the instant he freed it, slapping wetly against her stomach.

Bridgette closed her eyes, drawing in a deep breath before looking up at him. "I could help you out with that."

A blowjob. He was barely hanging on to his control, and she wanted to give him a blowjob.

"Next time. Some time, but now…"

He slid his palms up her thighs, grazing his thumbs over her mound. Slick fluid covered his skin, and he couldn't stop from shoving his hand beneath her ass and pulling her forward as he thrust inside, burying himself to the hilt.

Bridgette gasped as her head tilted back, the cords in her neck straining. Sam didn't move, didn't fucking breathe, as her wet heat engulfed him. He stared at where they were joined, her groin crushed against his. Fire licked down his spine and into his sac, threatening to end their encounter with his first stroke.

He forced himself to hold still, allow her time to adjust, when he realized he hadn't put on a condom. A laugh sounded in his head, and he knew his buddy was mocking his carelessness, yet, again.

Sam dragged his gaze upward, meeting hers when she lowered her head. Her pupils were blown wide, her skin now a beautiful shade of pink. Her chest heaved against his with every gasping inhale as she wrapped her arms around his neck, pulling him closer.

She nipped at his earlobe, her breath cooling his damp flesh. "God, please, Sam. Move."

He clenched his teeth when she tightened around him, squeezing him so hard he thought his shaft would simply explode. "I have condoms. I swear I do. Shit, they might even be flavored, but... They aren't helping us much sitting in my damn wallet and not on my dick. I'm clean. Get tested regularly, but... I never forget protection, until, apparently, now. With you. And once I move..."

Her expression softened, her lips curling up into a

sexy smile. "I'm on birth control. And I'm clean. I've never gone without before, either. So…"

He leaned his head back until he made eye contact. "Are you saying we can go bareback? Every time?" Just the thought had his cock pulsing inside her.

She moaned, angling her head to the side as if asking him to lick her nape. "Damn, you're big."

He complied, tasting the hint of salt on her skin. "Answer me because I can't hold off much longer."

"Yes. God, yes."

He snapped. The heat, the wet glide of her sex, the give of her flesh around his overloaded his senses, and he let loose—thrusting into her as he held her on the edge of the counter. Bridgette clung to him, crossing her ankles behind his back and using them to tilt her pelvis —meet every punishing stroke. He slid one palm under her ass, holding her steady as his other hand cupped her neck, allowing him to claim her mouth.

He swallowed her raspy pleas, finally easing back enough to stare at her. "Only the first round. God, what you do to me."

He lowered his forehead to hers, wondering if she was half as close as he was, when she gasped then arched back. Male pride swelled in his chest as her eyes rolled slightly, her walls contracting around his shaft.

"Oh, yeah, darling. Come all over me."

A rush of warm fluid sent him over. He slammed into her a few more times then stiffened, holding himself still as his release shot forward, emptying inside her in a series of hard spurts. Sweat slicked his skin, the steam from the shower curling around them.

Sam closed his eyes, lost in the racing of his heart

and the steady wash of breath against his shoulder. He just prayed he hadn't been too rough. He was supposed to be proving he could be trusted, not fucking her against any handy surface. But...damn.

He drew in a shaky breath, easing back enough to stare down at her. "You okay?"

She blinked open her eyes, looking up at him as if he was the answer to something she'd been searching for, before chuckling. "Not a virgin, Sam. So, yeah. I'm fine. Better than fine, actually. Especially if you're going to hold true to your word and that was only round one, because..." She licked her bottom lip. "That wasn't close to being enough."

"Was that your way of saying you didn't enjoy yourself? Are you questioning my ability to please you?"

"Paranoid much? That was mind blowing, but..." Her chin quivered. "I need more. More time with you. I don't want this to be over, yet."

"Nowhere close to over, Bridg. Which means, it's time for a shower, and this time, I'm gonna make you scream."

CHAPTER ELEVEN

This time, I'm going to make you scream.

His words repeated inside Bridgette's head, making it hard to move the few steps over to the shower. Usually, overt challenges like that struck a nerve. Made her back away—distance herself from any chance of a confrontation. But the way Sam said it—gravelly tones in a low, raspy voice that ignited the desire just starting to cool in the pit of her stomach—hit a different nerve. The one she'd buried that night with Brock. The part of her that longed for more than just passing encounters orchestrated around her obvious issues.

This time, she wanted everything.

Wanted to trace every inch of Sam's body. Feel him give himself over to her. But more than anything, she wanted to give herself completely to him. Have him hold her close as he slid into her, their gazes locked, only his face and incredibly wide shoulders visible in her field of view. She wanted to know what it was like to have his weight pressed against her, holding her in place with nothing but his cock moving inside her.

A shiver beaded her skin with bumps. What the hell was wrong with her? Less than twenty minutes ago, she'd had her own version of a panic attack because Sam had been in that exact position—on his elbows above her, his body long and hard against hers. Yet, one quick round of sex, and everything had changed.

Not everything. Just her. Though, she doubted she'd actually changed. More that she'd stopped fighting her attraction. And it wasn't the sex that had undone her, it had been that first kiss. As soon as his lips had touched hers, the walls she'd spent the past several years building had crumbled, leaving her exposed. It should have frightened her, but all she felt was relief.

Sam's hand landed on the small of her back, guiding her over to the shower. That's when she realized he hadn't demolished the walls as much as he'd scaled them then made his way inside. Like a key fitting into a lock. Only one possible combination.

"Cold?"

She glanced at him. God, the man was gorgeous. Firm muscles beneath taut, sun-kissed skin. He wasn't jarhead big. He was tightly strung, like a man who could move fast without compromising his strength. And she couldn't wait to run her tongue all over his body.

Her gaze drifted to his groin. Even semi-erect, he was large. Far thicker than the other men she'd been with. Just another reason no one else had ever seemed to measure up. They'd been judged against an impossible standard.

Sam laughed. "You keep looking at me like that and we won't make it into the shower before I wrap you around me, again."

Her breath caught. He was serious. The way his gaze bored into hers. The firm line of his shoulders. The tension in his muscles. He was holding on but barely.

She wet her lip, groaning when he leaned in just enough to have her trace his, as well. He nodded at the tub, and she managed to scramble over the side without falling on her face. Not that she would have with Sam's hand wrapped around her arm—as if he was afraid she'd vanish if he let go. But she considered it a win, seeing as her knees felt as if they might buckle at any moment.

Sam stepped in behind her, pulling her back against his chest before turning her into the spray. Warm water cascaded over her skin, easing the strain in her muscles —strain she hadn't realized was there. She relaxed, leaning against him as he grabbed a bar of soap and ran it across her stomach.

He hummed against her neck, dipping down to suck at her flesh, his hand still making lazy circles across her body, leaving a trail of suds. "Christ, you're beautiful. I love the way you fit against me." He swirled his soapy fingers up one side then down the other, pausing at the raised scar on her left side. "Fucking bastard."

She placed her hand over his, glancing at him across her shoulder. "What did you say earlier? Ancient history?"

"Not the same. I chose to enlist. I knew full well what could happen. What I'd signed up for. That I might not make it out alive—or that I might have to live with the kind of injuries that scar you forever. This...this was because some sick prick thought he owned you. It's not remotely the same, and if he ever comes after you, again…"

He didn't finish. He didn't need to. Bridgette knew how it ended. With Brock dead, his blood staining Sam's soul for the rest of his life. Not that Sam seemed to be worried about the state of his soul. Maybe he'd lost too much of it overseas. Buried it along with Gray after their last mission. Either way, she didn't want to think about Brock or how her work put her at risk. She wanted to live in the moment. Savor it. Have something other than regret to look back on when this assignment was over, and Sam moved on.

Sam nuzzled her neck. "Sorry. That's not the train of conversation that's going to lead to more of you writhing in my arms. It just guts me to think you went through all of that alone. That you didn't feel you could tell anyone. Call on someone for help."

Call on me.

He didn't say it, but the unspoken thought hung between them, tightening her chest as tears gathered in her eyes.

Bridgette turned in his arms, sliding her hands up to his shoulders. "It might have been a little late, but I told you. And I'm not alone, right now."

She slanted her mouth over his, allowing him to expend some of the energy straining his muscles. If she'd learned anything about the man he'd become it was that he felt a soul-deep need to protect the people around him. And just because he wasn't in the military any longer didn't mean he'd been able to shut that side of him off. It was in his blood.

Sam slid his palms along her back, twisting them then pressing her against the wall before freezing. He pulled away, muttering something under his breath as he forced his hands to his sides.

"Sam?"

"Let's get clean, so we can get dirty, again. Because being inside you with nothing between us…"

His nostrils flared, and his cock twitched, hardening under her gaze. She held out her hand, motioning for him to give her the soap. He arched his brow but handed her the bar, smiling when she rubbed it across his chest, covering every inch of skin she could reach.

"Damn. You are one fine looking man. I can't imagine how long it took you to get this ripped."

He snorted, palming her hips as she continued down his ribs. "You'd be surprised how quickly things change when you're busting your ass twenty hours a day."

She paused, looking up at him. "Did you ever question yourself? Wonder if you had what it took to make it?"

As soon as the question slipped out, she regretted it. No way a man like Sam had ever doubted anything. Not with all he'd accomplished. After their unlikely reunion, she'd researched what it took to become an Army Ranger. To say she'd been humbled was an understatement. And projecting her own insecurities on him wasn't getting them any closer to round two.

Sam gave her a squeeze. "Lost count of the number of times I told Gray we should just pack it in. Run away to some beach and drink Mia Tais. He'd always laugh and say, hell yeah, we'll quit tomorrow. But tomorrow never seemed to come."

She froze. "Really?"

"Everyone has doubts, darling. Success is pushing through despite them." He tilted his head. "Have you been having doubts?"

She snorted, rubbing her hands across his stomach. "Don't get me wrong. The satisfaction of putting scum like Stevens where he belongs is indescribable. But lately, I feel like I'm just going through the motions. Doing what I'm expected to do. I used to get this rush. Now...sometimes when I get a new case, I just find it hard to breathe." She shrugged. "Forget it. I'm sure it's just the stress."

Sam grabbed her hands, holding them still until she gazed up at him. "It's never too late to find a new passion. You know that, right? Life's too short to spend it following a dream you no longer believe in."

"Not all of us get a second chance."

"You're right. You have to make it, yourself. Speaking of second chances... You'd best get the important parts clean before I realize how much I love the thought of my cum dripping down your legs for the foreseeable future."

She inhaled, quickly cleaning the rest of him before dropping her hand to his cock. Sam clenched his jaw as she ran her fingers up and down his length, cleaning away the evidence of their combined releases. His shaft thickened, resting hot and hard in her palm as she shifted enough to wash away the soap.

She licked her lips, wanting nothing more than to drop to her knees and make him lose control, again. "Tell me, Sam. How much would you like to see your cum dripping from my mouth? Splattered across my chest?"

The muscle in his temple jumped as his fingers flexed at her hips. "Bridgette."

"Do you know how much I want to taste you? Watch you give yourself to me? I bet I could make you see stars."

He stopped her from kneeling in front of him. "Soon, darling, I promise, but first..." He blew out a forced breath as his muscles tensed. "I need you. I need to feel you clenched around me, your flesh hot and wet against mine. I..."

She released his cock, then claimed his mouth, moaning when he squeezed one hand between them to finish cleaning her off. Then he spun her around, holding her body flush to his as he angled her toward the wall.

His lips caressed her neck. "Is this too close?"

She shook her head, the answer stuck in her throat as desire burned through her veins.

He chuckled. "Speechless? That's a new one. Put your hands against the wall to brace yourself. That's it." He bit at her shoulder muscle once she'd complied. "Now lift one leg and put it on the back ledge."

He helped her move, keeping one large hand wrapped around her torso and across her shoulder as the other slipped beneath her thigh. His fingers slid through her folds, gathering her moisture then rubbing it around her clit. Pleasure billowed out from his touch, stealing her next breath as another release coiled tight in her core.

Sam hummed. "God, so fucking wet. I can't believe I

get to have you like this. Bare. All that slippery fluid covering my skin, burning me like a brand across my flesh. I could lose myself in you and never want to be found."

He dipped two fingers inside her, then swirled them around her nub. "I want you to come for me. I want to feel you contract around me, hear you shout my name. I want you to give me everything."

He nudged her sex then thrust hard, once again, filling her to the edge of pain, while his finger kept rubbing her clit. Dots raced across her vision as her orgasm quickly gained strength, taking her to the brink in a matter of moments.

Sam set up a steady rhythm, making her body shimmy with every upward stroke. When he'd made it obvious he planned on pounding into her in the shower, she'd imagined something more primal—her ass in the air with her hands braced on the edge as he took what he wanted without any kind of romantic connection. But the way he held her against him—his arms surrounding her, his lips pressed against her neck—it shifted something inside her. And for the first time in years, she could imagine a future with more than just her job as her focus. That there was someone she trusted enough to help shape how the rest of her life played out.

The thought intensified the heat rolling through her body, perching her on the edge—so close to going over but not quite able to fall. She clamped her hands around Sam's arm, digging her nails into his flesh as every muscle clenched tight.

"Now, Bridg. Scream for me."

He thrust hard, flicking his finger across her bud at

the same time he bit her shoulder, again. Her breath locked in her chest, squeezing to the point she thought she might pass out, before careening her over. Sam's name sounded around them, though she wasn't convinced she'd actually shouted it or if she'd merely yelled it inside her head. Everything dimmed, collapsing into Sam's skin against hers, his cock exploding inside her.

Bridgette sagged against him, her chin resting on his arm, her legs shaking. Sam's choppy breaths raked across her ear, her name mixing in with the gasping pants. She let herself fade, confident he wouldn't let her fall, when he dropped a kiss on her shoulder.

"Easy, darling. I've got you."

She blinked, but opening her eyes seemed far too strenuous.

"Bridg? You still with me?"

She forced her eyelids apart, this time. "I hope those muscles aren't just for show, because I'm not sure I can move."

He chuckled. "It's okay. I'll move us. Let's just clean off, first."

She groaned. "That sounds like moving to me."

"I'll do all the work."

He eased free, and she had to bite her lip to keep from begging him to take her, again. To chase away the empty feeling that clung to her like a shroud. The one he'd lifted for those precious moments they'd been together.

Sam balanced their weight, covering her in soap then rinsing it off. He moved his arm between them, and she assumed he was cleaning himself before he placed the soap on the dish the shuffled them forward. The spray shut off, instantly cooling the air and beading her skin with goosebumps. She shivered, burrowing against him in the hopes of sharing his heat.

Sam shoved back the curtain then lifted her out, wrapping her in the towel they'd left on the counter. The terrycloth felt oddly rough against her flesh compared to Sam's skin, and she wondered if he'd agree to spend the rest of the day holding her on the bed, naked.

"Penny for your thoughts, darling?"

She jumped, looking up at him. God, had he somehow gotten sexier? Or was she finally seeing him— without the blinders of her past?

She smoothed her hands up his arms and across his shoulders. "I…"

How could she say that she felt as if she'd just jumped down the rabbit hole and emerged as someone she didn't recognize? That she was pretty sure she'd fallen in love with him, again? That she didn't want whatever was taking shape between them to end on the steps of the courthouse next week?

Sam frowned, palming her jaw. "Hey? You okay?"

She tiptoed up and kissed him. More sex she could handle. All these feelings…

He responded, lifting her against his chest then carrying into the other room. He placed her on her feet just long enough to remove her towel, then picked her up and laid her gently in the center of the bed. He took the time to fan her hair out behind her, trailing a single finger across her shoulder then down her arm as he straightened, the lethal gleam back in his eyes.

He swept his gaze the length of her. "Comfortable? Your hair not bunched beneath you?"

"Fine, why?"

"Because it's about time I made love to you. And it's gonna take the rest of the afternoon."

CHAPTER TWELVE

Sam was one lucky son of a bitch.

He knew it. Standing there, staring down at Bridgette spread out on the bed—her hair pooled around her, her skin still dotted with drops from the shower—made him acutely aware that he'd just gotten his second, "second chance". And this time, he wasn't going to screw it up. Run away when life got complicated. He'd spent the past dozen years entrenched in complicated. He knew his way around the board. Though, Bridgette was a whole other level of the damn thing—like a labyrinth with endless wrong turns. One he'd have to tread carefully around or risk scaring her off. Not that he wouldn't give chase. If the Army had taught him anything, it was that the best outcomes were wrought from laser determination. And Sam was completely focused on her.

Goosebumps rose along her skin, though he wasn't sure if it was from a chill or having him study her. Catalogue every dip, every curve. Every tiny freckle scattered across her flesh. He wanted to be able to close his eyes and see her perfectly. Conjure her in his mind as he'd done with Gray's ghost.

Bridgette snagged her lower lip, worrying it for a moment before arching a brow. "Everything okay?"

He smiled, feeling insanely free. Light, as if he'd shed a weight that had been holding him down. "Fucking awesome. You...I could stare at you all day and still find something new to impress me." He reached for one of her feet, cradling it in his palm. "Like your feet. They're so small. Dainty, almost. Each toe smaller than the next."

He kissed her arch then slid his hands up to her calf. "Your skin is so soft, and I bet you're sensitive here."

He leaned down and licked the patch of skin behind her knee, chuckling at the way she wiggled on the bed. "Maybe ticklish is a better description. And here..." He smoothed one finger up her inner thigh, lightly touching where her leg joined into her groin. "You're already wet, again."

She huffed. "How am I supposed to be dry when you're standing there, staring at me—naked. Have you looked in the mirror? You're an endless expanse of muscles and rippling flesh. Is it my turn, yet?"

"Soon. But first..."

He sank to his knees, ignoring the way the shag carpet rubbed his skin. It was scratchy, like raw wool, but he'd learned to live with discomfort, and he was pretty damn sure he wouldn't give a shit about his knees once he'd buried his face in her cleft. Bridgette inhaled when he slid his hands under her ass and tugged her to the edge of the bed, her sex perfectly positioned beneath his head. Her earthy musk filled his senses as more of her arousal coated her skin, making it shiny in the glaring light.

"Mmmm, you smell so good." He dipped down, licking a path through her slit. "Better than good."

Her breath hitched at the intimate contact, and she squeezed her thighs against his shoulders as her fingers landed in his hair. Her nails scraped along his scalp before she seemed to settle with the strands fisted around her grip.

"God, Sam, you're killing me."

He chuckled, gazing up at her across her body. "I think the word you're searching for is pleasing you." He flicked his tongue across her clit, grinning at the way her hips bucked, pressing her nub harder against his mouth. "So sensitive. Makes me wonder how long it's been since anyone touched you this way."

Her gaze snapped to his, the shift in her eyes sparking his primitive needs.

He arched a brow. "Well? How long?"

Her mouth opened and closed a few times, nothing but throaty moans making it past her lips.

He shook his head, rubbing his tongue up and down her folds before pausing, again.

She groaned. "Please, don't stop."

"Then answer my question. How? Long?"

She blinked, looking as if she couldn't quite follow his words before pressing her lips together. "A while. A long, long while. Now, please…"

He sucked at her clit, then swirled his tongue around it. "How long is that?"

"Does it matter?"

"I'm feeling acutely possessive, right now. So yes. It's important. I want to know how many guys have tasted you like this. Buried their faces in your dripping flesh as they got you off."

Her eyelids fluttered, but she managed to hold his gaze. "That wasn't what you asked."

"So, answer both." When she stared at him, he teased her with a hint of penetration, sinking just an inch of his finger inside her. "Bridgette."

"Hardly any. A few short-term affairs that never became anything when I was first in university. But after Brock, I haven't really trusted anyone enough to…"

He stilled as her voice just faded without finishing, cursing the Neanderthal side of him. He shouldn't have pushed, but then, his dick had clearly been doing the talking. Or maybe it was the part of him that hated the fact he'd ever let her go. Allowed any other man to touch what clearly felt like *his*.

Great. Now, he sounded like her prickish ex.

He back pedaled, hoping to put a better spin on it. "So, you're saying I'm special."

"You're way past special. Now, don't you have something better to do with your mouth than talk?"

"Do I?"

"Sam."

He smiled, ensuring she was watching as he drew his tongue between her folds, lapping at the moisture clinging to her skin. She tasted like honey and spice, with a touch of heat that made his dick throb. He couldn't remember the last time he'd enjoyed licking a woman this much. Probably hadn't since the last time he'd had his head between her thighs, her juice coating his tongue.

Bridgette's grip tightened, the slight sting against his scalp making him smile. She was close.

He hummed against her flesh, the tiny vibrations making her squirm even more. She tilted her hips when he pressed his finger inside her, doing her best to take him deeper. He followed her lead, pressing fully inside her then slowly retreating.

She huffed, crying out a raspy version of his name when he slammed back in with two fingers. "God, yes. Please, Sam."

He set up a slow rhythm, easing back enough to watch his flesh sink inside her only to emerge glistening with more arousal. "Christ, you're beautiful. So wet. I can't wait to feel you around me, again."

"You're the one drawing... Shit."

Her back arched off the bed, and he had to lay one forearm across her hips to keep her still—prevent her from taking control. He wasn't ready to move on, just yet. What if he never got to taste her, again? If this was nothing more than another safe one-off for her? If the only reason he was "special" was because they had history

Bridgette moaned, drawing his attention. A deep blush colored her skin as she writhed on the bed, looking incredibly desperate and sexy. Christ, he was a fucking goner.

He sighed. "Fine, come for me. But don't think this is the last time I'll have my face buried in your flesh."

She creamed his hand at his words, nodding her agreement before pressing her head into the mattress.

Her neck corded, every muscle straining as he kept her poised on the edge. He smiled, taking one more moment to memorize the scene. He wanted to remember the color of skin, highlighted by the mass of golden hair around her shoulders. The way her chest heaved as she struggled to breathe past the searing pleasure. How her breasts pointed toward the ceiling, the nipples beaded into hard points. He wanted to suck on them, but he was having a hard time focusing on anything other than his need to be inside her.

He increased his thrusts, hitting her G-spot as he crooked his fingers, then sucking hard on her clit. Bridgette stiffened, squeezing his shoulders with her thighs before shouting her release. Strong contractions pulled at his fingers, drawing them deeper as her entire body responded. Her muscles flexed beneath her flushed skin as her head thrashed from side to side. He lapped at the wash of fluid, content to spend the next hour with his tongue pressed against her wet flesh, when the pressure around his shoulders eased, and her thighs fell to the side as her fingers slid from his hair.

He dropped an open-mouthed kiss on her clit then lifted his head, staring up at her as she breathed through the last of her orgasm. Her chest heaved from the strain, each raspy inhalation sounding through the room.

Sam untangled himself from her legs, moving off to one side. He skimmed his fingers along her abdomen then up her ribs and across her chest, brushing her nipple as he settled in beside her, his weight braced on his elbow. Bridgette shivered, fluttering her eyelids as she tried to focus on him. It took a few moments before her gaze cleared, the small ring of blue more brilliant than before.

He dipped down, dropping a kiss on her nose. "God, you really are beautiful. I could watch you come for me all day long."

A contented smile curved her lips, and she looked genuinely happy. "Not sure I could do that again and stay conscious."

He shrugged. "I've trained in the art of patience. I'll keep you safe while you recover."

Her eyes widened, taking on a glassy appearance as she grazed her thumb across her jaw. "How about we play more during the next round?"

"That sounds like you have plans for now."

"I do. You, inside me. For as long as you can last."

He clenched his jaw to keep from pouncing on top of her and slamming inside. "Sounds like a challenge, too, darling."

"Not a challenge. Five minutes. An hour. I don't care. I just need you."

His heart skipped, taking up a shaky rhythm as he fought to swallow past the lump in his throat. He leaned forward, resting his forehead on hers. "God, Bridg."

She slipped her hand around his neck, holding him close as their breathing mixed. Time faded into the gentle scratch of her nails against his scalp and the warm press of her body against his. What he wouldn't give to slide on top of her. Gather her in his arms as he slid deep inside her. Watch her face as she gave herself to him. Though he didn't equate loving to position, with her…

He pushed away the hint of disappointment. Maybe with time, she'd come to trust him enough he could love her that way. Until then, he'd respect her limitations. The last thing he wanted was to hurt her.

Bridgette stared up at him as he eased back, her big eyes watching him. She snagged her bottom lip as tension strained her muscles.

Sam gave her a smile. "Easy, darling. I promised I wouldn't hurt you, and that includes breaking any of your conditions. So be a good girl, and roll onto your side for me."

She opened her mouth, then closed it, following his directions and rolling away from him. He snaked his hand across her waist then between her breasts, tugging her back tight against his chest. She wiggled her ass, rubbing it across his dick.

He tsked in her ear. "I'm trying to be romantic—as much as I can be without climbing on top of you. But if you keep tempting my control like that…"

She laughed, the easy sound kicking up his heart rate. God, what he wouldn't give to hear her laugh like that every day. To see her face light up and know he was the reason for the small lines around her eyes or the light flush on her skin.

He let the thought linger as he nudged her thighs apart then smoothed his hand down her torso and across her hip. "Lay your top leg over mine. Good."

He skimmed his palm lower, tracing her leg as far as he could reach before slowly making his way back up. He circled her hip bone, smiling at the way she twitched, then lowered his finger to her slit.

He moaned against her neck, licking at her sweat-damp skin. "You're even wetter. I thought I'd licked you dry, but you're proving me wrong." He dipped his finger through her folds, gathering moisture on the tip. "Maybe I should go back down—do my job properly this time."

She inhaled, glancing at him over her shoulder. Her lips were parted, her breath panting around them. She swallowed with effort, the red slashes across her cheeks making the rest of her flesh look paler. "Sam, please."

He grinned, knowing it would irritate her. "Please lick me, again?"

"Please fuck me before I decide to tie you to the bed."

"Hmm, interesting concept. And I might hold still long enough for you to do that—eventually."

He silenced her with a firm kiss, tangling his other hand in her hair to hold her captive. Bridgette ate at his mouth as she wrapped her arm around his ribs, tugging in an effort to pull him closer. He shifted as much as he could, thrusting the tip of his dick against her sex.

She moaned into his mouth, lifting her leg higher— giving him better access. He curled his hand under her thigh, holding her there as he tilted his pelvis then surged forward, plunging deep inside her in one long steady stroke. A muffled cry sounded against his lips before she arched into him, increasing his penetration. He flexed his fingers against her skin, wanting to dig them into her flesh but afraid he'd leave bruises. And he'd be damned before he did that.

Instead, he forced open his hand, pressing his palm against her mound as he tightened his grip in her hair, holding her still as he started a firm rhythm. Every stroke shimmied her body within his arms, the wet echo of his thrusts sounding around them.

Time bled into the rapid beat of her heart echoing inside his chest and the slick glide of her flesh against his. He focused on keeping his breathing even, resisting the urge to pound into her, until his unrelenting need burned hot beneath his skin.

He repositioned his hand, veeing his fingers around his dick where they were joined. "Fuck, Bridg. So tight. I don't know how you take me inside you."

Glazed eyes glanced over her shoulder at him, rolling slightly when he slammed into her. "So good. Please—don't stop."

"No way I'm stopping until you've gone over, again. I've got all day. All night, too, if necessary. I can hold off as long as I need until you come for me."

She shook her head, crying out when he pressed the heel of his hand against her clit. "Already came. A few times. I'm not sure... Yes!"

She dug her fingers into his hip as she tilted her groin, allowing him to move more freely. Her head bowed toward her chest, the inklings of her release contracting along his shaft. He fought the urge to finish, not wanting their time to end. She wasn't the only one who needed—more.

Searing heat flashed along his nerves, pooling in his sac when she inhaled then shattered in his arms. She was breathtaking. Skin flushed a deep red. Her peaked nipples pointing straight out and reminding him he still hadn't tasted them the way he should have.

Later.

And there would be a later. And another after that.

Endless laters, if he had a say. If she didn't bolt like she had after her other sexual encounters. If he meant more to her than a trustworthy friend to scratch a few itches she had neglected for years.

If she cared.

He cared. More than he should. More than was wise. Just…more.

Bridgette's breath hitched, and she clamped down around him. Hard.

He came. Jerking against her body, emptying inside her in long, crushing spurts. His muscles stiffened, holding him rigidly against her until the burning sensation raging beneath his skin diminished, allowing him to rest his forehead against her shoulder.

The scent of sex filled the air, the heady aroma swelling his chest. A part of him wanted to bang on it like a damn gorilla—a visual display of ownership. He'd marked her. Now, she belonged to him.

Right up until she smacked him upside the head for even thinking that way. Bridgette Hayward wasn't the kind of woman who wanted to "belong" to anyone. She wanted—no, needed—a partner. A man who wasn't afraid of her intelligence or tenacity. A man willing to let her fight her own battles—backing her up when the situation called for it.

He could be that man. Usually. Definitely when her life wasn't in danger. When there weren't daily threats recorded on her cell or waiting on her doorstep. But when there were…

He sighed. He could only temper his protective instincts so much. Not because she wasn't capable of taking care of herself. But because in some instances, his training overrode hers. He hadn't spent twelve years slogging through mud and dirt, dragging his ass across enemy lines without developing a skillset designed to address the kind of trouble shadowing her. It didn't mean more than the obvious. He'd been trained to kill. Had killed in the line of duty. And he'd kill, again, if it meant she'd live.

If that made him more of the asshole bodyguard than the charming cook, so be it. Her safety outweighed her pride. Even if it meant he'd lose her.

God, he hoped he wouldn't. Not that he really had her. At least, not yet. But his time would be better spent charming her. Showing her he was a man of his word. One worthy of being more than just her bodyguard.

Bridgette released a shaky breath, burrowing against him as she sagged in his arms. He dropped a kiss on her neck, smiling at the resulting shiver.

"Are you okay, Bridg?"

She hummed, snuggling even closer.

He chuckled. "Come on. Another quick shower then you can sleep in my arms while I order us some dinner."

Her nose scrunched up. "Sleep, first. Shower and food later."

"You won't get a proper sleep with your thighs all sticky. I promise, we'll come straight back."

She pried open one eyelid, glancing back at him. "You'll do all the work, again?"

"Of course. Consider it part of my duties."

"I sure hope this isn't a regular duty with other clients."

"Just you, darling. I swear." He nuzzled her shoulder,

kissing his way up to her earlobe. "So was that a yes to the shower?"

"Yes, as long as you'll hold me after."

"Deal."

He eased free, cursing the way his stomach dropped from the loss of contact. Things were getting far more complicated than he'd ever imagined, and he hadn't even figured out who was after her, yet.

CHAPTER THIRTEEN

Bridgette sat in the passenger side of her Jeep, staring at the entrance to the Blue Moose tavern. It looked friendly, the front area brightly lit with white Christmas lights glittering from the eaves. Even the strings on the trees scattered across the lawn were still twinkling, and she couldn't help but wonder if the owners kept the lights up year 'round, or if they just hadn't gotten around to turning them off, yet. Not that she was complaining. The white color made the icy snow sparkle while chasing away most of the shadows—the kind she'd hidden in that night in the garage.

Guilt scratched at the edge of her conscience. She still hadn't told Sam about the incident, and a part of her worried that she was putting him at greater risk simply through omission of the truth. That knowing some black-clad freak had hunted her through her office building then into the garage would change his perception of the case. Alter whatever criteria he was using to list the possible suspects.

At first, she'd kept it hidden as a matter of principle. She hadn't wanted Sam's protection, hadn't thought it was necessary—especially when nothing had happened since she'd left Seattle. Even seeing the new set of photos hadn't unnerved her too much. No note attached. No creepy message. It seemed to reinforce her belief that it had been an isolated incident. An opportunistic event.

Then, they'd had to move because of the possible security leak. That's when she'd started wondering. Started questioning her choices. But every time she'd tried to tell him, her throat had closed around the words. She just wasn't sure if she was afraid of how he'd react or how she would. Other than her friend Jack, she hadn't told anyone about being followed. Sure, the police had a file—one she was certain Sam had already commandeered, not that she wanted to know how he'd gotten it. But she hadn't mentioned the armed assailant in her report to the cops. Not when she couldn't be sure Stevens didn't have connections that wore badges. And she hadn't known any of the officers long enough to vouch that they couldn't be bought.

Everyone had a price. Almost everyone. Men like Jack and Sam usually paid with their lives to remain honorable.

But after spending the afternoon in Sam's arms, feeling safe for the first time in years, she'd started questioning her reasons. Sam had proven he could be trusted. Had already gone to extreme lengths to ensure her safety. Yet, a part of her just couldn't take that final step. Whether it was years of being self-reliant or a deep-seated belief that in the end, everyone would eventually betray her, wasn't clear. All she knew was that she was walking a razor's edge with no way to get off.

She groaned inwardly. Who was she kidding? She hadn't told him because she knew he'd be angry—not that she'd blame him. He had every right to be angry. Keeping the incident a secret was foolish. Borderline suicidal, especially when she knew it was important. She fully expected him to lose his shit. Which was exactly why the words wouldn't dislodge from her throat. While she didn't actually believe he'd ever hurt her—strike out in anger like Brock had—the traumatized part of her just couldn't take that risk. Couldn't stop the images from materializing inside her head whenever she thought about confessing. And cowardly or not, she'd chosen to play it safe.

Sam nudged her shoulder, gaining her attention. His lips were pursed into a slight frown, the skin over his nose bunched. "You okay?"

She looked over at him—blue eyes intent on her—and she knew she could spend the rest of her life staring at him and never tire of what she saw. That it was only a matter of time before her brain caught up with her heart, and she let those three little words slip—ones she'd sworn she'd never say, again.

Though, if she were being honest, she'd never truly loved Brock. She thought she had at the time, but she'd discovered it had been the thought of him she'd been enamored with. The idea of having someone to spend her future with. Thank god, she hadn't made any kind of plans with him. Had discovered what kind of monster he was before they'd started making a permanent life together. Things could have turned out far worse.

She sighed. Maybe she was the problem. Maybe she was incapable of loving someone else. Sam had alluded to the fact the other day, and while she'd brushed it off, she couldn't deny he had a point. In retrospect, she hadn't really loved anyone, other than him. But they'd been eighteen—love struck. A time where every emotion was felt to the extreme. And now…

It had been so long since she'd let herself feel anything, she couldn't trust her feelings. Trust her heart, despite the way it pounded in her chest at the thought of Sam leaving. The empty feeling that gnawed at her stomach as she counted down the days until the trial began, and their affair ended.

Sam's frown deepened. "Bridg?"

She mustered a smile, hoping it was somewhat convincing. "Sorry. Guess I drifted into thought."

"Do I want to know what you were thinking?"

"Probably not."

His eyes narrowed. "I'll keep you safe. You know that, right? Even here."

Her chest tightened. Shit, now he thought she doubted his abilities. "I wasn't worried—"

"I'd say we could just bail, but I really need to talk to Hank, and I think you need to get out before you go stir crazy. Maybe have a quick snack. You didn't eat much of that salad you ordered. But we won't stay long."

She sighed then placed her hand over his. "If you must know, I was thinking about all the filthy things I'd like to do to you. After all, it still hasn't been my turn, yet."

The tension bled from his muscles as a wicked smile curved his lips. Sex was a great distraction, and one that obviously worked on him. "In that case, we'll make this even quicker. And if you're a good girl, I might just let you have your turn."

"If I'm a good girl, you won't enjoy my turn half as much."

He laughed, the rich sound wrapping around her. God, he was irresistible when he laughed like that. The sound coming from somewhere deep inside as his lips curved into a smile and the fine lines around his eyes crinkling.

He leaned forward, stopping a breath away. "You do me in with nothing more than a smile or a touch. *Anything* else will far exceed expectations."

"Don't set the bar too low, baby. I like a good challenge."

Those perfectly full lips lifted. "Then consider it set to the level of your last orgasm. I'm fairly certain you came close to passing out."

She reached forward, cupping his length through his pants. "I'll take that deal."

She kissed him, slanting her lips over his then licking her way inside. Sam responded, sliding his hand back behind her head—holding her tight as he ravished her mouth. Kissing the corners a few times then delving back inside. She lost track of time, of the light snow slowly falling from the inky sky, until Sam finally pulled back.

He thumbed the edge of her mouth. "Think you can hold that thought for an hour or so?"

"Sure. Besides, I can always excuse myself and take

care of business on my own in the washroom, if needed."

The muscle in Sam's temple jumped, and she resisted the laugh that clawed at her chest. She hadn't met a man, yet, that didn't seem fascinated by the thought of a woman touching herself. And Sam Montgomery was obviously no exception.

He hissed out a breath through clenched teeth. "You did that on purpose."

"Consider it foreplay. After all, I have a benchmark to meet, now."

He shook his head in mock indignation, reaching for the handle. "Ready to go inside?"

She nodded, the heady rush from kissing him draining instantly. She didn't know what it was about going inside that bothered her. Though, it was more likely the people she was meeting than the actual establishment. Hank Patterson and some of his men from Brotherhood Protectors. The same guy who had dug into her past. Who might know far more about her than she liked.

The lawyer side of her hated that. Having someone know more about her than she did about them. It was her job to dig up every piece of information she could. To know the people she was dealing with down to the size of briefs they wore. Going in blind...

She groaned inwardly, again. God, how long had she been isolating herself that she'd forgotten how to be social? Hank and his men weren't defendants she was trying to prosecute. They were Sam's coworkers. His friends. She needed to respect that.

Her door opened, once again, bringing her back from

her thoughts. Sam smiled as he held out his hand to her. She took it, ignoring the jolt of heat that passed between them as he maneuvered her against his side, holding her close. Though it was genuinely romantic, she knew Sam had ulterior motives, like being her first line of defense.

She swallowed against the punch of fear and guilt to her stomach. She couldn't think about Sam getting hurt. Having his blood on her hands because he'd taken a bullet meant for her. It messed with her brain—the one part of her she relied on to function when her heart seemed to have a mind of its own.

She sighed. Fear or not, she needed to tell him. Everything. As soon as this meeting was over, she'd come clean about the armed asshole, and anything else she might have left out. Risk his reaction because Sam deserved her honesty. Hell, he deserved a lot more.

Her chest tightened as she followed his lead, moving with him whenever he adjusted their position—no doubt blocking her body with his. It wasn't until they'd walked through the tavern doors that he seemed to relax a bit. Though, Sam relaxed equated to anyone else on high alert. He just made it appear more natural. Fool people into thinking he wasn't prepared to launch an attack, which he was. She could tell by the firm press of his muscles, and the way he constantly scoured the room.

A large man near the back of the tavern stood, motioning for them to join him. She suspected it was Hank Patterson, boss and creator of Brotherhood Protectors. Her stomach roiled, despite her previous pep talk to relax. But knowing most of the discussion would encompass her life, unnerved her.

Sam leaned in closer. "Easy, Bridg. We're all friends here."

She nodded, though she suspected Sam saw through it. *His* friends, maybe. She didn't have friends, or at least, very few.

The large man gave her a smile. "Thought you two were going to ditch us. The name's Hank Patterson. It's a pleasure to finally meet you, Counselor."

Bridgette chuckled. "Bridgette is fine."

Hank pointed to the guy next to him. "In that case, Bridgette Hayward, this is Alex Davila, but everyone just calls him Taz, and the guy next to him is Joseph Kuntz, or Kujo for short."

The man he'd called Kujo sighed. "You can call me Joe if the nickname bothers you."

She smiled politely. "Kujo's fine."

Hank motioned for them to sit as he eyed the other men. "Let's remember the lady's an assistant U.S. Attorney and act appropriately."

She waved her hand. "Not tonight, gentlemen. So please, don't treat me with kid gloves." She pointed to an empty chair next to Sam. "Are you expecting someone else?"

Hank grinned. "That's a surprise for Midnight."

She frowned. "Midnight?"

Hank's gaze swung to Sam. "You didn't tell her?"

Bridgette glanced at Sam, arching a brow. "Your nickname's Midnight?"

Sam shrugged. "All of the guys get called something. And yeah, mine's Midnight." He smoothed his hand over her shoulder as he smiled. "But I've been Sam to you since I was twelve."

A wave of heat followed the light caress, making it suddenly hard to breathe. One touch, and the rest of the world disappeared. Vaporized for all she knew. There was just Sam and heat.

She managed to regain a bit of her composure, winking slyly at him. "I can adapt, *Midnight*."

Sam rolled his eyes. "How do you manage to make it sound…juvenile?"

"It's a gift." She slid onto the wooden chair, still looking at Sam. "So why Midnight?" She inhaled. "Oh, wait, I think I know. Barrow, Alaska, right?"

Hank laughed. "Seems she's got you figured out, Midnight. Nickname and all."

Sam glared at the man. "That's right. Laugh it up, *Montana*."

Bridgette smiled, relaxing at the easy banter that continued around the table. Maybe the men weren't quite as intimidating as she'd imagined they'd be. Though, just staring at them sent a shiver down her spine. Heavily muscled with the same, intense body language Sam had, they looked as if they were ready to brawl at a moment's notice. Or maybe start one just to practice their fighting skills. Either way, she couldn't imagine anyone willingly going up against them. Which might be why Hank's company had grown so quickly. Though, she hadn't dug up too much information when she'd researched Brotherhood Protectors, she'd learned enough to know that the number of employees had skyrocketed in an incredibly short period of time.

Ex-special ops men as bodyguards and security

personnel. Of course, his business was thriving. The men all gave off the same vibe—"don't fuck with me". The kind cops and federal agents shared, only these guys took it to a whole new level. She just hadn't realized how strong Sam's was until he was seated with the others. That the stoic attitude she'd assumed was practiced determination was actually his way of warding off anyone who didn't belong. Any threat. An age-old symbol of a true warrior. And Sam had it in spades.

He glanced at her, and, for a moment, any trace of the hardened soldier vanished—replaced by a warm, dare she say loving, smile. The kind that lit up his face and made the multicolored neon lights around them dim. What she wouldn't give to have him smile like that at her every day. To wake up to him grinning down at her—fall asleep with his curved lips pressed against her forehead. To feel safe. Always.

Sam leaned in, close. Too close if he were merely her bodyguard. And she doubted the men would miss the way he reached up and tucked her hair behind her ear. If Sam had wanted to keep their new status as lovers a secret, he'd just blown it. "They won't bite, you know, even if they look like they could."

That gravelly voice wove around her, reminding her of how they'd spent the afternoon.

She nodded. "I know."

"And yet, you look as if you're about to face a firing squad."

She spared the other men a quick glance. "A firing squad of questions."

"They'll be discreet. Nothing you say here will be repeated."

"But they'll know. About everything. Until the other night, only a couple of cops, some hospital staff and Jack knew about Brock. Now..." She rubbed her arms, suddenly chilled.

He sighed. "I'm sorry."

She shrugged. There wasn't anything he could say to make her comfortable with talking about that night. Make it any less of a spotlight on her one true failure. Just thinking about how the others would look at her—a combination of pity and sorrow—made her skin crawl. Made the room feel as if it was closing in on her, much like it had the night they'd watched that stupid horror movie.

Sam's large hand landed on her thigh. "Breathe, darling. I'm right here."

She swallowed despite the choking lump in her throat and nodded, again. Breathe. It sounded so easy, yet, her lungs burned as she struggled to gasp in any amount of oxygen. Sam leaned in closer, when a shadow passed over them. She glanced over her shoulder, tilting her head back until she could finally see the guy's face.

He was bigger than Sam—broader. More body-builder muscly than Sam's tightly coiled strength, but the guy had similar dark hair and handsome symmetrical features. He looked slightly taller, with close-cropped hair and several days' worth of growth on his jaw. The bottom half of a tattoo colored his skin on his left bicep, the swirling design most likely some kind of military emblem.

He smiled, his stunning green eyes crinkling around the edges as he clapped an incredibly huge hand on Sam's back. "Midnight. Damn you're a sight. Hank said he'd sweet-talked you into joining up, but I had to see for myself."

Sam's eyes rounded before he laughed, surging to his feet then clasping the other man on the back. "God damn, Ice. Thought you were against indulging in furloughs, you ornery son of a bitch."

The guy—Ice—returned the gesture, nearly lifting Sam off his feet before releasing him. "You haven't changed a bit, other than looking shaggy as hell. Don't they have barbers in this town?"

"Why? So I can look like a cue ball, like you?"

Ice tipped his head and laughed. "I believe you meant badass. Because that's how I look." His gaze drifted to her and lingered. He wet his lips, backing up enough to give her a flourished bow. "Russel Foster at your service." He looked up, thumbing at Sam. "You are far too fine to be hanging around with this jackass."

Bridgette grinned, heat creeping up her cheeks as everyone stared at her. She extended her hand. "Bridgette Hayward."

Russel froze, glancing at Sam. "Bridgette? As in *the* Bridgette? The one Sam's been pinning over for... forever?"

Sam punched his friend in the shoulder. Hard. "Shut the fuck up." He focused on her. "He's an ass. A lying ass."

Russel rubbed her arm, though judging by the size of him, he probably hadn't felt anything. "An ass, definitely. But I'm not lying." He moved closer to her. "Sam, here, mumbles in his sleep. And I've heard your name more than a few times. But he never said too

much when we asked him about it. I can see why, now."
He whistled. "You're way out of his league."

Sam groaned. "Could you make this situation any more awkward?"

"Just wait. I haven't even warmed up yet."

CHAPTER FOURTEEN

Sam stared at his buddy. He hadn't seen Russel since the night of his last jump—the night his life had taken a distinctive turn. But Sam had to admit, the guy looked great. Strong as ever, and he certainly hadn't lost his touch with the ladies, the red blush staining Bridg's cheeks proof enough. The guy could sweet-talk a nun into his bed—probably had on more than one occasion. Though, Sam couldn't imagine what had dragged Russel halfway across the world. Sam hadn't been exaggerating. Russel only took vacation time when the air force threatened to boot his ass out, otherwise.

Sam gave the other man a shove, motioning to the seat next to him. "Are you gonna sit and tell me why you're here or just stand there, staring at the lady?"

Russel glanced at Bridg, again. "View's incredible, but yeah, I'll sit. As I recall, you still owe me a beer."

"More like a case." He reclaimed his chair, looking over at Bridgette. Though, he suspected she wouldn't ask, he knew she was dying to hear how he and Ice were connected. And after all she'd had to share, it didn't seem like that much of a sacrifice.

Russel stayed standing long enough to shake the other men's hands. Apparently, he already knew the rest of Hank's crew, which added another layer of mystery, before sliding into his chair. He stopped a pretty blonde waitress as she walked past, ordering a round of sodas for the table then focused on Sam.

Russel smiled. "You look great, Midnight. Really great. I'm glad civilian life didn't knock you on your ass."

Sam motioned to Hank. "Pretty sure it would have had me by the balls if Hank hadn't thrown me a lifeline."

Hank held up his hands. "I simply offered you a job. You're the one who's made it work."

"Trust me, that job offer saved my life as much as jackass, here, did." Sam turned to Bridgette. "Ice is an Air Force PJ, also knows as a Combat Rescue Medic. He's the guy who recused my ass when the jump went sideways, and I landed on the wrong side of a very volatile border. Never would have made it out alive if he hadn't been there."

Bridgette's eyes widened, then softened. She swung her gaze over to Russel. "Thank you for bringing Sam back in one piece."

Russel snorted. "No problem. Guys like him deserve whatever chance I can give them. I'm just sorry I couldn't save everyone that night."

Sam swallowed against the instant rush of guilt, fighting the pain prickling his eyes with unshed tears. Now wasn't the time to lose it. Or to focus on Gray.

Bridgette needed Sam's full attention or he'd fail, again.

She placed her small hand over his and squeezed. She didn't reply to Ice, just nodded. And damn if Sam's heart didn't swell a bit. He didn't know how she seemed to understand what he needed, but he wasn't going to question his good fortune.

He cleared his throat, hoping to change the direction of the conversation onto something far less dangerous than his state of mind.

He gave Ice a playful shove. "So, what the hell are you doing stateside? Last I heard, you were belly deep in the Afghan desert, working on your tan."

The smile on Ice's face faltered, and he glanced around the table, again, before laying his forearms on the shiny surface. "I was until a couple of weeks ago."

Sam stilled. He recognized the look on his friend's face. The hard tone of his voice. Whatever had happened, it hadn't ended well.

Ice pursed his lips. "Let's just say, I'm taking some of that stored up time and using it to explore other options. In case I need a Hail Mary."

Hank shifted back in his seat. "Door's open, Ice. We could use a man with your talents in our ranks. Though, I'll understand if you'd prefer to stay strictly on the medic side of things. Can't imagine you'd have a hard time finding a job."

Ice's jaw muscle twitched. "I guess that all depends on what the review board thinks." He waved his hand. "Which isn't why we're here." He looked over at Bridgette. "I understand you've been getting threats."

Bridgette fidgeted in her seat, eyes wide, the white

unnaturally bright. "The people I try to prosecute don't generally appreciate my efforts."

Sam hid his grin. Even noticeably unnerved, she handled herself like a professional. He laid his arm along the back of her chair, smiling at her when she looked at him.

Ice gave him an arched brow but didn't comment. "Hank says someone broke into your house earlier. That Midnight's moved you to a temporary location as a precaution. That's smart. Keep whoever's after you adapting. Don't suppose you know who it is, yet?"

Sam sighed. "As you can imagine, the list is long. Her current case involves Alexander Stevens. The man's head of one of the largest drug syndicates on the west coast. His resources are virtually unlimited."

"So, he's number one on the list?"

"Makes sense he'd hire a few thugs, or maybe even professionals, to convince Bridg to lose evidence or drop the case, but..." Sam glanced at Bridgette, aware this was the part she'd been dreading. "There's another possibility that's been nagging at me since Bridg told me about it the other night. It's personal and probably nothing. Still, I was hoping your contacts might have a way of getting more intel, Hank."

Hank narrowed his eyes, shifting his gaze between Sam and Bridgette. "Who are we talking about?"

Bridgette's chair scarped back, the harsh sound drawing everyone's attention. She fiddled with her purse as she shuffled from foot to foot. "I need to use the ladies' room. Why don't you continue without me? I already know how the story ends."

Sam pushed to his feet beside her. "I'll come with you."

She snorted. "I've been going potty by myself since I was two. Got it covered."

"I meant, I'll stand outside the door and wait."

The color drained from her face as she surveyed the rest of the men then focused back on him. "Sam, I—"

"I'll be her gallant knight." Ice rose from his chair. "It'll give me time to convince her I'm a much better catch than you."

Sam chuckled. "You'll have all of five minutes."

"Great. That'll give me four minutes to spare." He moved behind Sam, offering Bridgette the crook of his elbow.

Bridgette stared at them as if they'd all grown extra heads. "I'm going to the bathroom. In the middle of a crowded bar. What the hell do you think's gonna happen that I need military backup?"

Sam stood beside his buddy. "That's why Ice is going along. So nothing happens."

She tilted her head, looking pissed and relieved at the same time. "I can knock some drunk cowboy on his ass if he tries anything. You know I can."

"Unfortunately, the men who are after you aren't drunk, and they aren't looking to pinch your ass."

"Sam's right." Hank clasped his hands on the table. "Sadie's stalker tried to abduct her from that same washroom. You'd be surprised how vulnerable you really are. All the ways a person could drag you out of here without going out that front door."

Bridgette blew out an exasperated breath. "Don't

you boys ever get tired of thinking about exit points and sight lines?"

Sam smiled. "You're just as bad. Always looking at the legal side of things. Besides, Ice could use his ego bumped down a few notches. But reject him nicely, darling."

She rolled her eyes, took Ice's elbow then moved off through the crowd. Sam watched until the couple disappeared around the far corner then turned back to the men at the table.

Kujo leaned forward and folded his hands on the table. "Don't take this wrong, Midnight, but I'd say your girl left so she didn't have to be here when you told us about this other suspect."

Sam suppressed the hint of a smile. She wasn't his girl. Not in the sense he wanted her to be. But he liked the way it sounded. Loved it, in fact. "It's extremely personal, and something she views as a failing on her part, even though it wasn't. Either way, I assured her that nothing I tell you will ever be repeated."

Kujo snorted. "Pretty sure we can all keep a secret."

Sam met each of the men's steady gazes then went into an abridged version of what Brock Worthington had done, and how the case had ended with nothing but contradictory circumstantial evidence.

Hank leaned back in his chair, taking a short pull of the pop bottle the waitress had placed in front of him. "I agree Worthington is a bastard, and I'd personally love to cap his ass. I'm just not sure he'd take these kinds of risks when nothing new has been brought to light. Bridgette doesn't have a better chance of winning against him, now, than she did before, even with her new vocation."

"I know. It's just..." Sam scrubbed a hand down his face. "Something feels...off. The photos that were sent to her house seem different. Not that I can pinpoint exactly what's bugging me. It's more just this underlying feeling."

Kujo nodded. "Instinct. Hard to ignore when it's kept you alive so long. But it sounds like what Worthington did was opportunistic. She was alone, he was pissed. Not sure he'd screw that up by coming after her, again, especially if she doesn't have any new evidence. And with his father's resources, it would take something pretty damning to prosecute him."

Sam sighed. He'd told himself all of that and more. "Agreed. But I'd appreciate it if you'd have him checked out, Hank."

Hank nodded. "Will do. We'll have to tread lightly, though. Senator Dwayne Worthington isn't the kind of man you want to cross, and if he were to discover we were investigating his son without any kind of real evidence he'd done something..."

"Understood." Sam glanced up, quickly standing as Ice and Bridgette returned.

She stopped beside him, looking around the table. "Was I gone long enough for you to tell them about Brock, or should I pretend to powder my nose some more?"

He took her arm from Ice's elbow, tugging her a bit closer. "Nothing to be ashamed of. He's a monster."

Hank banged a fist on the table. "Damn straight. And while we'll quietly check out his whereabouts, I'm sure this is the act of a couple of Stevens' thugs. Gang bangers. Nothing Sam can't handle in his sleep."

Her brow furrowed, and she stared at him for a moment, looking as if she was going to say something, when Ice nudged him.

The man leaned in close. "Possible hostile. Black vest at the bar. Some kind of green lettering. Bastard stood and stared at the woman's washroom the entire time Bridgette was in there. He must have known I was in the shadows because he stayed at the end of the hallway."

Sam nodded, making a point of turning to face Ice before glancing over his shoulder. The man Ice had described was sitting at the bar, occasionally looking their way. He had something in his hand, though it was too far for Sam to see clearly.

He twisted toward Hank. "He's got a device in his hand. Wanna bet it's a camera?"

Hank made a few hand signals, and Kujo and Taz got up, each going separate ways. Taz made for the restrooms while Kujo snagged a nearby waitress, whispering something into her ear. She nodded and they moved off together toward the bar.

Sam leaned over to Bridgette. "You recognize the man in the black vest?"

She swallowed, waiting for a few moments before giving the guy a passing glance. Her brow furrowed before she focused on Sam. "I don't recognize his face, but the green lettering on his vest is common among Stevens' representatives. It's a symbol indicating he's a drug dealer."

Sam clenched his jaw. "Stick to my side like glue. Ice."

The large man slid in beside her. Ice didn't grab her arm or make a scene. He simply blended, which still amazed Sam. The guy was over six feet tall and heavily muscled—had to be in order to carry downed soldiers back to the rendezvous point—and yet he moved with the easy grace of a guy half his size. One that could slip under the radar. And nothing got to him. He was stone cold calm.

Sam gripped Bridgette's hand. "We'll take the long way to the door then straight to the Jeep. If I yell 'incoming'—"

"I hit the ground. No questions."

"That's my girl. If anything happens to me, you stay with Ice, hear me?"

Her face got impossibly whiter, but she nodded, eyes glassy.

He smiled. "Everything's going to be fine. Promise."

"There's something I need—"

He silenced her with a finger. "We'll talk once we're clear."

He straightened. He didn't have time to talk—not when Vest Guy could be calling in reinforcements. Or getting ready to open fire on a defenseless crowd. While it wasn't likely he'd been packing a semi-automatic under his shirt, Sam didn't like leaving anything to chance. He needed to get Bridg out of there. Get to a place where he had control of the situation, again, instead of constantly adapting. They needed to be on the offensive.

He moved, walking toward the dance floor then over

to the band. He stood for a few moments, pretending to watch the group play before circling back toward the entrance. Hank had Taz and Kujo covering the alternate exits, while Sam and Russel escorted her out the front. It was a risky play, but then any exit was just as likely to be covered. But this was the shortest route to the Jeep. Though, he'd check the damn thing for any sign of tampering before he jumped inside.

Bridgette didn't speak, following him as if she'd been one of his teammates the past twelve years. She moved silently, seamlessly adjusting to any shift in his direction. Thank god, she'd worn sensible boots and not something that would twist her ankle if she had to run. People swarmed around them, dancing, drinking. He swore he saw those green letters on every damn jacket or vest that darted past him.

A man appeared in front of him. Big. Brawny with a shaved head and similar black vest. He drew his hand out of his pocket, a flash of something silver glinting off the overhead lights.

Sam lunged into him, knocking the guy's arm to the side then using his other to slice it across the other man's shoulder, tripping the stranger onto his ass. Another step and Sam was hovering over top him, his hands fisted in the downy vest, his foot pinning the guy's arm to the ground.

The stranger's eyes rounded, his mouth hanging open in apparent shock. Sam glanced at the outstretched arm, cursing under his breath at the broken vape pen clutched between the man's fingers.

Sam leaned in closer. "This is a no smoking establishment."

The man nodded, offering the pieces over to Sam. "Take them. My wife wants me to quit, anyway."

Sam straightened, then turned, stepping over the guy still spread eagle on the floor then continuing toward the door. A few people had stopped dancing or drinking to watch the exchange, though the crowd seemed oddly detached. As if guys got knocked on their ass every night.

Hell, maybe they did. Sam didn't care. He was focused on the doorway. Vest guy was gone. Either out the door or hiding in the shadows. Sam paused at the threshold, peering through the frosted glass. The distorted parking lot looked deserted. Cold. A new layer of snow sticking to every surface, making it glitter from the white Christmas lights.

Good. He'd be able to tell if anyone had gotten close to Bridgette's Jeep. He signaled to Ice then opened the door, bracing against the gust of icy wind. He scanned the area. Knowing Hank, he was off to his left, securing that side of the lot. Taz had one of the rear exits and Kujo was most likely circling the perimeter. Not full cover, but better than if it had just been him.

He urged her closer, trying to speak just loud enough she could hear. "Stay close. When we reach the Jeep, stand with Ice while I do a quick check. Then we're in and out of here."

"Back to the hotel?"

He sighed, and she simply nodded. They couldn't chance it. He'd send one of the guys later. After midnight. Ice could be in and out silently. Quickly. Without anyone noticing he'd been there. Any of the other men could.

For now, they'd worry about getting clear then decide where to go. Hopefully, Hank could pull another miracle out of his ass.

Sam stalked forward—body tense. His muscles primed for battle. He listened for any noise that sounded unusual as he searched the ground for prints. Something to suggest he was walking into an ambush.

The wind whipped hard pellets across his face, stinging his bare skin. Tiny snow devils danced across the lot, stopping and starting with each gust. He kept moving, closing in on the vehicle when a small red dot landed on the snow, then lifted to Bridgette's chest.

"Sniper."

He turned, taking her to the ground as pain tore through his arm. He didn't wait, rolling her across the ground a few times before levering up. Ice was there, hefting Bridgette over his shoulder while yanking Sam the rest of the way up. They ducked behind a truck, a puff of snow next to his foot marking another shot.

Ice lowered Bridgette to her feet then pressed his back to the side of the truck. "The fucker can't be that far off. Not in this weather. Probably using a thermal scope to try and track us in the snowstorm." He nodded at Sam. "How's the arm?"

"Been worse."

Bridgette gasped, placing her hand over her mouth. She was obviously holding something back, but now wasn't the time to worry. If the shooter hadn't mistakenly missed his mark that first time and bounced the laser scope off the snow...

Push it aside, Sammy. That's the past. Focus on the present or you could lose her.

He mentally flipped off the inner voice, then reached for the truck's side mirror. He snapped off the plate then held it up, trying to get a bead on the sniper. Judging on the angle, the guy had to be across the main road. Probably between the buildings on the opposite side of the street. Maybe inside one.

Another flicker of red flashed on the mirror.

Sam dropped the mirror, cursing the metallic ping of the next round bouncing off the hood of the truck. The bastard had missed. Could have been the snow. The wind numbing the guy's fingers. Or maybe he wasn't that great a shot.

Movement in his peripheral vision had Sam looking toward the sides of the tavern. Hank was covering the left, Kujo the right. That left Taz. Either he was still guarding the rear or he was circling around—getting a better angle on the son of a bitch pinning them down.

Sam glanced at Ice. The man muttered under his breath as he shook his head then stopped and nodded. They needed a decoy. Anything to confuse the guy long enough for one of them to get to him. Sam signaled his intentions, inching toward the bumper when a truck jumped the curb and barreled through the lot, the man from the bar manning the wheel. He angled it toward them, lowering his window as he aimed a muzzle their way.

Sam shoved Bridg beneath him, drawing his M9 on the way down. He fired. Hit a bit wide, grazing the guy's shoulder as he veered to his right. Snow sprayed across them, the wet slush soaking through Sam's clothes as the truck picked up speed, fishtailing out of the lot then disappearing into the storm.

An eerie quiet descended over the lot, the steady swirl of snow quickly covering them. Ice moved first, motioning them to stay down as he peeked over the truck. A hushed curse drifted to them before his buddy straightened. He offered Sam his hand, helping him and Bridgette up.

Sam looked toward the buildings, sighing as Taz picked his way down the small embankment on the other side of the road then across the street.

He made his way over to the group, holding out his gloved hand. "Found these beside that small partial wall next to the store. Guy must have been perched on it. Not much of a rise, but enough to give him the advantage. A couple were still warm, but he was gone by the time I got there. I tried to follow, but the damn storm is covering his tracks faster than I can make out the next one."

Sam patted Taz's shoulder, glancing at the others as they ran to join them. "You got the bastard to stop shooting at us. That's a win in my books." Sam turned to Hank. "You know the local sheriff. Do you think he'd be willing to run ballistics on those? There could be a partial print. Either way, it can't hurt."

Hank reached into his pocket and removed a small sandwich bag. "I knew carrying these things around would eventually come in handy. I'll take them over, now. See if he can have some info by morning. In the meantime, I want you to stay at my place."

Bridgette shook her head. "You have a child. I won't put your family at risk."

"Sadie and Emma are in Los Angeles. Some big charity event. Swede and Ally are with her. They're well protected. So, the house is empty. The rest of us will take shifts walking the perimeter, tonight. Maybe we'll get lucky, and the bastards will make a play. Walk right into our hands. Either way, we'll move you both, again, tomorrow."

Sam gave Hank a smile. "Thanks. I owe you one."

"Don't mention it." He looked around at the blowing snow. "Let's get you back inside. I'm sure we can use their office. Have Ice patch you up. Then, we'll convoy back to my place. Give your admirers more than a few targets to choose from. Should confuse them long enough to allow you both safe passage. After that, we'll have your back."

Sam kept hold of Bridgette's arm as they headed back inside. The stakes had just been raised, and he'd be damned if he was going to lose this round.

CHAPTER FIFTEEN

"Here we are."

Bridgette jumped at the sound of Sam's voice, looking over at him as the Jeep stopped in front of a large ranch. He'd mentioned the name of it—Oak something—but most of his words had gotten lost in the steady strum of her pulse in her head. She'd felt as if the vehicle, itself, had been beating right along with her heart, drowning out everything but the rush of blood and the frantic gasp of her breath.

Sam had seemed strangely detached as Russel—Ice had cleaned the gaping wound on his arm then taped it up. Ice had said something about stitches, but Sam had waved it off, telling the other man just to bandage it.

Bridgette had sat in one of the chairs, staring at the blood-soaked gauze Ice had piled in a bowl, wondering how they all stayed so calm. Sam had been shot. Shot. Yet, they all acted as if he'd merely cut himself shaving.

She'd done her best to hide the way her hands

trembled, holding them tight in her lap. They'd been shaking since she'd stepped back inside the tavern, despite the increased warmth. Now, she was sitting in the passenger side of her Jeep, staring up at Hank's home, hoping it wouldn't get ruined if someone came gunning for her.

She closed her eyes. Two men had actually tried to kill her. Kill anyone associated with her. They hadn't just followed her through the building—though she'd suspected the masked guy from the garage was there to kill her, she'd never had proof. Not like tonight. Tonight proved these weren't idle threats any longer. They were concrete. As real as the white bandage beneath Sam's shirt.

They should talk. They *needed* to talk. And they would—as soon as she *could* talk, because right now, talking was beyond her. Breathing without begging for an oxygen mask was her shining accomplishment.

"Hey." Sam placed his hand on her thigh. "Are you okay?"

She forced herself to look at him. To smile. To do anything but let the scream clawing at her throat echo around them. She was supposed to be tough. Cutthroat. Not whimpering in the corner.

"Fine."

She'd managed a word. Only one, but she'd spoken without completely falling apart. Not that he believed her. He saw through the token reply. She knew he did. The way his eyes narrowed, and his mouth twitched. He knew she was lying, but he let it go. Gave her a smile then turned off the engine. He was at her door before she'd realized he'd even left the vehicle. It was as if time was starting and stopping for her while the rest of the world kept moving, giving her only fragments of what was really occurring around her.

Sam offered her his hand, keeping her tucked into his side as they made their way inside. He asked her something—she thought it involved food—but she shook her head. Whatever he thought she needed above being wrapped in his arms wasn't important.

He didn't speak, leading her through a series of dark rooms until he reached a door down a long hallway on the upper floor. He pushed it open, then turned on a muted light, revealing a well-appointed bedroom. She walked woodenly toward the bed, sitting on the comfortable mattress as Sam crouched in front of her. It took a few moments to realize he'd removed her boots.

Another time slip.

She blinked, and he was sitting beside her, toeing off his boots. The house was quiet, as if someone had wrapped a blanket around the outside. Maybe they had. Or maybe she was losing what was left of her sanity.

Strong hands engulfed hers, drawing her out of her thoughts. She looked up at Sam. God, he was handsome. Tousled hair, blue eyes staring at her, the color oddly vibrant in the dull glow. His mouth quirked, the hint of a smile dropping her stomach.

He released one hand, lifting it to tuck her hair back then brush the edge of her jaw. "It's normal."

She frowned, certain she'd missed half of what he'd said. "What's normal?"

God, her voice sounded as if she'd swallowed glass. As if it was taking all her strength just to whisper.

Sam pulled her close, resting his forehead on hers. "Feeling scattered. Like you're passing in and out of consciousness without closing your eyes. It's a byproduct of the adrenaline, fear, relief. It happens sometimes after a firefight. You get used to it."

She didn't want to get used to it. Didn't want to consider that her future was more of what had happened tonight. That she'd have to spend her life watching over her back.

She shook her head. "I don't know how you did it. How you *do* it. The noise. The blood. I didn't even see that red dot until you were shoving me out of the way." She managed to raise one hand and place it above his injury. "You took a bullet for me."

"It's just a graze."

"Don't. Don't trivialize what you did tonight. What you all did. God, Sam."

She wrapped her arms around his waist, holding tight as he embraced her. Tears threatened, but she didn't have the strength to cry. She'd cried enough. Tonight, she wanted to live. Wanted to bleed what she could out of every second. And that meant making herself vulnerable. Giving everything to Sam, without any guarantee he wouldn't shove it back at her once this was over. But it didn't matter because she knew she'd regret holding back more than she would getting hurt.

Sam whispered soothing words, stroking her hair as he rocked her back and forth. He smiled down at her when she eased back, dropping a chaste kiss on her nose. "How about some hot tea? It'll calm your nerves."

She held tight, refusing to let him move. "I don't want tea. Or warm milk. Or a shot of Hank's finest whiskey. I just want you. Making love to me. All night if you can manage it."

Sam cupped her chin. "You were just involved in a shootout. You're scared. Raw. The last thing you need is for me to take advantage of that."

"You're right. I am scared. And raw. If you hadn't been there. If my dad hadn't hired you. If I'd tried to handle this all on my own because I thought it was just a ploy... I was wrong. So, terribly wrong. But that doesn't mean I don't know what I need. Right here. Tonight. I'm not asking for promises. I'm just asking for one night."

"You know I want you. That I care—more than care." He gazed out the window, brow furrowed, lips pressed into a thin line.

Bridgette palmed his jaw, turning him back toward her. "Hank said they'd be patrolling the perimeter. All night. The house is alarmed, and I'm sure you'll have one of your guns tucked under the pillow. Not sure I could get any safer."

"No one's getting past Hank. Or anyone else. We're safe for a few hours at least. It's just..." He sighed. "You've already had a bad experience with a man taking advantage. I don't—"

She silenced him with a kiss. Slid her mouth over his then licked at the seam, delving inside when he opened for her. She didn't rush, giving him time to make peace with letting his guard down. Though, she knew a part of him would still be alert. Focused on their surroundings instead of her. But she could live with that. Share that bit of him that was determined to keep her safe. It was the rest of him, she needed.

Sam moaned into her mouth, taking control of the kiss. He dipped her head back, using the position to lower her gently to the bed. She moved with him, pulling him on top of her once her back hit the mattress. Sam stilled, obviously worried about breaking her condition of not being trapped. But she didn't feel trapped. In fact, she felt free. Free of the fear she'd been carrying around since that night. As if she'd reclaimed the part of her Brock had taken away. Left in a pool of blood on her apartment floor.

Sam eased back enough to make eye contact. "I thought this made you uncomfortable?"

"Do I look uncomfortable?" She smiled when he shook his head. "Stop worrying, and love me."

His jaw clenched at her words, then he was kissing her. Tangling his tongue with hers, his body crushing her into the mattress. She held him close, savoring the feel of his weight on top of her. The way his heart echoed inside her chest or how he made her feel encased. Protected.

He rolled onto one elbow, reaching for her with his left arm.

She stopped him, looking pointedly at his biceps. "This must hurt—"

"Not nearly as much as when I thought you might get shot. That..." He laid his forehead on hers, again, the gesture far more intimate this time. "All those years. All those missions, and tonight was the first time I was truly afraid. So, using my left arm to get you naked— barely registers."

She didn't argue, lifting and twisting enough to help him strip her down between drugging kisses. She tugged at his shirt, ripping the seam in an effort to yank it over his head. He chuckled against her belly, glancing up at her before bending his head.

She pulled harder, finally slipping his shirt over his head. It landed somewhere behind him, the soft rustle of it pooling on the hardwood floors making her shiver. She reached for his pants, but she'd never free them without him standing up.

Sam seemed reluctant to move as he kissed his way across her hip to her mound. He flicked his tongue between her folds, making her arch in response. "So fucking beautiful."

She fisted his hair, holding it firm until he looked up at her, again. "Stand up for me."

"Soon."

"Now." She huffed. "I still want you over me. Moving inside me while we're laying a breath apart. Letting me get you naked will only speed that along."

And if she got a few minutes to play—to taste him the way she'd been dying to—it was only fair.

Sam stilled, obviously torn between wanting to take things at his pace and allowing her this concession. It wasn't as if he couldn't strip off his pants himself. She had no doubts he could slip out of his jeans then into her faster than she could scoot off the bed. But she wanted the pleasure of undressing him, herself. Of watching him respond to her touch, her voice.

The muscle in Sam's temple jumped then he was moving—gaining his feet then helping her shuffle to the edge of the bed. He remained silent, watching her through narrowed eyes as she unbuckled his belt then opened the fly. His cock pulsed against the cotton briefs, the heavy length already bulging out of the opening.

She smiled as she hooked her fingers around the band and pulled them down his legs, taking his briefs and socks along with the denim. A quick shift of his feet and he was bare. Gloriously naked. Hard. Weeping with anticipation.

She hummed, skimming her palms up his thighs until she reached the base of his shaft. The thick length hardened further under her gaze, more drops of slippery fluid beading from the tip.

She leaned in, blowing a warm breath across the head then smiling when it flared. "Do you know how long I've wanted to lick you? Feel you move inside my mouth? You haven't been very fair."

Sam's fingers carded into her hair. "Fair doesn't make you scream out your release."

"That's where you're wrong. Pleasing you is just as exciting. Just as satisfying. I bet you taste even better than I remember." She ran her tongue across the smooth skin, humming at the salty flavor of him. "I was right."

Sam's grip tightened. "This isn't helping me get you on your back with my dick deep inside you."

She clenched her thighs at the image that materialized in her head. "Oh, but it is. I'll be more than ready if you let me indulge just a bit."

"You're already more than ready."

There was no denying it. She was. Wet. Hot. So needy it hurt. But she wanted this moment with Sam even more. A memory she'd carry with her if the future didn't work out the way she hoped.

If he left.

When he left. That was the reality.

She blocked out the negative thoughts. Tonight was about living. Loving. There wasn't room for anything that didn't bring them pleasure.

She licked him, again, swirling her tongue across the thick head then taking it inside her mouth. She couldn't take all of him. Not without choking. But the length she could accommodate—it was heaven. Or sin. Both, she supposed. It made her feel powerful. Sexy. Hearing Sam moan above her, his hips jerking of their own accord, his fingers flexing against her scalp, sending tiny stinging jolts straight to her sex…

It was better than she remembered. More intense, as if she'd found a way to turn up all the colors. Make everything more vibrant. Even his scent was headier. More tempting.

Bridgette took her time, rediscovering every hard inch of him. She let her hands smooth over his ribs and abdomen, skirting past the scar he didn't want to acknowledge. The one she knew he must have gotten the night he'd lost Gray. She didn't want to give him any reason to stop. To distance himself. He'd be doing that soon enough. Once the trial began, and she'd be damned if she'd lose what could be her last chance to savor him.

Sam growled out a raspy version of her name, getting her to look up. His eyes were heavy lidded, his nostrils flaring. A red hue slashed across his cheekbones as the loud echo of his throaty inhalations sounded around them. He was close.

She smiled then bobbed down his length, taking as much of him to the back of her throat as she could. Sam gave a strangled shout, tilting his hips a bit in an effort to go deeper.

"God, Bridgette. I won't last long if you keep sucking on me like that."

She shrugged, not wanting to release him. He still didn't understand that she didn't want him to last. She wanted him to lose control. To fuck her mouth like he'd claimed her body earlier. Then, she'd run her hands over his body, learning every new dip and plane, until he'd recovered enough to continue.

He grunted, tugging on her hair. "Don't want to finish like this. Need. You."

She looked up his body to meet his gaze. His jaw was clenched, the cords in his neck straining. His eyes had an edge to them—hunger. Lust. Maybe a combination of the two.

"Bridgette." He released one hand in order to trace where her lips touched his cock. "I'm too close. Too wired from the shootout. Thinking you could've gotten killed…"

She eased back, dragging her tongue along his length one more time before letting him slip free. Sam hooked her arms, lifting her then taking her down on the mattress. He moved over top, wedged her knees apart then pushed into her. Pleasure seared across her skin, her body already on the verge of release.

Sam stilled, dropping onto his elbows then gathering her close. He placed his forehead on hers as a shiver shook through him.

"God, Bridg. What you do to me. Loving you like this. Bare. You beneath me. Shit." He tilted his hips, slowly easing out then surging back in. "So wet. I love that you're always ready for me."

He moved, again. Slightly harder. Faster. She wrapped her legs around his thighs, crossing her ankles behind his back and using them to draw him deeper. He moaned, claiming her mouth as he increased his pace.

Tongues met then tangled, mimicking the way their bodies moved. Sliding over each other, then parting just enough to breathe before coming together, again. Pillows got knocked off the bed as their movements shimmied them across the mattress, bunching the blankets beneath her back.

She didn't care. Not with Sam looming over her, gazes locked, his fingers still wrapped around her shoulders as he pounded into her. It was an odd mix of sensual and savage. Gravelly whispers followed by guttural moans. He was a different man than before. Still safe. Still attentive to her needs, but intense. A hint of wild in his scent, like a tamed bear suddenly set free.

He was driven. Borderline obsessive in his need to have her. He was pumping harder, blurring the view beyond his shoulder into a wash of shadows. Heat poured off him in waves, making the air heavy. Hard to breathe.

She clung tighter, dangling on the edge of her release. Helpless to fall forward or pull back. He consumed her, and for the first time in years, it didn't scare her. Didn't make her want to curl in on herself. She'd done this to him. Pushed him past his limits. And it felt powerful.

Pleasure tore through her, stealing her breath as her climax came crashing down. She shouted his name, pulsing around him, gripping him so tightly he had to push onto his hands to keep moving. Four more thrusts, then stillness.

His body stiffened, the bands of muscles flexing as he hovered over her, holding his breath.

His cock swelled then he came. Hips jerking against her groin, hoarse versions of her name breaking the silence. He shuddered through several contractions then collapsed on top of her. Spent.

Bridgette wrapped her arms around him, palms pressed against his skin as he panted through a series of rough breaths. Tears burned her eyes, slowly tracking down her cheeks. It had been too much and yet, not enough. Never enough with Sam. He kissed her neck, then stilled, muttering under his breath before pushing onto one elbow.

She shook her head, urging him back down. "Don't go. Not yet."

He nuzzled her nose, his chest still heaving against hers. "Not going anywhere. I'm just…worried. I was too rough, wasn't I? Fuck."

She slid one hand over his shoulder to his chin. "You were perfect. Just the right amount of rough."

"Then why are your cheeks damp? And it's not sweat."

"Because you made me see stars."

"Or because I scared you."

"That's not the word I would have chosen."

He arched a brow.

She smiled. "Cherished. Loved. Those are closer."

He pursed his lips then rested his head on hers. "Bridg."

She closed her eyes, breathing him in. She didn't know how this was going to play out, but for tonight, he belonged to her.

CHAPTER SIXTEEN

Sam sat in a chair beside the bed, watching Bridgette sleep. She'd passed out in his arms exactly one minute after he'd whispered her name, and she'd barely moved all night.

The after-effects of adrenaline overload. It had kept her sharp during their altercation with the gunmen. Had been part of the reason they'd needed to blow off steam the moment he'd walked her through the door. But now...

Now, the high was over, nothing but bone-deep weariness left. Fucking the last of her strength away hadn't helped her combat the lulling effect, either.

Loving. He was supposed to love her fears away, not take her like some kind of junkie in need of a fix.

He tensed his jaw, scanning the yard for any movement. Though it was still storming out, the snow held that eerie glowing quality to it that seemed to light up patches the landscape with only a hint of daylight brightening the horizon.

He glanced back at her, noting the small hickey at the base of her neck. He'd been rough. Demanding. Claiming her as if he'd had something to prove. Ownership to stake. It wasn't like him. He'd never been one to think in those terms. Drag his knuckles on the ground and beat on his chest. He respected women. Respected *her*. Her intelligence. Her bravery. Her determination. It amazed him. But then she'd pulled him over top of her, and he'd seen red. His own version of a bull in a ring.

He was blowing it. He knew she didn't go for that kind of guy. No woman in her right mind would. And yet, he couldn't help the urge to mark her. A visible sign to any other man that she was already taken.

You mean like a ring, jackass?

Sam cursed Gray's ghostly voice. He'd been strangely silent the past few days, and Sam had hoped it meant he was finally making progress. Learning to leave that night in the past. Forgive himself.

It didn't help that Gray was right. Again. The proper route would be to get down on one knee and ask her to marry him. Give her a civilized display of his love instead of trying to leave some kind of sexual tattoo. Bridgette deserved that. She deserved more.

He studied her. Hair spread out in a golden curtain about her shoulders, long, dark eyelashes resting on creamy skin. God, she was breathtaking. And remembering how she'd moved beneath him—insisted he make love to her with his body crushing hers into the bed—it had messed with his brain. Or maybe he'd shut the damn thing off. Listened to his dick, instead. A bad habit where she was concerned.

He'd make it up to her. As soon as he and others had taken care of the men hunting her, he'd go shopping. Get something unique, like her, then beg her to spend the rest of her life with him. He wasn't sure how the details would work out. Her life in Seattle. His life in Montana. But he'd find a way. *Make* a way.

If she said yes.

He wanted to think it was a given. That she'd been showing him this was far more than scratching an itch. But a part of him realized she could do so much better than an ex-soldier still trying to make peace with his past, who had a ghost as a conscience.

His phone buzzed, dancing the unit across the small side table. He swiped his finger across the glass, keeping his voice low. "Something brewing, Hank?"

"Movement. Near the barn. One hostile, so far. But if he's coming after Bridgette here, no way this guy is alone. Thinking any others are spreading out. Trying to cover as many exit strategies as possible. Betting there's at least one taking up a sniper position, though, the snow's going to make it harder than shit to get a clear sight line. I've got your buddy Ice circling around." Hank chuckled. "Looks like I'm gonna have to pay the guy, and he hasn't even agreed to come on board, yet."

"He'll never take your money. Guy's got too big of a heart. Might sway his decision, though." Sam checked his gun then slipped on his boots. "I'll get Bridgette up. We'll meet you out back. I'd like her to be safe before we take on these boys."

"Roger. Kujo's got a truck waiting. He can see her to safety while we end this. Backdoor in five."

Sam shoved his phone in his pocket then sat on the

edge of the bed. He hated to wake her, but leaving her here, even with one of his teammates, didn't feel right. Too many variables. Hadn't Sadie's attacker blown up the house? Better to remove her from the equation, then he, Ice and Hank could go hunting.

He cupped her shoulder giving her a gentle shake. "Hey, darling. We need to go."

She blinked then jolted upright, tossing half the blanket on the floor. Sam reached for her, holding her tight until she focused on him.

He smiled. "I didn't mean to scare you. You okay, now?"

She looked around the room then back at him, nodding.

He sighed. She'd been doing that a lot. Visual cues instead of speaking to him. Not that her responses weren't accurate or informative enough. A nod obviously meant yes. But he hated knowing she was scared. That she wouldn't talk in case he heard the quiver in her voice or the noticeably higher octave. That she was worried he'd think she was weak. She wasn't. Not in the least.

He thumbed her cheek. "There's movement outside. We're going to get you dressed, then we'll head for the backdoor. Kujo's waiting to take you to safety while we deal with these men. End this."

She opened her mouth, but he placed his finger over her lips, stopping her.

"I know. You hate other people putting their lives at risk for yours. But...that's our job. No different than you taking on mob syndicates in the courtroom. Come on."

She waited until he'd moved his finger. "Sam. I really should mention—"

"Hold that thought until after you're safe. We don't have time to get into a discussion, now. But I promise we'll talk, after. About anything you want. Okay?"

She pursed her lips but nodded, again, quickly dressing then following him out of the room. She stayed close, like at the bar, once again, shadowing his every move. They walked quickly, making their way downstairs then avoiding any windows as they headed toward the rear of the house.

He led her into the living room, sticking to the inner wall. The front window exploded, spraying glass across the open space. A dull thud hit the wall between them, chipping off bits of drywall.

"Stay down." Sam shoved Bridgett's head down then pulled her back the way they'd come.

He retraced his steps, heading for the kitchen. Hank had mentioned something about an arsenal in the basement, but without the code or Hank's thumb print, it wasn't an option. Though outside was risky, Sam couldn't chance these men would destroy the house to get to her.

He stopped before entering the other room, glancing at the windows. The kitchen was on the opposite side of the house, but if Stevens had sent more than two men…

More glass broke in the living room. Risks or not, they had to move.

"We'll head out through the side door. Stay between me and the house. Keep your head down and your feet moving. If I get hit, run in a zig-zag pattern toward the closest cover. If you think someone's chasing you, keep running. Don't stop and hide until Ice or Hank catch up. Understand?"

Another nod.

"Words, darling. I want to hear you say it."

Red crept up her cheeks as her lips pulled tight. "Yes, Sam. I understand."

"Good girl. Ready?"

He took off, not waiting for her to answer. They didn't have time to wait if she wasn't. Bridgette kept the pace, darting across the kitchen then out the door once he'd done a quick scan of the area. They hugged the side of the house, sticking to the deepest shadows as they made their way around front.

Sam crouched next to the corner, motioning for her to stay as he took a quick peek around the side. Falling snow hid most of the driveway and yard, dulling any sounds that might have carried across the open space. He searched for tracks, but with the wind kicking up the top layer, any prints had been blasted away.

Sam focused on her Jeep. It was a good hundred yards across the lawn then over to the driveway. And nothing but wide open space the entire way. He glanced at Bridgette. She was fast. But that was a long stretch with only a couple of handguns and a knife for protection. They couldn't go up against a rifle in the hands of the right man. And after the shot through the window, he had to assume at least one of the men had some training.

Sam backed up when something glinted off to his left. He ducked as a chip of wood siding from the corner of the house pelted his face. "Move."

He pulled her toward the rear. They'd backtrack

halfway then make a run for the fence line and follow it over to one of Hank's sheds. From there, they could make for the narrow line of trees that ran to the edge of the long, winding driveway. Either Kujo or Ice would anticipate Sam making a play for the Jeep. They'd be there to back him up. He'd bet his life on it.

Bridgette didn't question him, shifting with him when he turned toward the out-building. She stayed low, moving faster than he'd predicted as he angled them behind a slight rise. It wasn't much, but with the swirling snow, it might mask their thermal signatures enough to get them to the shed.

Another missed shot puffed a clump of snow into the air just as they reached the small wooden building. Sam ushered Bridgette behind the right side, moving in beside her. She pressed her back against the wood once they'd taken shelter behind the wall, looking at him for guidance.

He scanned the area, catching a glimpse of the far side of the barn situated behind the house. Damn. Hadn't Hank said the initial movement had been beside the barn? And if he could see even a portion of it through the snow…

"Rear. Now. Then follow me over to the trees. We'll make our way to the Jeep from there."

He took off, pausing just long enough to clear the area before running for the trees. There was a moment of eerie silence, as if everything had stopped moving except them and the falling snow, before the rest of the world came rushing back. They hit the trees as gunshots sounded behind them.

Sam tugged Bridgette to the ground with him,

ignoring the bite of snow and ice. He'd spent years of his life cold. He could handle a few minutes thigh deep in it. Pockets of muzzle fire lit up the shadows, each flash a visual pinpoint of one of the men. Sam studied the movements, analyzing directions and speeds.

He'd bet his ass the two marks closest to the house were Hank and either Ice or Kujo. That meant one of them was still in the wind—hopefully tracking down one of the snipers. It also meant Sam didn't have a lot of backup handy until his buddies had eliminated their threats.

Bridgette palmed his shoulder, gaining his attention. "I don't understand. If they wanted me dead, they've had plenty of opportunities before I came to Montana. Why wait until now? Until I have all of this protection?"

He sighed, hearing the guilt in her voice. "I don't know, but I'd guess the fact the trial is next week and they haven't been able to scare you off the case, yet, is a pretty big factor. Makes me think they've decided if they can't intimidate you, they'll have to kill you before proceedings begin."

She frowned, looking as if she had more to say, but nodded instead. He wondered what was going through her head. Why she'd seemed off since the gunfight last night—other than the obvious—when he caught a flicker of movement way off to their right.

Sam motioned for her to shuffle behind a tree, using the one beside hers to hide his presence. He peered around the trunk, watching the area about fifty yards off. Darkness clung to every surface, that eerie glow from the snow creating large shadows across the icy surface. He waited, unmoving, until one of the shadows shifted.

Got ya.

He thought about drawing his gun, but without a suppressor, he'd announce their location. And he couldn't chance exposing Bridgette until he had backup. He had no idea how many bastards were combing the ranch, gunning for them. And he'd be damned if he'd risk her safety for an easy solution.

He reached for the Ka-Bar on his belt, then signaled Bridgette to stay. Her eyes widened as her gaze landed on the knife, some of the color draining from her face. He waited until she'd nodded, then moved, slowly making his way from tree to tree as he stalked the man shuffling through the forest. He'd try to avoid killing the bastard, but if it came down to Bridg's safety—no hesitation. No regrets.

The guy was tall, agile, and dressed in winter camo. Probably thought he was fucking invisible. Sam smiled smugly. Maybe to deer and his gang buddies, but Sam wasn't a weekend warrior. He'd bled. Had infiltrated compounds and eliminated threats without anyone knowing he'd been there. This...this was *his* sandbox, and he was definitely king.

He flanked the guy. Asshole was careless. Leaving a trail anyone could follow. Relying on the wind to wipe it away. Not enough of a breeze in the trees. Not even close.

Sam waited behind a tree, breath held. The guy was making a cloud around his head with every exhalation—like a fucking cigarette trail. He walked woodenly.

Probably wasn't accustomed to the thick snow. Amateur.

The jerk walked right up to Sam and still didn't see him. Didn't hear Sam take the one step needed to intercept him. Even as Sam grabbed the guy's neck, holding him tight as the choke hold rendered the creep unconscious, Sam doubted the idiot had a clue what was happening.

Sam duck taped the man's mouth shut, bound his hands with a set of zip straps, then made his way back to Bridgette. She hadn't moved, her attention glued to where Sam had disappeared. She swallowed hard when he slipped back into his position, her gaze sweeping his body.

She was looking for blood. He knew it.

He gave her a nod, then signaled his intentions. She trailed behind him, silent. Snow fell around them, dampening every noise. Nothing carried, as if someone had turned down the volume. He maneuvered through the brush, picking a path that afforded them the most cover while leaving the least amount of tracks. He couldn't prevent all of them, but he'd be vigilant—make sure nothing came at them from behind.

They'd covered half the distance when he stopped, dragging her back into the snow. Two men moved along the tree line not too far in front of them, their dark silhouettes just visible between the trunks as they patrolled the area.

Shit. He'd counted three other men earlier, besides the two he suspected were Hank and Ice. That meant at least six marks. One down. Five unknown. Maybe more.

He scanned the area, leading Bridgette over to a

large bush fronted by a boulder. She bit her lip when he motioned for her to stay, glancing toward the clearing.

He gave her an encouraging smile then moved off—stalking between the low branches with ease. He drew his knife. He didn't have time to take them out separately, which meant one of them was going to bleed. Though, he'd do his best to curb his natural reflexes and not go for a neck strike. He watched the men. The one off to his right was slower. He hesitated. Moved more cautiously. Definitely the weaker of the two. Sam would take the guy's partner out, first.

Sam readied his knife, holding the silver blade between his fingers. He waited until the stronger guy turned, then flicked his wrist. The knife glinted once, then it was wedged deep between in the man's shoulder blades, dropping the guy to his knees. Blood washed down his white camo jacket, dripping onto the snow. His partner turned, giving Sam the chance to step out—release some of his frustrations as he pounded on the guy, watching him drop. Red drops sprayed across the white surface, a small pool next to the guy's mouth.

Sam moved quickly, binding both then heading back to Bridgette. A voice stopped him before he'd reached her.

Fuck. She wasn't alone.

He ducked low, inching closer. He needed to see what he was up against. How to help her without making the situation worse. Icy pellets wiped his face as a strong gust swirled through the copse.

"I know you're behind that rock, bitch. Come out, and I might not kill everyone here."

The guy was off to the left. Big. Meaty. With an

AK47 clutched in his oversized hands. He had NVGs and a black ski mask.

Sam circled behind Bridgette's location. He didn't think she'd step out, but with other people's lives on the line, he couldn't be sure. No doubts she'd sacrifice her life for them.

The asshole fired off a few rounds, bouncing them off the boulder. One ricocheted and hit the tree next to Sam's shoulder. Close.

Movement by the bush. Shit. She was going to do it. Step out. Give herself over to the prick in the hopes he'd spare the rest of Sam's friends.

Sam ran to the next trunk, gun at the ready. The cold handle grounded him. Allowed him to focus on his mission instead of the icy fear beading his skin. Bridgette stepped out, revealing part of her side to the armed creep. The guy grinned and aimed.

Sam reacted. He didn't have a clear shot but fuck, he was taking one. Winging the bastard. Scaring him. Anything to give Sam more time. Time to get to Bridgette. He aimed but the guy was already reeling backwards, blood blooming on his shoulder. Sam snapped his gaze to Bridgette. Ice stood behind her, gun leveled at the masked bastard, a small tendril of smoke rising from the muzzle.

The band around Sam's chest loosened. He picked his way over to them. "Christ. You just aged me ten years."

Ice grinned. "If you hadn't left the damn house, I'd have had your back ten minutes ago."

"I couldn't chance they'd corner us. Blow up the

house to kill Bridgette." He focused on her. "When I thought you'd actually stepped out…"

She glanced at the man lying in the snow. "I'm not stupid. People like that don't leave survivors to testify against them. That's why they're so hard to convict."

"I know you're not stupid. But I also know you'd sacrifice yourself to save someone else." He released a slow breath, looking at Ice. "Update?"

"We bagged four by the barn. Two wounded, two unconscious. Heard chatter through their coms. Figure there's at least eight. I found the one you left in the snow. This one makes six."

"Eight, actually. Two more in the clearing. One's got a knife wound."

Ice grinned. "You were always partial to knives, Midnight. You were heading for the Jeep, right?"

"I want Bridgette clear. We can always chase these pricks down later. Her safety is my priority."

"Agreed. Hank and Kujo are clearing the house and the perimeter. I've got your six."

Sam gave Ice a smack on his back then reached for Bridgette's hand. It felt small in Sam's as he wove through the brush, avoiding where he'd downed the men. She didn't need to see that. She'd seen enough.

He stopped at the last tree before a large expanse of land loomed out in front of him. The driveway wove through it, the rest open until they reached the road. The vehicles were off to the left—dark mounds covered in a layer of snow. Only fifty yards from here, but just as risky. And once he started the Jeep, they'd be instant targets if there were any other men still hiding nearby.

Ice shuffled in beside him. "I can make a run for it.

Bring the Jeep closer and block any possible crossfire from the other side."

"And get caught in that crossfire. You're the medic. You know as well as I do you're the last one to engage in the fight. Your primary duty is keeping your ass intact so you can treat everyone else."

"This isn't a covert mission. We're equals."

"You're still a medic. Nothing's changed."

Ice grunted, staring at the space between them and the vehicle. Sam knew what he was thinking—it was fifty yards worth of target shooting if the others hadn't taken care of the sniper. Or snipers. No way to tell for sure if it was one, two or twenty.

Sam scanned the opposite side of the copse, figuring out the best nesting areas if he were the one holed up in the snow, waiting. Watching. The open space made it hard to hide without being buried beneath the surface, but there were a few places that drew his attention. If he used those to base his tactics on, he'd be better prepared.

He glanced at his buddy. "I'll make a run for the Jeep."

Ice drew his weapon. "Only one gunshot wound per customer, per visit, and you already claimed yours. So, you'd best keep your ass in one piece."

Sam nodded, giving Bridgette's hand a squeeze. He knew by the lack of color in her cheeks and the rapid pace of her breaths, she didn't like the plan. But letting her get shot wasn't an option.

"I'll be fine. Just be ready when I pull up. Listen to Ice. He'll keep you safe until you can jump into the passenger side."

A nod. Fuck. He really hated this. Couldn't tell if she was giving him the silent treatment because he'd somehow pissed her off—all this testosterone Army Ranger crap he was doing to keep her alive but arguably sounding like a drill sergeant who thought she wasn't capable of figuring anything out for herself—or because she was scared shitless. The kind of scared where people shut down.

She didn't look as if she'd shut down. She was scanning the area, pausing at the spots he'd already identified as possible hot zones. Her eyes were clear. Focused. Her muscles tensed, but in a way that suggested she was primed for battle. Not at all what he'd expect if she was merely going through the motions.

He cursed. He could worry about what was bothering her later. First, he had to ensure they had a later.

Sam took one last look then ran. Zig-zagging across the ground as best he could, punching through the top layer with every step. The snow tugged at his legs, but he forced them forward. If he slowed down, he'd be an easy target. As it was, his dark leather jacket already stood out against the dawning light and the unearthly glow of the white flakes. Amidst the trees, he'd blended. Out here—glaringly obvious.

He lunged to his right, hitting the surface when a shot exploded the spot he would have stepped in if he'd gone left. A loud report echoed behind him—Ice returning fire. Maybe trying to draw the sniper's attention.

Shit. Even if Ice had moved away from Bridgette, she'd be at risk.

Sam pushed himself up then took off, again. He gave up running in a pattern, electing to head straight toward the Jeep then diving into the snow after several steps. He'd wait until Ice would fire then run, again, repeating the process until he reached the vehicle.

Another shot hit the other side, the dull impact shaking the chassis. Damn. He'd have to get her Jeep repaired. No way he wanted her looking at bullet holes every day. A constant reminder of what she'd gone through—what she might go through over and over because she'd dedicated her life to putting scum behind bars. The kind that hired a small army of thugs to hunt her down.

The thought made it hard to breathe. Hard to focus on unlocking the door. The realization that she'd have to face this, again—maybe alone—messed with his brain. Blocked the signals from getting through. All he could see was Bridgette. Alone. Dead.

Not on his watch. Fuckers were welcome to try, but they'd never lay another finger on her. Period.

He tried the key, but the lock wouldn't budge. Most likely frozen shut. He grabbed his gun, raising the butt end of the handle above the glass, when shots echoed from the house. A second later, Hank and Kujo emerged from the sides of the home, rifles notched in their shoulders. They fired, again, then ran over to the vehicles, taking up point on his position.

Sam waited, searching for a glimpse of the sniper. Nothing moved. Nothing sounded in the early morning gray. He edged closer, looking through the windows for cover, when a distant engine growled to life.

Hank and Kujo must have heard it, too. They sprinted forward, fanning out to either side. Sam positioned himself between them, Beretta raised, half praying the sick creep would pop up out of the snow and Sam would have a justified reason to fire. To ensure Bridgette's life wasn't challenged, again.

They ran until they reached the road, two tracks carved in the snow their only prize. Red tail lights disappeared over a hill in the distance, and Sam knew it was the bastard's truck.

They surveyed the marks, deciding to head back. Tread prints wouldn't do much good when they didn't have any other deciding factors. Hank would call it in. Have forensics make casts, just in case. But right now, the battle was over.

Sam backtracked, steering off to the right when he came upon another set of prints. They were faint. Hard to follow, but he managed to track them to a small dugout—the sniper's nest. It was crude—definitely not military grade—but effective. It had hidden the guy well enough he'd escaped.

Sam crouched low, using the tip of his knife to lift the edges of the branches the sniper had laid across the snow for insulation. Something sparkled amidst the green. Sam snagged the object, holding it up by a silver ring with the end of his blade.

Hank knelt beside him. "What's that?"

Sam turned it over with the knife. "Looks like a lighter, but I'm pretty damn sure it's a key fob. For a very expensive car." He moved it closer. "Recognize the insignia?"

"Corvette. Bet my ass it's a Stingray. Either way, might help us get a lead on this guy."

Sam smiled. Murder attempt avoided, and a possible lead on the guy or guys who got away. Maybe this hadn't been the train wreck Sam feared it had been. In fact, they might have gotten their first real break.

CHAPTER SEVENTEEN

Bridgette sat in Hank's kitchen, coffee mug clasped between her hands, the steam distorting the couple of bubbles that floated across the brown surface. She'd been staring at it ever since Sam had given it to her after things had quieted down, and the police and paramedics had left with the men they'd apprehended. She didn't know how long it had been, just that she couldn't seem to focus on anything else—as if the coffee held the answers to all the questions tumbling through her head.

Eight men. Nine if you counted the one who'd gotten away. All coming for her.

If anyone had suggested Alex Stevens would send an arsenal of gang members to kill her a couple of weeks ago, she would have laughed at the idea. Hell, she would have laughed at it two days ago. It was just too... surreal.

She forced herself to swallow, biting back the gagging cough that threatened to rasp free. The last thing she needed was to have the men look at her as if she'd completely lost her mind. Lost her ability to drink a simple cup of coffee. God knew, she'd already given them plenty to question.

Bridgette cringed inwardly when she reran her actions from this morning. It was bad enough she'd been borderline catatonic last night. Had needed Sam to vanquish her demons—had begged him to make love to her. But this morning...

She'd been fine—had managed to remain calm—until the sniper had landed a slug in the wall between them. After that... She remembered going through the motions. Following Sam outside. Weaving their way through the forest. Waiting as he eliminated one threat after another. When he'd told her to run if he got hit, she'd thought he was being overly dramatic. A way to scare her into following his orders without thought, without question.

She'd been wrong. Again.

He'd been serious. Deadly serious, it had turned out. The men had been armed—willing to kill anyone and everyone who got in their way. If Sam and the others weren't trained soldiers—if they hadn't faced far graver situations on the battlefield—they all could have been killed. And it would have been her fault.

The guilt. The shame over not telling Sam about the incident in her office building. The fear of having more blood on her hands. All of it had come crashing down on her as the first bullet had struck the drywall.

After that...she'd barely spoken. Barely done anything other than comply. But not because she'd tuned out due to fear. That bullet had somehow flicked a switch inside her brain, and all the memories from that night with Brock had come flooding back. She remembered it vividly, now.

The force of his knuckles against her jaw. The crushing blow of the shelf against her head. How his boot had struck the same spot on her ribs five times before he'd been satisfied she wasn't getting up. Every detail, every second imprinted on her brain. But it wasn't just his actions.

She remembered his words. How he'd raged above her, pointing out every weakness, every flaw he'd obviously found in her. How she'd betrayed him. Teased him. He'd straddled her multiple times, ripping at her clothes, calling her a slut. Then he'd vanished, and she'd thought he'd left, only to blink to find him standing over her, again. He said he needed to take extreme measures to ensure she didn't do this to another man. That it was his responsibility to put her in her place. To make an example out of her.

The knife had glinted off the one lamp she'd left on so she wouldn't come home to a dark room. So she'd feel a sense of security. The blade had burned going in. But cold, not hot. They'd found a small wedge of the tip embedded in one of her ribs. She still had that piece. The only link to a crime that would forever remain unsolved in the eyes of the law. Three years of law school and six more working as an attorney, and she still couldn't prove anything.

He'd won.

A hot drop splashed onto her pants, and she shook away the thoughts, cursing when she realized she'd split coffee on herself. That her damn hands were trembling so bad she'd sloshed liquid over the lip. She needed to get a grip. Stop letting the past interact with the present. She'd already had a few fleeting flashbacks during their escape. She didn't need any more.

Bridgette placed the cup on the table, finally dragging her gaze to the window. Snow still fell in lazy fat flakes from the sky, erasing the evidence from their encounter. Soon, even the blood would be covered.

She swallowed, feeling her throat ease slightly. Unlike that night, today hadn't ended in tragedy. Thanks to Sam and the others, justice had prevailed. They'd not only stopped the attempt on her life, they'd greatly diminished Stevens' ranks. And if she played her cards right—did the one thing she was good at—she'd have more ammunition to throw his way.

While Sam could outsmart the enemy in a war zone, she could make the devil, himself, sign over his soul as part of a deal. That's why she'd gotten a shot at the U.S. Attorney's office. She had a knack for getting people to talk. To swing deals that benefitted her client. In the past, it had profitted the defendant but now... Now, she played for the other side and stopped at nothing to get the conviction she deserved.

Eight men. She'd bet her ass she'd get at least four of them to agree to testify against Stevens. True, she might have to swallow enough of her pride to offer witness security, but they were just pawns. Small fish in an ocean of sharks. And she wanted the mother-fucking alpha shark. The guy behind more death and destruction than all of his minions combined.

If that meant some of these men wouldn't have to pay for trying to kill her—trying to kill Sam and the others—she could live with that. As long as Stevens paid.

"Can I get you more coffee?"

Bridgette gasped, startling to her feet as she snapped up her gaze. Her chair fell against the wall, and she had to scramble to right it before it crashed to the floor. Ice stood at the side of the table, brows drawn together, a red hue on his cheeks.

He muttered something under his breath as he raised his hands palms up. "Whoa. Sorry, Bridgette. I didn't mean to scare you."

She released a shaky breath, leaning against the wall in the hopes of staying on her feet. "I didn't hear you come in."

He grimaced. "Old habits. Noise gets you killed."

"Right." She smoothed the wrinkles on her shirt, cursing at the way her hands trembled. "Everything okay in there? You guys have been talking for hours."

"Tying up loose ends. We'd hate to miss something and put you at risk."

"You're worried about the man or men that got away. That they might try, again."

Ice's lips twitched into a smile. "They can try all they want, sweetheart. They won't get past us."

"Sweetheart?" Sam punched Ice in the shoulder as he moved in beside him. "Are you making moves on my girl?"

His girl.

Her stomach somersaulted. God, she hoped his claim was true. But he'd been noticeably distant since they'd returned. Though, it was probably more that he'd been immersed in work—tracking down leads—than he was avoiding her. But she also knew he was itching to find out why she'd been so quiet. Why she hadn't challenged any of his orders earlier. But she hadn't been able to voice her reasons, yet. Wasn't sure she was ready to tell him everything—how every shot had flashed an image from that fateful night. That she was drowning in guilt over keeping secrets. That a part of her was still scared shitless that making him angry would lead to reenactment of that night.

It was stupid. She knew it was. She believed whole heartedly that none of the men in the house would ever hit a woman out of rage—least of all Sam. But it was hard silencing the voice in her head—the one that had worked hard to keep her safe since Brock. That had been the reason she hadn't given up.

But Sam deserved to know. She knew that. And as soon as her brain finished processing everything, she'd tell him.

Ice merely shrugged. "I know a catch when I see it. And I'm not above trying to convince her I'm the smarter choice."

Sam snorted. "Right. Have you forgotten that weekend in Paris?"

The color drained from Ice's face. "You wouldn't."

"Try me, big guy. Besides, I come bearing good news. We found a key card in one of the thug's pockets for a hotel in Livingston. The sheriff there just swarmed the place, and he found our missing guy. Black truck out front has matching treads. Thinking this is over. And once you work your magic on those men…"

Sam whistled. "Stevens won't be able to touch you

with a ten-foot pole without being charged with even more atrocities. Looks like you won, darling."

His words bounced around in her head for a few moments before slowly sinking in. They'd caught the other man. The nightmare was over. Or at least, this one was over. Sam was right. Once Stevens learned his attempt had not only failed, but his men had been arrested—he wouldn't be able to risk another attempt on her life. It would be too obvious. And it could be the difference between being put away for life or getting the death penalty. Something she hadn't been pushing for, so far, but she knew her replacement—Jeremey Brenner —would. Especially if she was killed.

The thought made her pause. She hadn't considered that before. Hadn't thought through how the trial would change if Stevens had managed to kill her. Which only confused things more. Why would Stevens want her dead if her successor would seek a harsher sentence?

Ice yelling a hearty, "Hell yeah," interrupted her line of thought.

Sam's smile faded a bit as he stared at her. "You okay?"

She plastered on one of her fake smiles. "Fine. I guess I'm just...surprised. In shock, maybe. After everything, to hear you say I'm safe—"

"Theoretically. I'm still going to shadow you until the trial starts and your office has police protection. But it looks promising."

"Of course." She wanted to ask what happened after that, but Hank yelled for Sam and Ice to join him in the other room.

She mouthed her thanks, again, watching them

leave. The tension in her shoulders eased slightly, and she sank into the chair. She could think through things, later. Puzzle out the aspects that were still bothering her when her mind had cleared. After she'd told Sam everything, because if she had any hopes of continuing what they had started, she didn't want to keep secrets from him.

Not anymore.

A genuine smile curved her lips. She'd make it up to him. And she'd start by asking him to teach her a tougher form of self-defense. Maybe how to shoot better. Not that Jack had been lacking, but Sam definitely had a few scary tricks up his sleeve. Ones she could learn to make herself a harder target for anyone else who might come gunning for her.

She stood, finally feeling more like her old self. It was time to take back her life. Make plans for the future that involved more than just endless cases. If she played her cards right, Sam wouldn't be a distant memory once the trial started. He'd be part of her life. Part of her future memories.

Warmth spread through her chest at the thought, and she realized she was ready. Scared but ready.

She felt lighter as she headed for the other room. She wasn't sure what the men were talking about, but she needed a few moments alone with Sam. Surely the others would understand, especially with everything winding down.

She picked her way down the hall, their low gravelly voices finally rising above indistinct murmurs. She slowed as she neared, Hank's words bringing her to a halt.

"I can't believe how close we came to not being involved in this one. Can you imagine how it would have gone down if George Hayward hadn't hired you? If Bridgette had managed to kick your ass out?"

She frowned. True, she hadn't understood how severe the situation truly was, but there was something in his tone that put her hackles up. Made her stay in the shadows lining the hallway.

"Can we not go there?" Sam's voice sounded strained. "Just thinking about Bridg facing those monsters alone…" He sighed. "I'll have nightmares. Guaranteed."

"Good job you're such a sweet talker." Ice crooned the words, and she suspected he was goading Sam.

"Jealous, buddy?"

"Fuck, yeah, despite the fact you only convinced her because you got lucky. You do realize you can't charm every client into your bed as a means of getting their cooperation, right? Though, it worked like a hot damn."

Her stomach dropped, followed by her heart. Had she heard Ice right? Had he really implied Sam had only slept with her as a means of getting her compliance?

Sam chuckled. "Extreme circumstances call for extreme measures. And I wasn't going to lose this one, no matter what it took."

Ice replied, but she didn't hear the words. It was just noise mixing in with the frantic thrash of her heart. The hallway narrowed, and for a moment, she thought she might pass out. Heat billowed up from her feet, and she had to brace her hand on the wall to stay upright.

Extreme circumstances. That's what he'd said. That *she'd* required extreme measures. Just like Brock…

Bridgette took a stumbling step toward the kitchen. She couldn't talk, could barely breathe. Voices mixed together—Sam's and Brock's—but it was Brock's sadistic laugh that echoed in her head. That faded the hallway into ghosted images of that night. The knife glinting above her. Her blood smearing across the floor as she forced herself to crawl over to her phone. She tried to push them out, but it only blurred her vision more. Mixed old and new memories together until she couldn't separate the two.

It was happening, again. Sam had been playing her. All this time. Using their history, their obvious attraction, as a means of controlling her. He'd said he cared, but he'd meant about his job. About the success of his mission. That's what it came down to. A mission, and she'd been it. It wasn't love for him. Wasn't a future in the making. It was a means to an end. And she'd fallen for it. Had believed every word. Every caress. No wonder he'd been distant. He was buying time until he could break it off. Let her down easy.

She shuffled back, finding herself standing by the side door. Her bag with her laptop and purse was sitting on the counter. One of the men must have brought it in after going back to their hotel last night, just as Sam had promised. The keys to the Jeep were lying beside it. Why wouldn't they be? Sam had her full cooperation. She'd personally promised him she wouldn't try to ditch him. It was the last thing he'd suspect, especially after everything that had gone down.

She grabbed the keys, tossed her bag strap over her shoulder, then slowly opened the door. Not a creak. Not a hint of a sound as she stepped outside, shutting away the murmur of voices just drifting down the hall.

She moved quickly, sticking to the side of the house as they'd done earlier. She paused when she reached the corner, looking at the windows fronting the yard. She smiled. Hank had boarded over the broken glass, which meant they couldn't see her without moving to another room.

Or opening the door. Which could happen if they heard the engine.

Snow fell harder around her as she ran across the yard, moving to Hank's truck, first. She knelt beside one tire, quickly removing the cap then pushing on the valve, letting out some of the air. She repeated the same procedure on Ice and Kujo's vehicles. Though, she suspected it wouldn't take long for the men to change the tires or pump them back up, it would be enough to give her a head start.

Sam wasn't the only one who knew how to drive in the snow or make good time. She'd been raised in Montana, and her Jeep hadn't let her down, yet. A quick stop in Livingston to pick up a few things she needed for work that she'd left behind, and she'd be off.

Home. Seattle. Alone.

A hint of doubt scratched at her consciousness, but she ignored it. Sam, himself, had said it was over. Sure, he'd said he'd stay with her until the trial, but she knew it was mostly for show. Proof for her father he'd gotten his money's worth from Brotherhood Protectors.

She darted over to her Jeep. Thankfully, it had warmed up enough the locks had thawed since Sam had tried it earlier. The seat creaked as she leaned it forward in order to toss her bag in the back before slipping in behind the wheel. A way of nausea rolled through her stomach as she put the key in the ignition.

It felt wrong. Running away. Regardless of his intentions, Sam and his buddies had saved her life. Maybe if she went in, confronted Sam...

The sick feeling increased. How could she face Sam and not hear those words ringing in her head? Not feel her chest constrict as she tried to breathe? Maybe in time, but right now—she was raw. Like there was a live wire sparking against her skin.

She started the car then threw the gear shift into reverse. She backed up carefully, avoiding over-revving the engine as she spun the vehicle around then took off, not even glancing in her rear-view mirror.

The old Bridgette was back. Cold. Calculating. Cutthroat. And she wasn't going anywhere, again.

CHAPTER EIGHTEEN

Sam sat in Ice's passenger seat. Fuming.

It had been thirty minutes since he'd last seen Bridgette in the kitchen, and they were just heading out after her, now.

He clenched his fists. He didn't know if he was angry or scared, but damn it, whatever it was, it was eating at his gut. At his sanity. What the fuck was she thinking?

He didn't know. Didn't have a clue why she'd taken off. He'd gotten a strange feeling while talking with Hank and the others in his living room. As if they were being watched. But when Sam had decided to check up on her, Hank's phone had rung. The sheriff had called back.

After running background checks on the men, he hadn't found any of them that owned a Corvette. Stingray or otherwise. The news had prickled another sense—the one that told him things might not be as picture perfect as they'd thought. That's when he'd gone in search of Bridgette.

Finding her bag missing from the kitchen hadn't worried him, initially. He'd assumed she'd headed upstairs for a shower. It wasn't until he'd searched the house that the inklings of panic had set in. Then he'd gone outside, and his heart had stopped. Just stopped beating. Or it had been going so damn fast he hadn't been able to feel it. Either way, he'd realized his mistake too late.

Ice slapped him on the thigh. "Stop mulling it all over in your head. It's driving me nuts listening to you growl."

"I'm not growling."

"Right. And I'm the fucking tooth fairy."

"What the fuck was she thinking?"

Ice shrugged. "You say that like I understand women any better than you. There's a reason I'm alone, Midnight."

"But we're talking her safety. Shit, we just took down nine men. Nine mother fuckers that were ready to put a bullet between her pretty blue eyes. And she ditches me? Lets the air out of everyone else's tires so she'd get more of a head start?"

"You did suggest that it was over."

"I said 'theoretically'. But that's beside the point. She promised me she wouldn't run. To. My. Face."

Ice nodded, traveling for a while in silence before glancing at Sam. "She still not picking up?"

"Voicemail."

Ice pursed his lips, taking the next exit toward Livingston. "Maybe this isn't about the case. Maybe this is personal. Did you do or say anything that might have upset her?"

"I haven't had a chance to talk to her since the shootout. So, unless she's pissed because we *haven't* talked, I don't see how I've upset her. I thought…"

He thought they had something special. That this was the beginning of the rest of their lives. Together. How had he read things so wrong? Read *her* so wrong? He knew she'd been distant, but he'd chalked it up to the trauma. Being caught in the midst of two shootouts in less than twenty-four hours. That, coupled with some lingering guilt about ever doubting she needed protection, had seemed like a viable reason for her somber mood.

Obviously, he'd been wrong. Monumentally wrong. The only saving grace was that she hadn't taken off her necklace. Had most likely forgotten he could track her by it. And the dot on his phone told him everything he needed to know.

She was headed back to Livingston. Then, most likely, on to Seattle.

"Try her, again."

Sam grunted but hit her contact number. It rang, the sound fisting his hands. He went to tap the disconnect when her shaky voice answered.

"Please, stop calling, Sam."

He froze for a moment. He hadn't really believed she'd pick up. Not after trying a couple dozen times, already. "What the hell do you think you're doing?" He cursed the hard edge in his voice. Great. He finally gets through, and the first thing he does is yell at her.

He heard her swallow, the sound thick. Shaky. "Bridgette? Are you crying? Shit, are you hurt? Pull—"

"No. You don't get to ask me that after what you said. You don't get to say shit."

He pulled the phone away, looking at it as if it might give him the answers because he didn't have a clue what she was talking about. "After what I said? What the hell did I say that made you ditch me? Just hours after nearly getting killed?"

A sniff. Damn. She was crying.

He tamped down his anger. This wasn't like her. Something was wrong. "Darling, please—"

"Don't call me that. Just… I'm fine. Thank you for everything you did, everything your friends did. I know I can never repay you or them. Never say thank you enough, but it's over. I'll ask for police protection once I'm back just to be safe. But your *job* is done."

Job? Did she seriously think she was nothing but a job to him? Hadn't he told her he cared? That he more than cared?

"Is this about last night? Was it too much? Did I scare you? You could have told me."

"Too much?" She snorted, but he heard the thickness in her voice. The wavering pitch. "I trusted you. I let you hold me down. You knew what that meant to me. You should have just come clean, then."

Sam glanced at Ice, arching a brow, wondering if Bridgette was talking in a different language. "I don't understand what you mean by coming clean. Of course, I know what holding you like that meant to you. It meant just as much to me."

Silence. Dead silence.

"Bridgette?"

"Extreme measures, huh?"

He froze. Again. "What did you say?"

"You heard me. And I heard you. I guess I was wrong before. You do understand women. Whatever they taught you in Army Ranger school…you aced it. Because I believed every word. Congratulations, soldier. Mission accomplished."

Shit. "Bridgette. It's not like that. I didn't—"

The line went dead.

"Bridgette!"

He called her back, cursing when it went to voicemail, again. This couldn't be happening.

"Midnight."

He stared at the phone, watching the dot move closer to her home. Closer to leaving him for good. He could follow her, but once she got back to Seattle—once she arranged for police protection and didn't need him anymore—he'd be hard pressed to win her back. Hell, he'd be hard pressed, now, but at least he might have a shot. A chance to explain in private.

"Sam!"

He glanced over at Ice. Had he just called him Sam? The guys never did that unless it was during introductions.

Ice shook his head. "Snap the fuck out of it. We'll explain everything to her. Fuck, it's my fault. If I hadn't teased you…" He glanced over at Sam. "I didn't know she was listening. That she'd heard."

"It's not your fault. It's mine."

"I was the one who brought up you sleeping with other clients. Christ, I'm an idiot. She obviously didn't hear anything after that or she would have realized it was a joke."

"I didn't tell her."

Ice frowned, glancing quickly at him before concentrating on the road. "Tell her what?"

Sam just stared at him.

"Oh. You didn't tell her that you love her."

"The night she was attacked. It's left some... lingering issues. Intimacy issues. But last night..." He slammed his fist on his thigh, wishing it hurt a lot more than it did. "She took a risk. A huge risk. I knew it. I knew it meant more than her trusting me. She was telling me she loved me. Not with words. With her actions—fuck they were screaming it at me. And what did I do? I told her I cared."

He slammed his hand against the window, this time, embracing the sting that shot up his arm. "I actually used that word. I said 'I cared about her'. Then I pounded into her as if my fucking life depended on it instead of showing her I'd gotten the message."

He hung his head. "This is all on me. Like that jump. I saw Gray stumble. Saw his hand twitch. He even said he felt invincible. I knew something was up. But then the PT tech said Gray was fine, and I just let it go." He closed his eyes. "Let him step out into the dark. I could have stopped him. I was standing right there."

Ice remained quiet, nothing but the rumble of the tires on the snow sounding inside the vehicle. The roads were getting worse, slowing them down. At this rate, Bridgette would be long gone before they made it to Livingston.

A few minutes passed before his buddy shook his head. "So, that's what this is really about." He slowed a bit in order to gaze over at Sam for more than just a second before turning back to the road and picking up speed. "You gotta let that go, Midnight. Gray's death wasn't your fault."

He held up his hand, cutting off Sam's reply. "He was a fucking Army Ranger. He'd made a hundred HAHO jumps just like that one. He had to know something was off, but he chose to jump. To ignore the symptoms and put everyone else at risk. Probably not consciously. But that doesn't change the fact that he did. And you did everything you could to save his ass. But sometimes…shit just happens. Time to bury it. Send his ghost to the other side for good."

Sam stared at him. Fuck, when had he become this open book?

Ice chuckled. "Close your mouth before your face gets stuck that way. I'm not blind. Been on almost as many missions with you as the rest of your unit. Not sure why I seemed to get stuck with your sorry ass all the time, but I know that look in your eyes. See it in the mirror, myself. But there comes a time when we gotta move forward. Bridgette's your new mission." He punched Sam in the shoulder. "So, suit up, and let's go get the little minx before she makes me drive all the way to fucking Seattle." He winked at Sam. "I hate Seattle. All that rain."

Some of the tension eased. Not much, but enough that Sam was able to breathe. "Well, if you'd stop driving like a pussy, we'd be in Livingston, already."

Ice smiled. "You know I love it when you talk dirty to me."

"Then you'll go apeshit when I tell you to—"

A blast of music drowned out his voice. He looked at

his phone, frowning at the unknown number. "Montgomery."

A throat cleared on the other end. "Is this Sam Montgomery? First Lieutenant Samuel Montgomery?"

"Used to be. Who's this?"

"Jack Taylor. Special Agent Jack Taylor. George Hayward gave me your number."

Sam glanced at Ice then put the call on speaker, even though Ice had seemed to hear every word between him and Bridgette. "You're Bridg's FBI friend. She... mentioned you a few times."

"That sounds perfectly ominous."

"You seem to be one of the few people she trusts. That says a lot. What can I do for you?"

"I've been trying to reach Bridgette, but her phone goes straight to voicemail. It's vital I speak with her. Immediately."

The hairs on Sam's neck stood up. He knew that tone. It meant trouble. "She's driving back to Livingston to pick up some of her belongings. I'm with Russel Foster. He's an Air Force PJ. Tough as nails. Trustworthy. I've got you on speaker, just so you know. We're not too far behind her. Had a couple of loose ends to tie up. Just took down a squad of Stevens' men during an attempt on Bridgette's life. Looks like the worst is over."

Silence. Again.

"Jack? You still there?"

"There's been a...development. One I'm concerned about." The man's sigh echoed through the cab. "How much do you know about a guy named Brock Worthington?"

The name nearly set Sam off, and he had to consciously clench his muscles to keep from slamming his fist against the dash. "He's Senator Worthington's son, and also happens to be the sick son of a bitch who put Bridg in the hospital." Dead man walking if Sam had his way.

"I see she told you. Then, you're aware I've been keeping tabs on him. On the family. Just in case anything developed that might give Bridgette a chance at nailing his ass for what he did. Or if he decided there needed to be a round two."

Not as long as Sam was able to breathe. "She mentioned that, which I appreciate. Bridgette has a hard time asking for help. Seems to think she has to do everything herself to prove she's strong."

"Agreed. Which is why I dug a bit deeper after the incident in her building. The way she described the guy who'd followed her—it didn't sound like a gang member to me. Creeped me the hell out, to be honest."

A dull roar sounded in Sam's ears, and he had to focus on each finger in order to release his death grip on his phone. "What did you say?"

Another length of silence. "Shit. She didn't tell you about it. About being followed. Hunted, really. How the guy had been masked. Had a big gun with a suppressor. That he'd shot up her Jeep."

A mix of white-hot anger and fear scorched through his body, making it hard to breathe. To sit there without punching everything in sight. Suppressors weren't standard fair for drug dealers and gang members. "I read the report on the Jeep. It didn't mention any bullets."

"They never found any inside, so they marked it

down as vandalism. Fucking rookies. Thankfully, she gave half of the photos and the note the bastard had left on her desk to me before heading home to Montana. She's smart. Thought my department might have more resources to unearth some evidence. ID the prick."

Christ, this just got worse the more Jack talked. "He'd left her photos? And a note? What the fuck did it say?"

"I'm coming for you."

"Damn it. I knew she was hiding stuff from me, but I thought she'd come clean. No wonder she's been distant the past twenty-four hours. She's feeling guilty about not telling me. About how it might have influenced a few important decisions." He pushed his hand through his hair. "You think Worthington's the guy behind the mask?"

"The fact she can still press charges makes him a suspect in my books every time she gets threatened." Jack mumbled under his breath. "She needs to find a new vocation. But...so far my suspicions have never panned out."

"That implies they've panned out this time."

"The day she got those photos, a Bureau task force raided a health club in the posher side of town. It was being used as a waylay point for drugs, weapons, sex trade workers. Anything and everything that makes your skin crawl. The club is owned by a shell company that leads back to—"

"Brock Worthington."

"And his father. We've suspected for years that Senator Worthington was involved in arms dealings, human trafficking, and money laundering. But haven't been able to connect him to anything. This bust—it's huge. Not only does it implicate the senator in illegal undertakings, the drugs they found tie him back to Alex Stevens. With Stevens' trial on the horizon, the team bagged and tagged everything. Every toothpick, every damn condom in the machines. It's taken two months to catalogue everything and connect the dots, which is why it only popped up on my radar a couple of days ago. When I saw the report, I pulled a few strings. Finally got a list of their inventory. There's a knife listed on there with a photo."

Sam's blood turned to ice. Froze him from the inside out. He tried to form a sentence but only managed to repeat the word, "Knife."

Jack sighed, again. "I know how you feel. When I saw the photo with the tip of the blade broken off—the same fucking type that had disappeared from the hospital... It took me ten minutes to remember how to breathe. I got clearance to retrieve the knife this morning, since it's not really vital to either case. It had been packed away in an old tool box in a safe. Probably been there since that night. It's the one. I'll bet my life on it."

Sam swallowed in the hopes of getting his damn throat to work. "Bridgette doesn't know, yet, does she?"

"No way she could have. The team organizing Stevens' case didn't have all the information from the new bust that's relevant to her case until a few days ago when it got put into evidence. They were going to walk her through everything once she'd returned. Which means—"

"Only Brock knew the significance of it before

Stevens' lawyers would have gotten notice of the new evidence. Only he and his father knew it could tie them to Stevens' drug cartel, not to mention linking Brock back to Bridgette's assault. No way to avoid it this time. It all would have come out during the trial."

"Unless someone kills the only person that can substantiate the claims. Make the connections. But... I don't see Stevens caring if Worthington goes down. Not if he's already neck deep. Why not take a big political figure down with him?"

Ice cleared his throat. "But, then why did Stevens send all those men after her? A couple already admitted they were sent here by that bastard. Are hoping to cut deals."

Jack breathed into the phone. "I have no doubts Stevens sent most of the threats. Tried to get her to throw the case. But who's to say Stevens was the one who sent this last batch? If he's in bed with Worthington the way we think he is, the good senator could have been behind the latest contract. Made it appear like Alex Stevens had sent the orders. Bridgette hasn't sought the death penalty for him, yet. But if a U.S. Attorney ends up dead at the hands of his known associates..."

Sam growled. "It'd be the first thing her successor does. And if they don't have enough to charge Worthington, to actually prove he's a partner, Stevens dies, and Worthington's in the clear. That might explain why the previous threats were mostly for show. Those were the ones that actually came from Stevens."

Fuck. He'd had that hunch all along. That there might be more to this than a drug lord trying to intimidate an attorney. That it would be the perfect time to piggyback another agenda.

"I wouldn't be surprised if Worthington has some ace up his sleeve that's going to put his association with Stevens in question. The guy had deep pockets and enormous connections. The only thing he can't control is what Brock did to Bridgette. It's on record. We all know Dwayne Worthington bought his son's freedom. That knife will prove they lied. It's the proverbial smoking gun."

Sam glanced at the dot. It had stopped. She was home.

He bit back another curse. "Hey, Jack? I don't suppose you know what kind of car Brock drives?"

Jack snorted. "Funny you should ask. He drives a Stingray. Black. Kitted out. Reeks of blood money. Why?"

"Shit. We're almost in Livingston. Call whoever you trust that's close. Tell them to head to Bridgette's house. I'll call Hank. Get him to get his ass there any way he can. This isn't over."

CHAPTER NINETEEN

It meant just as much to me.

The words repeated in her head as Bridgette opened the door then stumbled inside. Bone weary. Wishing she could curl up in her bed for a week. Shut out the rest of the world. Shut out Sam's voice.

A shrill tone caught her off-guard, and she shrieked before she realized it was the damn alarm Sam had installed. She punched in the code, staring at the faceplate. Christ. He was everywhere. She'd inhaled his scent the entire drive back. She hadn't realized his cologne had been infused into her Jeep. That the air seemed saturated with a mix of male spice and cottonwood. That she'd be forced to breathe him in for the hour-long drive. Or that he'd left his station programmed into her radio. There was even a pair of his gloves on the back seat.

Just another reminder of how foolish she'd been. How easily she'd played into his hand. While she'd initially admired his mission-oriented way of thinking, now it left her feeling flat. Hollow. As if he'd taken part of her with him—stolen it in the night without her even realizing it. Maybe he had. Like all those missions he'd performed overseas where no one ever knew he'd been in and out.

The thought burned hot beneath her skin. She'd prided herself on being able to see through lines. Though flowery bullshit. Yet, she'd let Sam trick her. And not just once. Twice. All that talk about what had happened when they were teenagers—most likely just more lies. Fabrications designed to pull at her heartstrings. To make her trust him.

And she had. Like a freaking fish grabbing for a worm and not seeing the hook. She'd just latched on and let him reel her all the way in.

Only, it had been real for her. Other than not telling him about the incident in her building, she'd been completely honest with him. Bared a part of her soul she hadn't shown anyone. Ever. Confided secrets she'd never uttered aloud. And he'd made her feel...

That was her problem. She'd let herself *feel*. Had leaped blindly ahead, oblivious to the traps he'd set. She'd been reckless. Uninhibited. And now, she'd have to learn the lesson Brock had beaten into her all over, again.

Pain tightened her chest. Had it always been this hard to breathe? To focus? She knew Sam would follow. He was a soldier, and watching over her was his mission. Logic dictated that he wouldn't stop until she was back in Seattle, a token cop in tow. Which meant grabbing the few things she needed then heading out.

She probably could have done without the files.

Without her running shoes or boxing gloves. She could have bought new ones. But she'd driven here instinctively. Maybe it was because she wanted to say goodbye. See her grandmother's house one last time. Because after today, she wouldn't be coming back.

Montana would be nothing but memories. A view of snow-capped mountains and sprawling ranches reflected in her rear-view mirror. She'd let her father decide what to do with the house. As much as she'd hoped that one day, she might be able to make it her home, it wouldn't shock him when she didn't. She'd been gone for a dozen years. She'd been foolish to think she could have come back to stay. That her time here would offer her more than what it had—a place to hide.

It struck her that somewhere deep inside, she'd been secretly hoping for some kind of epiphany. That the pictures or the landscape would offer a solution that would ease the emptiness that had taken root inside her. That she'd find another path that didn't leave her feeling...

Damn. That word, again.

She swallowed the bitter taste of bile lingering in her throat as she quickly gathered the files she needed then returned to the kitchen. She set them on the counter, rooting under the sink for a plastic bag to keep them dry until she could transfer them to the carryall she'd left in her Jeep. All she needed were a few personal items, and she'd be gone. And in under ten minutes. If she took some of gravel roads instead of the main thoroughfare, she'd likely avoid any chance of running into Sam if he'd managed to make good time. Which he would. Probably had taken classes in that, too.

She straightened, plastic bag in hand, when the door at the side of the kitchen opened. A swirl of cold air rushed past her legs, the incessant beeping of the alarm stopping her cold.

It wasn't Sam. She knew it wasn't. He would have deactivated the alarm from his damn phone. Would have wanted the element of surprise. He wouldn't have given her a chance to prepare before the inevitable confrontation. Wasn't that how soldiers won battles? By out-thinking their opponent? Letting her believe she'd been quick enough, had successfully avoided him, only to jump out and prove her wrong?

The hairs on her neck prickled. A footstep sounded behind her. She recognized it. Whether outright or on some cellular level, she wasn't sure, but she knew she'd heard that same hollow tone before.

Following her in her office building.

Walking across the parking garage while she'd huddled behind the cars.

Pacing her living room floor before turning to kick her in the ribs.

She almost laughed. How had she not figured it all out? The way he'd let her get just far enough ahead that night to make her think she'd be safe. How he'd managed to stalk her without her noticing. Even the shape of his body beneath the black wardrobe. They'd all been clues he'd left for her. Ones she'd been too blind to see until just now. Until it was too late.

Bridgette took a deep breath, letting it slowly hiss out through her teeth. She waited for panic to set in, but all she felt was a numbing calm. As if her life had finally come full circle. "Hello, Brock."

The footsteps stopped. He was on the other side of the island. She didn't need to turn around to pinpoint his location. She knew by the squeaky wooden plank he'd just stepped on. The one her grandmother had always begged her grandfather to fix. She saw it all clearly in her mind. He'd be dressed similar to the night in her office building, only no mask. He wouldn't want to chance someone might spot a masked man going into her house. Brock wasn't stupid.

He'd have a gun. He wouldn't want to leave anything to chance this time. Wouldn't want to risk cutting himself or having to wrestle with her. He'd want the kill to be clean. Efficient. Too bad she didn't plan on making it easy for him.

A raspy chuckle sounded behind her. "How did you know it was me?"

She shrugged, making a point of grabbing the files before slowly turning to face him. He hadn't changed. Not really. Same pretty face. Square jaw. There were a few more lines around his eyes, but they were the same deep blue. The man was stunning. A monster, but definitely one of the most beautiful ones she'd ever encountered. The kind that got away with anything because he didn't look dangerous. Had enough money to buy any version of the truth he wanted.

She held her head high. "I just knew."

He smiled. A smug, vicious grin that beaded her skin with goosebumps. He was holding that large black gun with a suppressor. Sam would know what kind of handgun it was simply by looking at it. He'd know how many rounds the clip held, what the muzzle velocity was. Exactly where to hit a person to either maim or kill. Sam's gun had looked like an extension of his arm. As if he'd been born with the long cylindrical object fused to his hand. He hadn't thought about how to hold it, how to move with it primed and ready. He'd just done it. Naturally. Same with that massive knife he'd pulled out of some hidden holster.

Brock was nothing like Sam. Brock gripped the handle as if he expected the gun to jump out of his hand. Just standing there, she could tell he wasn't accustomed to the weight. To the feel of the metal grip against his palm. She had no doubt he'd killed before. Would kill, again. But he wasn't good at it. Whatever skill he'd acquired, he'd had to work for. He was nothing more than a bully with a lethal toy.

Brock leaned against the counter. He was enjoying this. He thought he had the upper hand. That he was in control. He wasn't. Not in the way he imagined.

He nodded at her. "You look good. Much better than the last time I saw you." Another cruel smile. "Do you remember?"

She relaxed her shoulders. She needed to be primed but calm. Needed to think five steps ahead while keeping him talking. Making him think the situation was going exactly the way he'd envisioned. She wasn't convinced she'd walk away from this alive. But she'd sure as hell make sure he burned for his crime. "I hadn't, until today. Funny how it all came back, now. Like an act of providence."

"A deadly one." He wet his lips. "God, you really are pretty. You've lost some weight. Look—harder, maybe.

But gorgeous. And you're a lawyer. A fucking assistant U.S. Attorney. Now *that*, I didn't see coming."

"Really? I thought you would have expected it. After all, you pushed me down that path. Made me what I am."

His smile broadened. "Did I? Guess it's true what they say about self-fulfilling prophecies. Here, I've been afraid you'd find a way to take me down, and my very actions are what put you in that exact position. Gave you the knowledge to seek revenge."

"I believe the word you're searching for is justice."

"However you want to look at it, baby." He sighed. "It's a fucking shame I didn't come here to get reacquainted. Where's your bodyguard?"

"Gone."

"Not wise, Bridgette. He was good. I knew as soon as I broke in here and caught a glimpse of him that he wasn't the kind of man I'd choose to fight. He's why I left. Why I switched to a long range rifle. I didn't want to get anywhere near that cowboy. You should have kept him close."

"And you should have made sure you killed me the first time. Big mistake on your part."

She swung her arm, launching the file folder at his head. He hadn't expected it. Had let his guard down, and the papers fluttered loose, covering his face as the edge of the folder caught him in the temple, slicing a line across his skin.

She ran, darting through the doorway and into the hall. She grabbed the small bookshelf beside the opening, tumbling it across the entranceway. The wood crashed to the floor, half the books and trinkets spilling onto the hardwood.

Brock yelled her name, the sound followed by a series of dull pops. Pain blossomed through her shoulder, knocking into the far wall. She hit hard, then tumbled onto her knees. Her vision blurred as the room swam for a few moments before mostly clearing. She pushed to her feet and managed to scramble to the stairs, taking them two at a time. More soft pops pelted the wall above her, and she ducked low, hoping to give him a smaller target.

Wood crashed in the distance as she raced down the hallway and into her bedroom, locking the door behind her. She knew it wouldn't hold him, but it might slow him down. Give her a chance to make her next move.

She darted to the window, breathing against the burning numbness settling in her left shoulder and down her arm. It felt heavy. Thick. And it took all her concentration to force that hand to grip the window and shove it open.

Footsteps pounding up the stairs, that hollow noise skittering down her spine. Like rats running between the floorboards.

She kicked out the screen then jumped through, sliding down the roofline as her door burst open, bouncing off the wall. She didn't try to catch herself, following the broken mesh over the side of the gutters and down to the ground.

There was a moment of silence as she seemed to hover in the air. She'd heard soldiers talk about how everything slowed down in battle. As if they were moving at half speed. This must be what it felt like.

Hanging there, watching the ground inch toward her, as the snowflakes hung in mid-air.

Then it was rushing back. Triple time. The snow-covered ground raced up and smashed into her with crushing force. The air left her lungs on a whoosh, as black dots danced across her vision. Pain flooded her system, the intensity preventing her from fading. She blinked, staring up at the roofline, then laughed.

So much for your clean, efficient kill, you fucking bastard. Bet your DNA is all over the house, now.

She smiled. Score one for the good guys. Brock would never clean everything up before Sam got there. And she knew he'd make sure Brock got what he deserved.

More footsteps. Breaking through the snow. Following the path around the house. He was taking the long route. Probably forgot there was a shed attached to that side. He'd have to detour around it. Jump that fence since she was sure the gate wouldn't open without being shoveled, first.

She used her right hand to drag herself onto her stomach then pulled her knees underneath her. Blood stained the snow. Bright. Red. Like a giant bullseye of where she'd landed.

Good. More evidence to convict Brock's ass. She hoped he choked on her blood.

The ground tilted beneath her as she staggered forward, tripping over her own feet. Each step felt harder. Slower. Until she realized she wasn't moving. She'd reached the side of the house fronting the street and had slumped against the siding. She tried to straighten, but her hand slipped on a window, leaving a bloody streak across the glass as she tumbled forward. Snow stung her exposed flesh, the icy drops trailing down her skin. But it faded, feeling almost warm as it settled around her neck.

The snow crunched beside her as a shadow blocked out the muted light, but it didn't matter. She'd won.

CHAPTER TWENTY

"This is taking too damn long."

Sam slammed his hand on his thigh as he watched the dot hover over the same spot on the map. Bridgette had been at her house nearly ten minutes, and he knew she'd be keeping track of the time. Rushing to leave on the chance he'd figured out her plan and was on his way.

He'd nearly jumped out of his seat when his phone had buzzed, signaling an alarm as she'd entered through the front. She'd reset the panel, but knowing she was already there—was preparing to run—had made him acutely aware of every passing second. And how they didn't have any left to spare.

Ice sighed. "Going as fast as I can, buddy, without crashing. Snow's thick. But we're close. Another five minutes."

"That's four minutes too long. She'll be gone. That's assuming Brock wasn't waiting for her."

His stomach clenched at the thought as the hairs on the back of his neck stood up. His skin felt tight, as if it didn't quite fit, and there was a light sheen of sweat dotting his flesh.

He hated feeling like this. Being afraid. He'd never balked at a mission. Never lost his cool. And yet, there he was, sweating like a pig, imagining every sick thing Brock could do to her if Sam didn't get there in time.

Ice nodded, expression flat. "You think he was the sniper that got away. That the other guy we found was just lucky on our part."

"Or part of Brock's plan to make us think it was over. That she was safe."

His phone sounded, again. Kitchen door bypass.

"Shit. Someone's there."

Ice fishtailed his truck around a corner, doing his best to keep up the speed. "How do you know?"

"The alarm for the kitchen door just went off. Only, whoever opened it, tried to bypass the code. I rigged it to beep then turn off so any intruder would think they'd disarmed it."

Ice hit the accelerator. "Just a few more minutes."

Sam didn't reply. They both knew Bridgette could be dead and Brock long gone in a *few more minutes*. Instead, Sam checked his gear, needing to do something besides scream silently inside his head. Ka-Bar, right holster. His M9 in the left. He removed it, checked the magazine. One in the chamber, another fourteen in the clip. He had two more clips in his pockets, and a Glock 19 strapped to his ankle. More firepower than he would need, and yet, it might not be enough to save her.

He glanced at the clock. Two minutes. He could infiltrate a compound, kill the guards, extradite a prisoner, and be out in that amount of time. And Bridgette was alone. With that sick son of a bitch.

It was Brock. Somehow, Sam knew. Felt it. Sixth sense or just logic, it didn't matter. It settled with unforgiving certainty in his chest. He could picture it. Visualize a dozen different ways it could play out. But they all ended the same. Bridgette dead.

Ice rounded another corner, closing in on her street. Three more minutes, maybe less. A large, black truck was parked on the side of the road, half hidden behind a bunch of scrubby bushes.

Brock's truck. The taillights looked the same as what Sam had watched disappear over the rise at Hank's ranch. Brock was smart. He'd ensured he and Stevens' men had the same make. Same model. Same damn tire tread.

Sam glanced at Ice. "See the truck."

Ice's lips were pursed into a grim line. "Looks the same as the one the sheriff found. Betting that's Brock's."

"No reason for a local to park it there. You ready?"

"Been ready since I had to change my tire." He gave a hint of a smile. "She's smart and resourceful. She won't be an easy target."

"She'll give him a beating. No doubt. Hard to outrun bullets, though."

More alarms flashed on his phone. Motions up the stairs then down the hallway, ending with the contact alarm on her bedroom window. There were a few moments of silence before another round lit up.

"There's something going down. I'm getting

multiple alarms. Windows. Doors. Now, a motion by the side gate."

Ice nodded, still barreling through the streets. If there'd been any speed traps, Sam doubted the cop could have kept up. "I know how much she means to you. How desperate you are to get to her, but... Don't go barging in there half-cocked with no plan. You can't help Bridgette if you let yourself get shot by some pansy-ass rich boy."

Alarm. Front door.

Sam clenched his teeth. "Completely focused."

To his credit, Ice didn't roll his eyes. He knew Sam was riding the edge. "Any chance he could turn this into a hostage situation if he knows we're coming?"

"He doesn't strike me as the type. He needs this to be anonymous. Have Stevens take the hit for killing her. Brock wouldn't do anything that could draw attention to himself. Though, I can see the bastard using her as a shield if he gets caught in there. Until he got the upper hand. Then he'd plan on killing everyone. No loose ends, this time." Sam stared at his buddy. "But I only need one inch of him visible to take a shot."

Ice nodded, again, swerving around another corner then homing in on the house. Trees and snow rushed past the windows, blurring into a wash of muted colors. He fishtailed it into her driveway, following Sam out while the chassis was still rocking to a full stop. Sam fanned to the right as Ice panned left, carefully stalking their way to the door. A bloody trail led toward the backyard, the front door slightly askew.

Sam focused on the mission. On silently pushing open the door then clearing the main room. On anything other than the possibility it was Bridgette's blood on the floor. Each drop bringing her closer to death.

Ice shadowed him. They moved seamlessly together. A well-oiled machine. A few hand signals and they'd cleared the next section, quickly bearing down on the kitchen. The odd smudged boot print marred the floor, the tread larger than Bridgette's.

The remains of one of her bookcases was scattered across the hardwood, surrounded by broken bits of pottery and chunks of wood. A few threads of fabric had gotten caught on the sharp edges, as if it had been used it to block the entrance. Though, it obviously hadn't done much more than slow the other person down as they'd kicked their way through.

Good girl. Make him work. Keep him off-kilter. Get him angry because he can't think straight when he's angry.

More blood.

Two distinct trails. One leading upstairs. The second back into the kitchen. There was a splatter on the far wall, half a bloody handprint on the floor. She'd been hit. But she'd managed to get away. That meant there was still time. Ice motioned to the entrance, carefully stepping over the debris.

"You'll fucking pay for making me chase you, baby."

They froze as the deep male voice echoed through the house. They were in the kitchen.

"I was going to make this painless, for old time's sake. One tap to the head. But now...now, I'm going to take my time while I watch you bleed out."

Ice palmed Sam's shoulder when he went to step through, shaking his head at him. Sam resisted the urge to knock off his buddy's hand. Ice was right. Barreling in blind wouldn't help her.

He made a series of signals, then quickly backtracked, disappearing around a corner. He was going outside—heading for the kitchen door.

Sam inched forward as he drew his knife, using the blade as a mirror to get a better look inside the room. Brock had Bridgette pinned against the wall on the far side of the kitchen, close to the other door. It was in a bit of a nook. Sam couldn't see much of her from this angle other than her left arm. The one dripping blood onto the floor.

He clenched his jaw to stop from acting impulsively. He didn't have a clear shot at Brock from this angle. Whether the guy had planned it that way or had gotten lucky by choosing the spot closest to the back door, Sam didn't know. But as it was, he'd have to shoot through Bridgette to hit Brock. No way Sam would do that. She'd already been compromised. But it also meant he had little chance of sneaking up on the bastard.

He scanned the room. Brock had left his Glock on the island. Big˙ sucker. Probably a twenty-three. Suppressor screwed into the threaded barrel. It packed a hell of a punch.

The fucker had to have a knife. Probably trying to recreate that first night. The ultimate payback in Brock's mind. Terrorize her before he killed her.

Asshole would pay.

Sam sheathed the blade, calmed his mind, then stepped out. "Let her go, Worthington."

Brock jumped, but not in the direction Sam had hoped would make this a simple take down. All he'd needed was for the jackass to look toward the door. One second, and Sam would have put a bullet between his eyes.

Instead, the other man ducked farther behind the corner, then spun Bridgette, holding the edge of an enormous blade across her throat as he hid behind her. It wasn't easy. The guy was nearly as tall as Sam, with wide shoulders and a muscular frame, but Brock managed to hunch down—eliminate any viable target that would end this rather than simply piss the guy off.

The only solid mark was the guy's hand, with his beefy fingers gripped around the knife's hilt. Sam could hit the fucker's knuckles. But this close, the bullet would go right through. Peg Bridg in the chest. Not an option.

He kept the gun leveled at Brock's head, not giving the guy an inch. "No way out. Drop the knife, and you might walk out of here alive. Might."

Brock cackled. No other way to describe the throaty sound that rasped out of his throat. "Drop your gun, and back the fuck up, or you'll watch me slit her throat."

Sam risked a glance at Bridgette. Blood soaked the left side of her shirt, smears of it across her neck and face. There was a bluish tinge around her lips, and a bruised look to the skin beneath her eyes.

She'd lost a lot of blood.

He went against the voice in his head and glanced at her eyes, inhaling sharply. Calm, almost cold. Not an ounce of fear. In fact, she looked at peace. That's when he realized, she hadn't planned on getting out of this alive. She'd fought back, had made the bastard chase her in order to leave clues—the partial bloody boot treads down the hall. The bits of fabric that had caught on the broken bookcase. And somewhere along the way, he'd scratched his left arm, the wound no doubt leaving small drops of blood on the floors or the snow. A thousand ways to place him at the house. Prove he'd killed her.

Fuck that. Brock could fry for his crimes, but there was no way Bridgette was dying. Not on Sam's watch.

"You touch her any more than you have, and I'll forget about the might."

"Make all the threats you want, cowboy. There's no way you can get off a shot without clipping her. And she's already halfway dead. Another hit, even a minor one, and you'll kill her." Brock yanked on her hair, scratching a line across her skin. "Put that fucking thing down, or I swear I'll gut her. You'll kill me, but you'll have to watch her die, first."

Sam held firm. He didn't need Brock to give him a target. He just needed to get the bastard to move his hand slightly. Remove the blade from in front of her throat and over to the side. Somewhere it wouldn't involuntarily hurt her when he went down. And the bastard was going down.

Sam smiled, slowly lowering his gun. "Fine. We'll play it your way."

Brock's muscles eased, and his hand drifted over. More. More. Just a little bit more...

Sam raised his gun then fired, hitting the creep in the wrist, paralyzing his hand, just as Ice barreled through the backdoor, clipping Brock in the back of the head. A red mist exploded in the room, shooting across the cupboards as Brock's body quivered then dropped. Hard.

The force knocked Bridgette backwards. Ice dove at her, catching her head in one outstretched hand before it had bounced off the floor. The reverberation from the shot lingered for a few more seconds, then silence.

Sam holstered his gun, then was clearing off the island with a sweep of his hand—tossing Brock's gun onto his corpse. Ice lifted her over, placing her on top then angling her onto her right side. Her skin was deathly pale, the red splotches of blood standing out in stark contrast. Her head lolled against the counter as her eyelids fluttered but didn't open.

Sam grabbed her hand, squeezing it to gain her attention. "Bridg."

She blinked a few times, half opening unfocused eyes before drifting off, again.

"Damn it, darling. Open your eyes. Look at me." Sam glanced up at Ice. "Russel. Brother, you have to save her."

Ice paused. Sam had only ever called him Russel during a mission once before, and he hadn't been able to save Gray that night. Ice nodded, searching through the drawers until he found a stack of tea towels.

He cut away her shirt, frowning when Bridg groaned as the fabric pulled a bit on her skin. "Shit. Hold these. Tight against the wounds. Two on the back, one on the front. Equal pressure both sides. I've got a medic bag in my truck. I'll be right back." He stopped in the doorway. "Tight, Sam."

Sam pressed on the padding until his damn hands cramped. Bridgette's eyes flew open, the whites cloudy.

Dull. She opened her mouth, took a few gasping breaths —sounding like each one would be her last. She managed to grab his wrist with her right hand, leaving a smear of blood and sweat on his skin.

He leaned over her. "I know it hurts. But we need to stop the bleeding."

Her eyes darted from side to side, and her tongue swept weakly across her lips. "Brock..."

"No longer a concern."

A small twitch of her lips. "Fucking...A..."

"Listen to you. A few weeks with an ex-soldier, and you've developed quite the potty mouth. No, no, no, darling. Stay with me."

Her eyelids fluttered, and her grip weakened.

"Bridgette!"

He put every ounce of command in his voice. The hard tone that had made new recruits scramble to attention. Bridgette barely opened her eyes.

"Eyes on me. I want to see those beautiful baby blues, okay? Russel's coming right back. He's got a magic kit with him. I've seen him scare soldiers back from the dead with it. So, just...keep your eyes on me. Just a bit longer. Give him a chance."

A hint of a smile this time. "Must...be serious." She coughed. Grimaced. Looking weaker by the second. She managed to lick her lips, staring up at him, glazed. Lids starting to close. "You called...him...Russel."

"Can't fool you." He leaned in closer. "Don't die on me. Please, Bridg."

Ice appeared in the doorway, huge black bag over one shoulder. He placed it next to her on the island, spreading open the sides. He motioned for Sam to release the back wad of towels, as Ice grabbed a bunch of supplies, working quickly. Then he leaned over her. "Hey, sweetheart. I'm going to walk you through this, okay?" He poured some liquid onto a pad. "This will cleanse your wound. It's gonna sting but only for a few moments."

Bridgette stiffened the second he touched her puckered skin, wiping away the top layer of dried blood and bits of material from her sweater. Her grip on Sam's wrist tightened, turning his skin white around her fingers as Russel worked on her wounds.

Sam bent close. "I'm right here."

She whimpered, and something turned over hard in his chest. He wanted to take it all away. Change places. He was the soldier. He was the one who was supposed to die like this. Not her. Not at the hands of some sick prick.

Ice sighed. "Great job. That part's over. Now, I'm gonna put on some coagulating powder. Nothing to it. It'll help stop the bleeding. Do you know what blood type you are?"

She was fading, eyelids drooping.

Ice did something—pushed on some part of her— and her eyelids fluttered open. "Bridgette? What blood type are you, sweetheart?"

Her lips formed an O, but the word barely registered.

"She's O, Ice."

He nodded. "Positive or negative?"

"Neg..." That's all she managed before it morphed into a groan.

"O negative. Got it, sweetheart." He looked up at Sam as he layered on some kind of bandage then started taping it in place. "You're O neg, aren't you, Midnight?"

"Yeah."

"Good. I've got help on the way, but...we might have to do a direct transfer. She's...dangerously close to hemorrhagic shock."

"How much do you think she's lost?"

"Over a liter."

Sam swallowed. How the fuck was she still conscious? Still breathing? He stared at her. Willed the pulse beneath her skin to keep fluttering. Those gasping, rough breaths to keep filling the room.

"We need to lay her flat, now. Let me deal with the through and through."

Sam helped ease her onto her back when Ice's words finally registered. "Through and through? How many times was she shot?"

Ice was already cleaning her wound. "Twice. One's still in there. Hopefully, it's in her scapula and didn't ricochet."

"And if it did?"

Ice gave him a cold stare but kept on working.

Sam lifted her hand, sandwiching it between his. "Bridgette. Eyes on me, beautiful."

It took her a few agonizing moments to work up the energy just to look at him.

He leaned in until his mouth was inches away. "Almost done. Then, it's just a ride, okay?"

She squeezed his hand. Barely noticeable, but he returned the light touch. "Not...your fault."

Tears burned behind his eyes. "We can discuss blame later. Just focus on staying here. With me."

"I'm...sorry, Sam." She gulped in air, but it didn't seem to do much good. "Should...have told...you. Never...should... have...ru—"

"It's okay. It's over, now. And you're going to be okay." He glanced desperately at his buddy. "Russel."

"She was shot point blank. We're lucky she's as stubborn as you are and wasn't killed outright." He cocked his head to the side. "Sirens. But she can't wait. I'm starting that transfusion."

Sam rolled up his sleeve. He'd give her every last drop if it would make a difference. Russel used another thick bandage and wrapped some kind of tape around her shoulder, keeping everything tight. It looked as if he'd stopped the bleeding, though, based on the white cast to her skin, she was already on the edge.

Sam squeezed her hand. No response. "Bridgette!"

A grimace. Nothing else.

Ice scraped a chair across the floor. "Sit."

Sam wasn't sure if he sat or if his knees just buckled, plunking him down in the chair. Russel wiped something on his arm, then there was a small prick. Sam glanced down, staring at the red-colored tube connecting his arm to hers. When had Ice gotten it all ready?

Shit. Sam was losing it. Losing pockets of time. Bits of his soul as he sat there, holding Bridgette's hand, wondering if this was the last time it would have any warmth. If he'd never get a chance to tell her how he felt.

Voices sounded in the background then the room exploded with people. Police. FBI. Hank and Taz appeared beyond Ice's shoulders, mouths pinched tight.

Ice was talking to everyone, recounting what had happened. Then he was giving a couple of paramedics the run down. Rattling off her vitals, not that Sam had even realized Ice had taken them. Sam had tunnel vision. Deadly, but he didn't care. He was focused on Bridgette. On not letting go of her hand. Not letting go of *her*.

He bent low, brushing his lips across her ear. "Don't you die on me. Not now. Because I love you, Bridg. And damn it, we're going to spend the next fifty years driving each other crazy. Do you hear me? I love you. And you're going to live so you can tell me you love me, too."

CHAPTER TWENTY-ONE

I love you.

Bridgette opened her eyes, a ghostly echo of Sam's voice filling her head. Her eyelids felt heavy, thick, and it took a while before she was able to blink away the fuzziness blurring the room, finally focusing on the beige-colored walls and the collection of flowers stacked along a narrow ledge. A steady beep sounded behind her, the noise disturbingly familiar. She waited, trying to place the rhythm, when it hit her.

Her heartbeat.

A hospital.

She inhaled as memories shuffled inside her mind, Sam's words playing in the background like a soundtrack. She'd been pinned against the wall, waiting for Brock to finally let her die, when Sam had shown up. He'd somehow tricked Brock into letting his guard down then…

She groaned, the barrage of disjointed images making her nauseous. It was like an array of snapshots flashing on and off. Sam and Russel trying to save her. Men surrounding her in the kitchen. Voices shouting in the background as flashlights shined in her eyes. There'd been big white lights on the ceiling. Men and women dressed in lab coats and scrubs. A room full of gleaming instruments. Then...

Here she was, laying in a hospital bed, her scattered memories set on repeat. Sam's words still looping inside her head. Those, she did remember. Vividly. Like a moment out of time where her mind wasn't burdened by the effects of blood loss or shock. He'd been holding her hand, begging—no ordering—her to stay with him. To not die. Then he'd said he loved her.

No hesitation. No awkward pauses. As if it was the easiest thing for him to admit.

She took a moment to breathe, to absorb the memory, when she noticed a warm feeling in her right hand. It took her a few seconds to shift her focus—actually look to her right. He was sprawled out in a chair at the side of her bed, one large, calloused hand holding hers. She'd never realized how big his palm was compared to hers until now. Until she stared at their joined hands. Marveled at the way he held hers firmly, yet gently. He could crush her fingers if he wanted to.

After what had felt like an hour focused on their hands, she managed to drag her gaze up his arm, over his shoulder, finally reaching his face. Eyes shut. Muscles lax. It was like staring at a photo. Perfection.

He didn't look like a hardened soldier sleeping in the chair, his legs crossed at the ankles, half of one butt cheek off the seat. He made the furniture seem small. Maybe it was. Or maybe she was finally seeing *him*. No filters. No past memories or future expectations blinding her. Just Sam Montgomery. Ex-Army Ranger, and the man she'd been in love with since she was eighteen years old.

She swallowed. It seemed so obvious, now. That she loved him. That she'd been in love with him all along, and she couldn't help but wonder why she'd resisted it. Why she hadn't told him. What she'd been afraid of. Then his eyelids fluttered, a few fleeting glimpses of blue, before he was staring back at her. Alert. Attention fully on her. And she forgot everything she'd been planning to say. It just vanished. Seared from her brain from the heat in his eyes. He looked like a man on a mission—one he didn't plan on failing.

Her fingers squeezed reflectively in his, and he bolted upright, leaning forward until his face filled her field of view.

He lifted their joined hands to his lips, placing a soft, sensual kiss on her knuckles. "Welcome back."

"Sam." She reached for his face. Was certain she'd lifted her other arm from her lap and angled it toward his jaw. But all that happened was a blinding jolt of pain that danced tiny specks across her vision. Then a dull roar sounded in her head, and the scenery swam.

"Whoa, easy there, slugger." Sam's other hand was on her chest, pressing her into the mattress. Keeping her down without causing more pain. "Your shoulder's a mess. Will be for a while, so...don't try to move it. In fact, don't try to move, period. At least, not without help for a bit. Okay?"

She nodded. She'd heard most of what he'd said until she'd found herself staring at his mouth. Watching the way it moved. Imagining it sliding over hers, his tongue softly stroking between her lips.

Sam smiled. He was breathtaking when he smiled. "I recognize that look. And you're a few weeks away from that kind of fun."

She frowned. "You..." She cleared her throat. God, her voice sounded like a combination of sandpaper and metal filings. "You can't...kiss me for a few weeks?"

He chuckled, nuzzling her nose. "Kissing, we can manage."

He paused a moment, his nose lightly brushing the side of hers before his mouth settled on her lips. He moved slowly, as if he thought any quick motion would hurt her. His lips molded to hers, lingering on the edge of sweetness before finally opening in invitation. She accepted, sweeping her tongue into his mouth—sighing as everything clicked into place like tumblers inside a lock. Sam moaned, lifting one hand and gently cupping the back of her head.

She let him brace her. Let him lead, smiling up at him when he finally eased back. The rest of the room faded in the background, her entire world focused on the blue of his eyes.

He caressed her cheek, shaking his head in mock frustration. "You'll have me breaking all the rules the doctors wrote down if you keep looking at me like that."

"Like what?"

His lips quirked. "Like you just found what you'd been searching for."

The tension bled from her muscles, and she knew he was right. That it was time. "Maybe because I have. I hadn't even realized I'd been looking. That there was something missing. But…" She smiled. "Didn't plan on it being six-feet of muscled Army Ranger, though."

His eyes narrowed as he reclaimed his seat. "Hold that thought for a moment. First, how much do you remember?"

She swallowed, praying she hadn't fabricated Sam telling her he loved her. That it wasn't fantasy intruding on the ugliness of reality. "Everything, I think. Right up until you and Russel showed up. It gets…blurry after that."

"Understandable. You lost over a liter of blood. I'm surprised you were even conscious." He smiled. "From the look of the house, you caught Brock off-guard."

"He thought I'd just stand there. Frozen."

"But you weren't going down without a fight, were you?"

"I didn't think I'd live to prosecute him, so I wanted to make damn sure someone else could." She gave his hand a squeeze. "I knew you'd eventually show up there, though, I didn't expect you that soon. Was it just a lucky guess I'd go back there?"

He lifted his hand, grazing it over the pendant resting against her chest. "I used my Hail Mary."

"The necklace." She shook her head. "I'd forgotten it was a tracking device. I'm glad you gave it to me."

He shrugged, gaze locking on hers. "Guess I knew it was only a matter of time before you ditched me."

She inhaled, cursing silently under her breath.

Sam snorted. "Betting you'd forgotten that part. Just like you'd forgotten to tell me some creep had hunted you through your office building then down to the garage? That he'd been armed and had popped a few bullets in your Jeep?"

She let her good shoulder slump. No use denying anything when he already knew the truth. "Did Hank tell you that?"

"Actually, your buddy Jack called. Had lots of interesting tidbits of information."

"Jack called you? Remind me to thank him properly, later."

"Oh, no. You don't get to blame him. He only mentioned it because it pertained to the case, and he thought you'd told me. And why wouldn't he? Only a fool would have kept that to themselves." When she didn't answer him, he arched a brow. "What? No comeback? No overly complicated excuses?"

"Why, when you're right? It was foolish. Not that I suspected it was Brock, but I should have come clean. At first, I justified it because I didn't really want your help. Didn't think you'd be around long enough to worry about it. Thought you were being overly dramatic. Then, after we had to move to the motel... I tried a couple of times, but it was always at the worst possible moment. When the world was going sideways on us. But I could have insisted." She sighed. "Honestly, by that time, I was just scared."

"Scared? Of what?"

"Of everything. Of looking like an idiot. Of having to admit I'd been wrong. That I would have died if I'd sent you away." She looked him in the eyes. "But mostly, that you'd be angry. Really, *really* angry."

He sat back, staring at her. "Oh, darling."

"I know you promised you'd never hurt me like that,

but... I'm not proud that a part of me was afraid. Afraid I'd given you more than enough reasons to..."

"To hurt you."

"I know you'd never hit me. I do. But it was easy to talk myself out of it. To tell myself I was just being safe. But all it did was put me in the very position I was trying to avoid. I'd gotten so good at being alone, at only depending on myself, that I'd forgotten there are evils in this world I'm simply not equipped to fight. That sometimes, I have to rely on someone else. That's not something I do willingly. And I knew if I let myself rely on you, if I got used to having you there, I wouldn't want you to leave."

She groaned as she pressed her head into the pillow. "Which only scared me more. It's one thing to secretly pine for someone. It's another when you realize you've been in love with them forever, but you have no idea how they feel or if there's any chance at a future together."

She met his gaze, wishing she could stare at her hands but aware she needed to tell him. Needed to see his reaction—good or bad. "I hadn't contemplated a future. Not a happy one. With a guy and a house and maybe a few kids driving me crazy. Testing even my lawyer's nerves. Not until you showed up. But I should have told you. Everything. From the start. Brock. The creepy note. The guy I thought was going to kill me. I can rationalize it away, but it was stupid. And I'm lucky you're as skilled as you are or I'd be dead. So, for what it's worth—I'm sorry. And I promise, if there's any kind of future for us, I won't keep secrets, again."

Sam sat there, lips slightly apart, eyes wide. He

looked as if he was going to talk then closed his mouth, still staring at her.

"Unless, you only said you loved me to make me fight? To keep me focused on something other than dying? Shit." She swallowed, trying to shrink into the bed. "Forget everything I just said. Other than the sorry, part. I—"

He kissed her. Leaned his chest lightly against hers, slid his hand behind her head and kissed her. Full tongue sweeping into her mouth, his breath hot against her skin. His fingers dug into scalp as if he could pull her closer. Kiss her deeper. No soft, sympathy kiss. It was sex without using the rest of their bodies.

Sam stayed close, his heavy pants raking across her chin, his gaze laser focused on her. "Do you really think I'm going to forget that you finally told me you love me? Do I look like an idiot?"

She did her best to breathe, finding it extremely difficult with Sam inches away, studying her every move. "But you didn't reply—"

"I was shocked. Twelve years in the service. Endless missions that rarely went as planned. There was always something that reared up—an unavoidable glitch we had to adapt to. And I've never been this—"

"Speechless?"

"Utterly surprised. There are a thousand reasons you deserve so much better, but I'll take my lucky breaks wherever I get them. Which reminds me. I owe you an apology, too."

She frowned. He owed her an apology?

He sighed, stroking his thumb along her jaw. "You left because you heard us talking. Heard Russel suggest

I used sex to get my clients to comply with my wishes, and then I agreed. Joked about doing anything to get you to trust me." His jaw clenched as his voice got choppy. Thick. "God, Bridgette. I didn't mean it like that. I'd never use sex like that, least of all on you. Never with you. But when you told me what you'd overheard... Shit. I can see how it sounded bad. *Really* fucking bad. I tried to explain, to apologize—"

She placed a gentle finger over his mouth. "It's okay. It wasn't all your fault. It just so happens Brock said something very similar that night he attacked me, and when I heard those same words—"

"Fuck. You had a flashback, and I sounded exactly like the prick who'd nearly killed you."

"You couldn't have known. But I got confused. Couldn't separate then and now, so I ran. I'm not proud of that fact. But at the time, it was the only option that made me feel as if I had any control left."

He closed his eyes, resting his forehead on hers. She let herself drift for a moment. Lost in the heat of his touch, the safety of his arms, until he eased back.

She cupped his jaw. "So...you're not mad?"

He chuckled. "Why be mad at you, when I can love you, instead?"

Her heart thumped hard in her chest. "Say it, again."

He smiled. "I love you, Bridg."

"Good because I love you, too, *Midnight*."

EPILOGUE

Eagle Rock, Montana. One month later...

Sam leaned against the wall, watching Bridgette rearrange the items on her desk for what had to be the hundredth time in the past ten minutes. He didn't miss the way her hands shook. Not much, but enough she'd nearly tipped over a collection of pens. Twice.

He crossed over to the desk and palmed the surface. "You're nervous, Counselor."

She immediately drew back her hands, the left arm moving stiffly. It was going to take a few more months before she'd have full range of motion back in her joint, but she'd healed faster than he'd expected. Had treated her physiotherapy sessions like a freaking mission from God. But it had gotten her functioning in half the time he'd anticipated. And he couldn't be prouder.

Bridgette pursed her pretty mouth. "Until two weeks

ago, I was an assistant United States Attorney. I don't get *nervous*."

He suppressed the smile tugging at his mouth. "So, you have an obsession with pen placement, then?"

She glanced at her desk then sighed as she pushed to her feet, rounding the desk until she could rest her ass against the edge. "This is all so...new."

He shuffled over until he was standing in front of her, hands lightly trailing up and down her arms. While she'd be adamant about quitting—about starting her own practice and heading a number of clinics that offered free services to women in need—he couldn't help but wonder if she felt trapped. If their relationship had colored her decision.

He didn't want her to have to be the one doing all the compromising. He'd told her he'd find a way to make it work. Travel as much as necessary because damn it, *she* was his life. His entire future. As much as he loved working at Brotherhood Protectors, he'd give it up. For her.

He'd climb Mount Everest for her.

But she'd insisted. Had reminded him that she'd already told him she'd been having doubts. Thoughts that her job wasn't the direction she wanted to keep going. And now she had a chance to make a change. She'd also poked him with one incredibly delicate finger and told him she'd kick his ass if he gave his job up for her.

He loved that about her. Her conviction. Her passion. He just worried she'd come to regret leaving her life in Seattle behind. That it would eventually be what tore them apart.

No way. He wouldn't let it. He didn't fail missions, and he'd already told her she was his. Period.

He gave her a smile when she stared up at him. "You know, if you're having second thoughts, you can still change your mind. Jeremy told you, point blank, that you'd always have a job there. If you called, they'd hire you back before you had a chance to say hello."

Her face scrunched up, forming sexy little lines above her nose. God, she was beautiful. "Is that what you think? I'm regretting my decision, already?"

"I'd understand if you'd come to realize it was just too much to give up. All your hard work to get there, and now you're giving it up. For me."

She laughed. Loud. Shaking her head before standing and wrapping her arms around his neck as his hands fell to her waist. "You know I love you, right?"

He nodded.

"Then I hope you wont be offended when I say that I didn't give up my job for you. Sure, us being together was one factor in my decision, but ultimately, I quit for me. Because while I was lying in that hospital bed, I realized something."

"And what was that?"

"That somewhere along the line, I'd ventured off the path and gotten lost in these dark woods. Not terrifying ones like in the movies, but ones that messed with my head. Made me forget why I'd become a lawyer in the first place."

"To seek justice."

She smiled. "Right. Justice, not vengeance. And while I can sugar-coat my response, or downright lie, working for the U.S. Attorney's office was all about vengeance. About making men like Brock pay. But not in the right way." She exhaled. "It's hard to explain. All I know is that as soon as I'd handed in my resignation, I felt...free. Like I'd found my way back."

The band around his chest loosened, and he realized he'd been scared. Afraid that maybe she'd regretted saying she wanted to live with him. Share their lives, and not just that she'd changed jobs. But staring down at her, seeing the gleam in her eyes, the easy smile on her face—it was crystal clear.

She looked happy. Radiant, in fact.

He rested his forehead on hers, breathing in the scent of her perfume mixed with the sweet essence that was just Bridgette. "So, why the rearranging of pens for ten minutes straight, then?"

Bridgette sighed, and he felt the tremble in her arms. Heard the shaky way her breath washed over his chin.

He pulled back. "Bridg? You okay?" He cursed, quietly. "It's too soon, isn't it? We can put off the opening. People will understand. The doctors—"

She silenced him with a finger then smiled. "I do love how you have a thousand answers just waiting before I get one out. Yes, I'm fine, and no, I don't want to put this off. I'm just...worried."

He kissed her finger then eased it away. "Worried about what?"

She lowered her arms then paced over to the wall before spinning and leaning her butt against it. "That I'll screw it up."

"Screw what up?" He chuckled. "Their cases?"

"It's not funny, Sam."

"I wasn't laughing at that. It's just..." He walked

over to her and copied her stance. "You used to put drug dealers and mafia bosses behind bars. This is nothing like that."

"That's my point. Before, I was representing the state. Sure, there were victims, but there was more at stake than the lives of a few people. It was doing a service for the greater good. But now..." She turned to look at him. "Now, I have to look a woman in the eyes and swear to her that her fuckhead boyfriend or husband or whoever it was who thought they had the right to use her as a punching bag—to terrorize her and her children—is going to get what he deserves. That I *will* personally put his ass away for a very long time and ensure she's safe."

Bridgette swallowed, coughing a bit as if she'd choked trying, before scrubbing a hand down her face. "God, listen to me. I sound like some crazy person with trauma issues." She snorted. "Which, I am, but still..."

Sam lifted his arm and wrapped it around her back, tugging her against him. "You're not crazy. And you sound passionate. Like someone who genuinely cares what happens to her clients."

He turned, pushing her back against the wall as he held her tight. She didn't even flinch, which told him so much more.

He nuzzled her nose. "You're going to be great."

She sniffed. "How can you be sure?"

"Because you've been there. You know what it feels like to be powerless. To spend years looking over your shoulder, wondering if some sick prick might be coming back for a second go at your life. Those aren't traits you learn in school. Or even in a courtroom. You've lived these women's lives. You get it. *Really* get it. And that's why you'll be amazing."

He dropped a kiss on her mouth. "Just remember one thing. You are *not* seeing to their safety. Hank has donated his company's services if any of these women are at risk. I've freed up my schedule for a couple of weeks, just in case." He thumbed her jaw. "You're not alone in this. It's a noble venture. We all want to help."

She smiled, and just like that, his stomach flip-flopped and his heart gave a hard thud. "Have I thanked you?"

"For what?"

"Everything. Saving my life. Helping me through physiotherapy. Finding this place and having it ready for me." She brushed her knuckles along his cheek. "For agreeing to shack up with me. That, alone, deserves a medal."

He grinned. "You are impossible to live with. All that love, all the time. It's killing me."

"Jackass."

"As long as I'm *your* jackass. Forever. Which reminds me…" He backed up, removed a velvet box from his pocket then got down on one knee. "This isn't a medal. Or quite as functional as a GPS necklace, but…it's an extension of my heart. The one you've had since we were eighteen. And I'd be honored if you'd wear it for the next seventy years."

Bridgette's eyes widened, then misted over, a few tears leaking onto her cheek as she stared at the ring. He'd opted for a tanzanite stone—something as rare as she was—on a simple platinum band.

She reached out and gently eased the ring out of the

box, staring at it in her hand for a few moments before sliding it on her finger. More tears fell before she gave him a smile. "It's stunning."

"Just like you. But you never answered my question, Counselor."

She quirked her lips, looking down at him. "I don't believe you actually asked me a question, soldier."

He laughed. "And you wonder if you'll do these women justice. Fine. Bridgette Louise Hayward..."

He smiled when she winced at her middle name. He knew she disliked it. "Will you marry me?"

She looked at the ring, then back at him, tilting her head as if she were actually thinking about it. "Yes, on one condition."

He stood, arching a brow.

"You promise the guys won't call me Mrs. Midnight."

He took her in his arms, sliding his mouth over hers for a long, slow kiss. Just thinking he'd get to do this for the rest of his life settled the butterflies in his stomach. Filled the empty space he'd lost to the desert. "I don't know. It has a nice ring to it. Mrs. Midnight."

"Sam."

"Fine. No, Mrs. Midnight. In fact, they already have a name for you."

She frowned as he released her, moving back over to her desk. "They do?"

"Yup."

"What name?"

"Sorry, that's privileged information. Can't break confidences."

"That's not funny...Midnight."

"Actually, if you could see your face right now…" He ducked when she launched a pen at him. "Temper, darling."

She took a step then stopped when the door opened and a woman appeared in the entrance. Shy. Obviously skittish. Bridgette's face softened, and she walked past him, glaring at him as she went by. "I'll find out."

He watched her interact, feeling his chest swell. The tenderness mixed with steel determination was quite the sight to behold.

He headed for the door, stopping beside them. "I'll see myself out. But remember, call me if anyone needs my services."

"Of course, Samuel."

He groaned. She knew he hated being called Samuel. "Ladies."

She blew him a kiss, then focused on her client. But he didn't miss the way she shivered. How she immediately rubbed her hands along her arms as she spoke to the woman then pointed to a coffee machine in the far corner. He took a step then stopped, spinning to face her. He shook his head, slipped out of his jacket then removed his sweater.

He closed the distance, handing it out to her. "You look cold. Guess you forgot to check that app you have on your phone. This should keep you warm until I come back to pick you up tonight."

Her eyes misted over as she inhaled against the fabric before pulling it over her head. It dwarfed her, but she looked perfect. "Does this mean I can start sleeping in your T-shirts?"

He damn near moaned out loud. "I'll personally put

this one on you *after* I've picked it up off the floor, tonight." He smiled at the way her eyes glazed for a moment then dropped a kiss on her cheek before continuing to the door.

"Sam."

He paused in the doorway, smiling at Bridgette as she stood there, grinning, his sweater falling halfway down her thighs. "Yes?"

"I love you. Midnight and all."

"Love you, too...*Rogue*."

CARVED IN ICE

BROTHERHOOD PROTECTORS WORLD

KRIS NORRIS

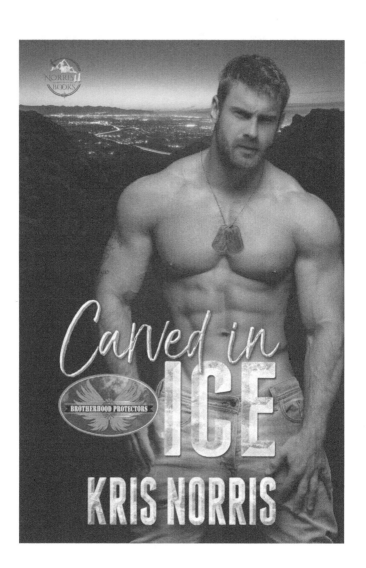

CARVED IN ICE

EXCERPT

"What can I get you?"

Russel focused on the woman standing behind the bar, a towel slung over one shoulder, her platinum-blonde hair swept up into a messy bun. Jet-black eyeliner ringed her eyes, highlighting the light blue of her irises.

He smiled. "Pale ale. Whatever's best out here."

She cocked one eyebrow then grabbed a bottle from beneath the counter. "Manny's is a local favorite." She cracked the cap off. "Glass?"

"No, ma'am."

"Ma'am? Wow, you really aren't from around here, are you?"

The truth hit home, only it wasn't just Seattle or Washington State that seemed alien. It was the whole package—civilian life. Christ, just thinking those two words made his skin crawl. After all his years in the service, he'd never imagined he'd be sitting in a bar, his career in the crapper, and his damn head so fucked up, he wasn't sure whether laugh about it or start a fight. Or maybe he'd come here hoping to hook up. A few rounds of hot sex generally took the edge off.

Right. As if sex was going to make him forget getting kicked out. Forget the stain on his record—the one that virtually erased all those years of risking his ass to save someone else's. That mocked the oath he'd lived by since joining. While a part of him had known the inevitable outcome a month ago, it hadn't lessened the stab of pain when he'd gotten the official ruling.

Russel forced a smile. "That obvious?"

The woman laughed. "No one says ma'am around here. At least, not without a thick southern accent. I get called babe. Darling, sometimes. Besides, you've got the look."

"The look?"

"There's a reason people pour out their hearts to bartenders, sweetie. We're pretty good at reading body language. The way you're scanning the bar, looking like you're about to jump out of your skin... Either you're a spy, or this isn't your usual scene." She stepped back, crossing her arms over her chest. "Let me guess. Based on your freakishly large frame, short hair, and what looks like possible dog tags around your neck, you're either a wrestling pro in town on a tour, or..." She grinned. "You're military."

He snorted, the word stinging the raw wound still bleeding beneath his skin. "Not anymore."

"Ouch. Doesn't sound like it ended well."

"Most things involving war don't."

"So, is this a stop on your way home?"

He shook his head. How did he say that he'd come

here to deliver a dying message to a dead soldier's wife? That every tear she'd cried had been like a knife across his flesh. That having her thank him for his kindness had cut deeper than his other-than-honorable discharge. She wouldn't have thanked him if she'd known he'd abandoned her husband's dead body in order to track down the men who'd captured his partner. That Russel had disobeyed direct orders in an effort to save a soul—atone for arriving too late. For not saving the other half of hers.

He worked up a quirk of his lips. "I had a promise to keep."

She frowned then sighed, leaning her elbows on the bar. "Sounds like you need more than just one beer. Like I said, I'm a pretty good listener. How about you and I..."

Her gaze drifted to somewhere over his right shoulder. "Shit."

Russel glanced behind him, but to him, it was just a sea of people—endless leather jackets, jeans and cowboy hats. Nothing looked out of place. Guys hitting on girls. A couple of boys shoving each other off to one side. Exactly what he'd expect in this kind of establishment.

He arched a brow. "Something wrong?"

The woman huffed, fluttering a few wispy hairs around her face. "I'll say. Looks like Red, over there, has some unwanted company. The kind that's gonna either break out into a brawl or get the cops showing up at my door. Maybe both."

He swiveled on the stool, searching the area more closely until he narrowed in on a pretty little redhead on the far side of the room. She had her hair in a similar bun, only half of hers had slipped out of the knot, cascading around her shoulders in a messy curtain of auburn curls. She was sitting alone at a table, nursing a drink, while three guys hovered around her. One of them slid his hand along her shoulder before she knocked it off, clearly mouthing for him to "fuck off".

Russel grinned. He had to hand it to her, she had guts. She didn't look big enough to take on one of the men, let alone all three. Though, he knew better than to judge people by their appearance. He'd witnessed more than a few female soldiers half his size kick guys on their asses without breaking a sweat. So, maybe the girl could handle herself.

The bartender muttered something under her breath then sighed. "Girls like that don't belong in this kind of place. Not alone, anyway. Most of the men that frequent this bar aren't the kind you want to take home—not unless you're a damn black belt. Or heavily armed."

"Do you know her?"

"She's like you. A first-timer. And the way she's been belting back those coolers, I'd say she's either going through a breakup or lost her job. She doesn't seem like the typical party crowd we get. Casual clothes. Very little makeup. Girl's out of her league, here."

She tossed the towel on the counter. "I'll grab one of my guys. Have them step in before it gets ugly. Or bloody."

Russel snagged the woman's wrist, giving her a genuine smile, this time. "No need. I've got this."

She tilted her head. "Looks, manners, and a gallant knight? You must have been some kind of soldier."

"Nothing special. Just did my job." He stood, reaching for his wallet. "How much do I owe you?"

She smiled and waved it off. "That one's on the house. Consider it a thank you for your service. Or, if that bothers you, it can be payment for helping me out."

Russel nodded. He didn't like getting special treatment, but he knew by the firm press of her shoulders that she wasn't going to take no for an answer. He turned, staring at the redhead, again. The guy who'd touched her had shuffled closer. He seemed determined to drape his arm around her shoulder, despite the way she continually batted away his advances. A light flush now colored her cheeks, and her back looked stiffer. A few more minutes, and Russel bet his ass things were going to get physical.

The guy bent lower and reached for her thigh, rewarded with a face full of whatever cooler she'd been drinking. He startled back, scrubbing his hand down his face before glaring at her. "Shit. Why the hell did you do that?"

She tightened her grip around the bottle, looking as if she was considering smashing it over the guy's head, when Russel moved into her sight line. She froze, her gaze shifting toward him. Her eyes widened as her head tilted back to meet his gaze, and her mouth gaped open slightly.

He smiled, hoping the simple gesture put her at ease, before addressing the men. "I don't want to speak for the lady, but I'm pretty sure that's the universal sign for all of you to get lost."

The guy glanced up. Whether it was Russel's size or how he carried himself, he wasn't sure, but the man

304 | CARVED IN ICE

straightened, nudging his buddies then lifting his chin higher. "You're right. You don't speak for her. So, why don't you go back to wherever you came from? We're in the middle of a conversation."

"You mean the one where she told you to 'fuck off' a few minutes ago?" He took a step closer, placing his beer bottle on the table. "As I see it, this can go down two ways. You boys can disappear on your own, or we can take this outside."

"You think you can take all three of us on? Alone?"

"It won't be a fair fight, but I can wait while you try to convince a few more of your friends to join in, if you'd like?"

A smile twitched the woman's mouth before a bemused chuckle made it past her pursed lips.

The guy behind her sneered, glancing between her and Russel a few times. "You must think you're something."

He reached for the woman a moment before Russel moved. Within seconds, he had the asshole off to the side and on his knees with his wrist bent backwards. The man grasped at Russel's arm in an attempt to release his hold, cursing when Russel increased the angle.

Russel leaned in, still eyeing the other men as he dragged the jerk toward him. "I don't think you understood me. Try to touch her, again, and I'll break more than your wrist. Now, I suggest you all leave."

The creep nodded, cradling his hand against his chest when Russel released it as he shoved him onto his ass. His buddies helped him up, all three giving Russel a wide berth as they headed for the door.

Russel waited until they'd stumbled outside before gazing down at the woman. "My apologies, ma'am. Men like that give the rest of us a bad name."

She stared up at him, blinking several times, before shaking her head. "You... I didn't even see you move. Then, you had his hand, and—"

"I hope I didn't frighten you."

"Hell, no. That..." She whistled. "Is it bad that I kinda wish they'd been stupid enough to go outside with you? Because I would have enjoyed watching them get their asses handed to them."

He chuckled. "For a moment, I thought you were gonna cold-cock that one creep with your cooler."

"I was." She motioned to the chair across from her. "Would you like to sit? Can I buy you another beer as a thank you?"

He scraped the chair out then slid onto the seat. "You don't have to thank me."

She scrunched up her nose. "Are you seriously for real? Is there a hidden camera or something?"

"You act as if no one else would have done that."

"That's because no one else would have, other than maybe one of the bouncers. Even then, he would have probably asked me to leave, too. Haven't you heard? Chivalry is dead, and nice guys are extinct."

He laughed. God, it felt good to do that. "So, you're saying I'm a throwback?"

"In a good way. Though, I'm surprised they tested you, because..." She waved at him.

"Because I'm freakishly large, as the bartender put it?"

Her lips quirked. "I wouldn't have used the word 'freakishly'."

Russel smiled as he leaned back in the chair. He couldn't remember the last time he'd enjoyed easy banter with a lady. "You're...unique."

She pouted. "Unique? Isn't that guy-speak for crazy?"

"It has multiple meanings."

She arched a brow as she copied his position. "Sure. Just like, 'she's got a great personality', right?"

He laughed harder when she made the air quotes with her fingers. "I was right. You are a ball-buster. So, tell me. If I hadn't happened along, what were you planning on doing, other than breaking the bottle over his head?"

Her lips lifted, and it was as if someone had beamed a spotlight on her. Her smile lit up her entire face, accentuating the even symmetry of her features and the devilish gleam in her eyes. Her insanely *green* eyes. Fuck, how had he missed that before? Missed how beautiful she was? How smooth her skin looked or how full her lips were?

Her smile flourished, and his damn chest gave a hard thump, as if his heart had just flipped over. "I'm not helpless. I can punch a guy without crying over breaking a nail. And I have a full can of mace in my purse. I only needed enough of a distraction to get some distance."

He leaned in, bracing his forearms on the table. "Let me get this straight. You were gonna hit that asshole over the head with your cooler bottle. Then, while he was working himself up into a lather, you were gonna slip out, punch anyone who got in your way then hold them all back with a can of mace?"

"Well, when you say it like that..." She scowled. "What else was I supposed to do?"

"How about not put yourself in this position to begin with?"

He sucked in a deep breath then eased back, taking another pull of his beer. He wasn't sure why he was so worked up, other than picturing all the ugly ways her night could have ended.

She stared at him for a while. "So, I'm not allowed to come out and have a few drinks by myself because I have a vagina?"

He choked on his beer, nearly spitting it across the table. Damn, he liked this woman. Feisty. Beautiful. A dangerous combination, but Russel wasn't known for shying away from danger. "You're right. It's not fair. But places like this don't care about equality. And guys like that take what they want without any regard to who they hurt in the process."

She leaned forward, this time, that green gaze locked on his. "Trust me. I'm *intimately* aware of what guys like that are capable of. I know the moment I step into a room who's safe and who isn't."

Russel studied her, her words making the hairs on his neck prickle. The bartender wasn't the only one who was good at reading people, and he knew there was far more to this woman than he'd initially thought.

"I see. So, who else in here is safe?"

"Besides you?" She chuckled as she leaned back, again. "No one."

"And you're sure about me? I could have chased those guys off so I could get you alone."

She snorted. "Please. Everything about you screams honorable. I wouldn't be surprised if it was tattooed across your chest."

Except for the part where the Air Force had deemed him anything but.

"Besides, it would be a pretty stupid move—making a scene like that—if you planned on being anything less than a gentleman." She nodded toward the bar. "I'm betting the bartender would remember you to a tee. She hasn't taken her eyes off you since you sat down."

He glanced over his shoulder, grinning at the blonde watching them from behind the counter. "You have a point. But, if you know how dangerous it is in here, why come in?"

She shrugged. "I wanted to go somewhere... different. Off-character, I suppose."

"You mean, somewhere you wouldn't be found."

Her expression sobered. "I just didn't want to bump into anyone I knew. Not tonight."

"Something happen tonight?"

"Do you always ask strangers this many questions? Christ, I don't even know your name."

He extended his hand. "Russel."

She stared at his palm then slowly placed her hand in his. "Quinn."

OTHER BOOKS BY KRIS NORRIS

SINGLES

CENTERFOLD

KEEPING FAITH

IRON WILL

MY SOUL TO KEEP

RICOCHET

ROPE'S END

SERIES

'TIL DEATH

1 - DEADLY VISION

2 - DEADLY OBSESSION

3 - DEADLY DECEPTION

BROTHERHOOD PROTECTORS ~ Elle James

1 - MIDNIGHT RANGER

2 – CARVED IN ICE

3 - GOING IN BLIND

COLLATERAL DAMAGE

1 - FORCE OF NATURE

DARK PROPHECY

4 - Reckoning

ABOUT THE AUTHOR

Author, single mother, slave to chaos—she's a jack-of-all-trades who's constantly looking for her ever elusive clone.

And don't forget to subscribe to her newsletter to get the latest scoop on new and upcoming releases as well as exclusive free reads.

https://www.subscribepage.com/krisnorris

Kris loves connecting with fellow book enthusiasts. You can find her on these social media platforms...

krisnorris.ca
contactme@krisnorris.ca

f facebook.com/kris.norris.731
X x.com/kris_norris
instagram.com/girlnovelist
a amazon.com/author/krisnorris

BROTHERHOOD PROTECTORS

ORIGINAL SERIES BY ELLE JAMES

Bayou Brotherhood Protectors

Remy (#1)

Gerard (#2)

Lucas (#3)

Beau (#4)

Rafael (#5)

Valentin (#6)

Landry (#7)

Simon (#8)

Maurice (#9)

Jacques (#10)

Brotherhood Protectors Yellowstone

Saving Kyla (#1)

Saving Chelsea (#2)

Saving Amanda (#3)

Saving Liliana (#4)

Saving Breely (#5)

Saving Savvie (#6)

Saving Jenna (#7)

Saving Peyton (#8)

Brotherhood Protectors Colorado

SEAL Salvation (#1)

Rocky Mountain Rescue (#2)

Ranger Redemption (#3)

Tactical Takeover (#4)

Colorado Conspiracy (#5)

Rocky Mountain Madness (#6)

Free Fall (#7)

Colorado Cold Case (#8)

Fool's Folly (#9)

Colorado Free Rein (#10)

Rocky Mountain Venom (#11)

High Country Hero (#12)

Brotherhood Protectors

Montana SEAL (#1)

Bride Protector SEAL (#2)

Montana D-Force (#3)

Cowboy D-Force (#4)

Montana Ranger (#5)

Montana Dog Soldier (#6)

Montana SEAL Daddy (#7)

Montana Ranger's Wedding Vow (#8)

Montana SEAL Undercover Daddy (#9)

Cape Cod SEAL Rescue (#10)

Montana SEAL Friendly Fire (#11)

Montana SEAL's Mail-Order Bride (#12)

SEAL Justice (#13)

ABOUT ELLE JAMES

ELLE JAMES also writing as MYLA JACKSON is a *New York Times* and *USA Today* Bestselling author of books including cowboys, intrigues and paranormal adventures that keep her readers on the edges of their seats. When she's not at her computer, she's traveling, snow skiing, boating, or riding her ATV, dreaming up new stories. Learn more about Elle James at www.ellejames.com

Website | Facebook | Twitter | GoodReads | Newsletter | BookBub | Amazon

Or visit her alter ego Myla Jackson at mylajackson.com
Website | Facebook | Twitter | Newsletter

Follow Me!
www.ellejames.com
ellejamesauthor@gmail.com